MORNINGSIDE
HEIGHTS

MORNINGSIDE HEIGHTS

Joshua Henkin

PANTHEON BOOKS

NEW YORK

All rights reserved. Published in the United States by Pantheon Books, a division of Penguin Random House LLC, New York, and distributed in Canada by Penguin Random House Canada Limited, Toronto.

Pantheon Books and colophon are registered trademarks of Penguin Random House LLC.

Library of Congress Cataloging-in-Publication Data
Name: Henkin, Joshua, author.
Title: Morningside Heights / Joshua Henkin.
Description: First edition. New York: Pantheon Books, 2021.
Identifiers: LCCN 2019034236 (print). LCCN 2019034237 (ebook).
ISBN 9781524748357 (hardcover). ISBN 9781524748364 (ebook).
Subjects: LCSH: Domestic fiction.
Classification: LCC PS3558.E49594 M67 2020 (print) |
LCC PS3558.E49594 (ebook) | DDC 813/.54—dc23
LC record available at lccn.loc.gov/2019034236
LC ebook record available at lccn.loc.gov/2019034237

www.pantheonbooks.com

Jacket design by Kelly Blair

Printed in the United States of America

First Edition

2 4 6 8 9 7 5 3 1

For Orly and Tamar

Part I

1

Growing up in Bexley, in the suburbs of Columbus, Pru had been drawn to the older boys, thinking they could take her far from home. Her father was from Brooklyn, her mother from Manhattan's Upper East Side, but they met in the middle of the country, in Ann Arbor, at a freshman mixer in 1944. Pru's father was studying engineering, and when he graduated he went to work for GM. But he wasn't cut out for the auto industry, for its assembly lines and economies of scale, and Pru's mother didn't like Detroit and its suburbs—Ten Mile Road, Eleven Mile Road, Twelve Mile Road—everything measured in a car. But Pru's father was happy in the Midwest, and when an opportunity arose in Columbus, he settled on it. And on Torah Academy, where Pru, as a kindergartner, was dropped off every morning at eight o'clock.

Pru liked the Hebrew songs, liked apples dipped in honey on Rosh Hashanah, liked staying home on Passover and eating matzo brei. But kindergarten became first grade became second became third, and she started to feel constrained. She had an older brother, Hank, but they weren't close; it was just her and the other students in her class. "Torah Academy's so Jewish," she told her parents.

"Well, it *is* a Jewish school," her mother said.

In eighth grade, on a trip to New York, the students were taken to the Streit's Matzo Factory, and to Ratner's for lunch. Years later, living in New York, Pru went out to La Difference, a kosher French restaurant, ostensibly high-end, but when she tasted her food, she told her friend Camille, "La Difference is this food sucks."

Pru's mother wasn't Orthodox—she'd agreed to keep a kosher home for Pru's father—and one time, a friend of Pru's saw Pru's mother at a restaurant eating breaded shrimp. When Pru confronted her, her mother said that when Pru turned eighteen she could eat as much breaded shrimp as she wanted to.

Was that why she was attracted to older men? If she couldn't be eighteen, she would go out with boys who were eighteen. In seventh grade, she dated a tenth grader, captain of the JV basketball team. In high school, she went out with a young man soon to graduate from Ohio State.

She was two months shy of her eighteenth birthday when she arrived at Yale in 1972. There was breaded shrimp to be had everywhere, but a curious thing happened those first few weeks at college. It wasn't that she missed her parents, though late at night, listening to her sleeping roommates, she would think of her family back in Ohio and grow teary-eyed. She lay in her dorm in her OHIOANS FOR MCGOVERN T-shirt while Derek and the Dominos looked down at her from the wall. She shivered: wasn't it supposed to be warmer on the East Coast? Fall had come early that year, and, walking across Old Campus, she was already wearing a parka. Torah Academy was eons ago—she'd gone to public high school, where her graduating class had been four hundred strong—but she wasn't prepared to be so far from home. Torah Academy had seemed too small and too Jewish; now Yale seemed too big and not Jewish enough.

She was no longer forced to keep kosher, but to her surprise, she continued to. Then spring came and along with it Passover, and she was answering questions from her secular Jewish friends, who weren't quite as secular as she'd thought. Why weren't peanuts kosher for Passover? Beer they understood, but corn and rice? And was it hypocritical to eat your cheeseburger on matzo?

She was again dating an older man, a graduate student in history, the president of the Yale chapter of SDS. Returning from services one Friday night, she joined him at an antiwar rally. *One, two, three, four, we don't want your fucking war! Ho, Ho, Ho Chi Minh, NLF is gonna win!* But when someone passed her the megaphone, she handed it back to him because she wasn't allowed to use a megaphone on Shabbat.

She did theater at Yale, and when she moved to New York she tried to make a go of it as an actor. Camille had done theater at Yale, too, and they dreamed of starring onstage together. They found an apartment in the West Village and worked as temps. When their bosses weren't looking, they would leave work early for auditions. "Ah, the casting couch," Camille said.

"Would you do that?" Pru said. "Sleep with someone to get a part?"

"Why not?"

Pru wondered: Was she less ambitious than Camille? Was she simply a prude?

One day, Camille announced that she was quitting theater. She was tired of temping, tired of auditioning for terrible parts. Secretly she'd applied to law school. She was starting NYU in the fall.

Maybe she was wrong, Pru thought: maybe *she* was the more ambitious one.

Or maybe she just clung to things. She had a new boyfriend, forty-seven when she was only twenty-two. "My God," she told Camille, as if she'd only just realized it. "Matthew's more than double my age."

"Well, good for you!" Camille said.

For a time there was talk about marrying Matthew. At least Matthew was talking about it, and Pru, flattered, started to talk about it, too. Convention be damned, she thought, even as she cleaved to her own conventions, keeping two sets of dishes, one for milk and one for meat, making sure on Friday evenings before the sun set to extinguish the joint she'd been smoking.

But eventually, she and Matthew broke up, and she moved uptown and started graduate school at Columbia, in the doctoral program in English literature.

Her first day of class she looked up from her seminar table and saw Spence Robin, her Shakespeare professor, enter the room. He was only six years older than she was, but he was the professor, Columbia's rising star, so when she passed him on a snowy afternoon outside Chock full o'Nuts, she glanced away.

"Are you pretending to be shy, Ms. Steiner?" That was how he addressed the class—Ms. Steiner, Mr. Jones, Mr. Thompson, Ms. Dunleavy—doing it with an edge of humor, as if it were a mild joke. "We do spend most of our day outside the classroom. It's not like we just materialize in Philosophy Hall."

A gale blew past them, and Spence's jacket collar flapped up to his ears. His shock of auburn hair was covered in snow, and Pru was tempted to offer him her hat. But her hat was pink, and if she gave it to him, then *she* would get covered in snow, and she knew he wouldn't countenance that.

They seated themselves in Chock full o'Nuts. "The coffee's terrible here," Spence said.

Pru agreed, though she was inured to terrible coffee. She drank terrible coffee most days, often from Chock full o'Nuts.

Spence removed a packet of peanuts. It was an old habit, he explained, a product of his fast metabolism. He'd been so thin as a boy he'd been sent to summer camp by the Fresh Air Fund, and when he failed to gain more than a few pounds, he got to stay for an extra two weeks.

The snow was falling harder now; at this rate, they'd be skiing home. Pru said, "Are we going to talk about *Coriolanus*?"

"Do you *want* to talk about *Coriolanus*?"

"As long as you don't make me recite." It was what Spence did in class, saying that word, *recite*, with the same little ironical smile he wore when he called her *Ms. Steiner*.

"How about you tell me where you're from?"

Under the influence of the coffee, and urged on by the wind coming through the open door, Pru started to loosen. She was from the suburbs of Columbus, she said.

"Sounds like a tautology to me."

She surprised herself by saying, "You little snob!"

"Little?"

It was true: he must have been six feet tall.

"And what's in the suburbs of Columbus?"

"Oh, just a bunch of complicated Jewish families like mine."

"Another tautology?"

"So you know about complicated Jewish families?"

"I come from one."

This surprised her. With his rangy, slender frame, his pale face, and thatch of red hair, he put her in mind of the Irish countryside.

And Spence—she thought of Spencer Tracy—not to mention his last name—Robin—well, you could have fooled her.

"My Christian name is Shulem," he said.

"That doesn't sound very Christian to me."

In kindergarten, he said, he'd changed his name to Spence. At five, he became an Anglo-Saxon, at six a Francophile. "It's the old immigrant story. I was trying to escape the Lower East Side."

"Well, you've done a good job." He was the youngest tenured member of the English department; the author, at thirty, of an award-winning book; a guest on PBS with Bill Moyers. "You're not still religious, are you?"

He laughed. His paternal grandfather had been a rabbi in Lithuania, but his parents' god had been Communism. He hadn't even been Bar Mitzvahed. One Yom Kippur, he'd gone to the Museum of Natural History to stare up at the great blue whale.

She told him about growing up Orthodox in the Midwest, how she'd moved to New York to become an actor. "So here I am," she said, as if everything she'd done—leaving Columbus, going to Yale, moving to New York to do theater—was in order to be seated where she was now, having coffee with Spence Robin.

"I could never be an actor," he said. "I don't like to perform."

"That's not what I heard." His lectures were said to be packed to the rafters; people were up in the nosebleed seats.

"Acting's different," he said. "I'm a shy man."

Yet here he was, talking to her—talking to this stranger.

But then he stopped talking, and she became shy herself. The snow had tapered off, and with the weather no longer keeping them indoors, she thought she should make her getaway. She got up, and he followed her.

"That's me," she said, in front of her building.

"And that's me." Spence pointed up Claremont Avenue. "If I work on my arm, I could throw snowballs at your balcony."

"I'd like that." And then, feeling foolish—she wanted him to throw snowballs at her balcony?—she rushed inside.

———

She started to run into him everywhere: in front of Daitch Shopwell, in front of Woolworth's, in front of the West End Bar.

"It seems our moons are in alignment."

She regarded him mildly. "I didn't realize you had a moon."

"I think you're following me," he said.

"Well, *I* think *you're* following *me*."

She saw him on Broadway, riding a moped, and she called out, "Hey, you! Hey, Spence! Hey, Professor Robin!"

He pulled over.

"The picture becomes clearer," she said. "You're the rock-star professor."

"Then you really don't know me."

"Then why the moped?"

"Because it gets me places."

She said, "Can I hop on?"

He took off his helmet and handed it to her.

"Shouldn't the driver wear a helmet?"

"In that case, you drive."

She'd never ridden a moped before, but if Spence could be reckless, so could she. Through the streets they went, the pavement slick like the back of a seal, the rain puddling in the gutters. She could feel his breath against her neck, his hands on her shoulders, large as lion's paws.

They parked in front of her building.

He said, "You took those streets like a native."

"I've always had a good sense of direction."

"Wasted on someone who lives in New York."

He leaned over and kissed her. He smelled of musk and cinnamon. She cupped her palm behind his neck and felt a line of perspiration, delicate as a silkworm. She rested her hand beneath his shoulder blades. She pressed her nose to his cheek.

She was neither the most nor the least talkative student in seminar, but at the next meeting she couldn't even look up. The class was discussing *Cymbeline*. Was that why no one else was talking, either? Because it was a difficult play? Or had the other girls kissed him, too?

Did he meet them all at Chock full o'Nuts? Did he sit across from them, eating peanuts?

Maybe she would have to drop the course. It was too bad: she loved Shakespeare.

The class ended at 4:00, and at 3:59 she was already out the door.

But when she stepped out of her building the next night, he was standing there, beside his moped.

"Oh," she said. "It's you."

"It's me," he agreed.

"I was wondering if you forgot about me."

"Forgot about you? I've been waiting here for the last two hours. You didn't tell me you were such a stowaway."

"You could have rung up."

"I thought it was better to smoke you out. I was getting ready to drive off." He pointed at the exhaust coming from his tailpipe.

"Do you want to come upstairs?"

"I thought you were leaving."

I was just going on an errand. It can wait."

"Okay," he said. "But first let me take you for a spin."

This time he drove, and as they sped along the streets, she pressed her nose to his neck, felt the hum of her breath against him.

When they got upstairs, she took him into the kitchen. "Are you hungry?" she said. "Would you like some food?" She removed leftovers from the fridge and placed them in the oven.

"I don't want to eat your dinner."

"There's enough for us both." She put some stew onto his plate, and some string beans and rice.

"You made this whole meal for yourself?"

"A person has to eat."

They ate and talked, while from outside on Broadway came the whoops of college kids and the pneumatic sigh of a stopping bus.

She had a loft bed raised almost to the ceiling. Seeing the ceiling fan swinging languidly on its hinge, Spence said, "Just don't go bolting up in the middle of the night. You're liable to get decapitated."

This time she initiated the kiss.

He pulled the chain on the ceiling fan and the clanking stopped. "Better?"

"Certainly safer." He'd heard of autoerotic suicide, but this would be something else.

They lay together: two halves of a clam. Outside she could hear a woman singing. "I'm knock-kneed," she said, and she knocked her knees against his. She rested her chin on the little triangle of flesh beneath his throat. She could feel his Adam's apple like a sparrow pulsing.

2

"So you're sleeping with your professor," Camille said. "Weren't you the one lecturing me about the casting couch?"

"I wasn't lecturing you," Pru said. "Spence isn't casting me in anything, besides."

"But he's giving you a grade. And letters of recommendation. Don't those professors get you jobs?"

Jobs? Pru wasn't even a semester into graduate school. She had more immediate concerns: she and Spence had to sneak around.

"I would think the sneaking around would be fun."

It was in a way. No holding hands above 59th Street. Even below 59th, they had to be careful. At the end of the day they would leave the library, making sure to walk several yards apart. "Shall we go north or shall we go south?" South meant Pru's apartment, north the extra hundred yards to Spence's, the two of them descending the hill past Chock full o'Nuts, hurtling down the cliff of 116th Street.

When she stayed over at Spence's place, Pru would leave in the morning while it was still dark out, and when Spence stayed over at her place, he would do the same thing. They would go to the Met or the Guggenheim, and she'd walk into the gallery from one entrance and he'd walk in from the other entrance. One time, she saw someone she recognized, and she ducked into the ladies' room.

When she spoke in seminar, half the time she forgot what she was saying. Was there a raised eyebrow? A smirk?

She and Spence would eat lunch at Woolworth's, the soda fountain gleaming across from them. "Be careful," she said. "Those security guards have eyes."

Years later Spence would say, "I can't believe I dated my graduate student."

"Not only that, you married her." But Pru didn't think anything of it at the time. It was the 1970s, she thought, looking back: a decade when no one knew anything.

Soon it was no touching above 72nd Street, then no touching above 96th Street, then no touching above 110th. One time, Spence grabbed her hand just blocks from campus and kissed her on the neck. Another time, she pinched him on the butt, which startled him: he liked to maintain a certain decorum.

But the next time, he was the one who pinched her.

"Maybe we should just tell people."

"We can't," he said. "I'm your professor."

Finally, at the department Christmas party, she'd had enough. Winter break was coming, 1979 was being ushered in, the age of disco was upon them. Music was playing, and the students had started to dance. Some of the professors were dancing, too, though not Spence; he was across the room, conferring with a colleague.

Pru handed him a glass of eggnog.

"I think it's spiked."

"Of course it's spiked. It's eggnog." She was standing beside the Christmas tree, and a couple of pine needles got lodged in her hair. "Dance with me."

He hesitated. "I'm not a good dancer."

"So what."

A graduate student brought out a broomstick, and everyone started to dance the Limbo.

"Look at Professor Robin!" someone called out. "He's dancing the Limbo!"

"Hey, check it out!" someone said. "Guess who's dancing with Pru!"

When the party was over, they walked across College Walk, Pru resting her hand on Spence's shoulder. Seeing them together, someone whistled.

———

Pru thought spring term would be easier: she wasn't in his class anymore. But in Philosophy Hall everyone looked at her differently. "Someone caught the big fish," a classmate said.

"I'm not even his student this semester."

But what about the next semester, and the semester after that? She wanted to study the Elizabethans, and if you did that at Columbia you did it with Spence Robin. Maybe she should transfer to NYU. But what good would transferring do? She could have transferred to Berkeley— she could have sailed clear across the world—and she would always be known as Spence's girlfriend.

"I hate it," she told him, out to dinner one night.

"Give it time," he said. "People will move on to other things. And you'll make your mark. I promise you."

She had a couple of glasses of wine and her mood calibrated. After dinner, they walked up Broadway, hand in hand.

They stood on the corner of 116th Street; gazing north, she could see the galaxy of lights strung like wire along the rooftops.

"Take a look," Spence said, and he opened his mouth so she could see inside. "There's not a filling in there. Not a penny's worth of orthodontia." He handed her his jacket. He was wearing loafers, a pair of slacks, an Oxford shirt tucked into them: not exactly running gear, but he took off. Across the Street he went and up Claremont Avenue, and Pru called out, "Spence, what in God's name are you doing?" but he was already gone, getting smaller as he went. She held his jacket in one hand while in her other hand she clutched her leftover pasta, which she was planning to eat for the next day's breakfast.

Then she heard her name being called ("Pru! Pru!"), and there he was, having run a square block, sprinting toward her in his loafers.

He placed her hand against his forehead. "I'm not even sweating. I'm in perfect health."

"Who said you weren't?"

"Look," he said, "I know I'm older than you."

"Not by much." Her last boyfriend had been more than double her age.

"Both my parents died young. My mother had cancer. My father had heart disease."

"I'm not worried about that." Years later, when Spence got sick, she would wonder whether he'd been warning her that night. But of what? He didn't have cancer or heart disease. He couldn't have known.

"I want to marry you, Pru."

"You do?"

"I'd marry you tomorrow. I'd marry you yesterday if I could."

3

Everything came in a rush after that, starting with meeting Spence's sister. "You must think it's strange you haven't met her."

Pru didn't think it was strange; Spence hadn't met her brother, either. The difference was, her brother was a banker in Hong Kong, and when Spence told her his sister lived in New York, she *did* think it was strange, because she'd been led to believe his sister was far away, that she was, for all intents and purposes, inaccessible.

"Enid's brain-damaged," Spence said. "She was in a car crash when she was sixteen. Drunk driving."

"She was drunk?"

"The other driver was. But she hung around with the wrong crowd. I was always waiting for something to happen to her." They were standing in the lobby of a nursing home, waiting for the elevator to take them up. "I was thirteen when she got hurt. It's the great sadness of my life."

They found Enid upstairs in the cafeteria, taking a stab at playing cards. She was thirty-three, but she looked as if she could have been sixty-three, her hands callused, her hair gray and slung unevenly in back. "Enid, this is my fiancée, Pru." But nothing registered on her, and the air in the room was thick and smelled of salami, and Pru thought she might retch.

On the subway home Spence was quiet. "I'm just carrying out my brotherly duty. Fifteen minutes and I'm gone."

"A lot of people don't even do that." Pru was thinking of Hank in Hong Kong, calling home just once a month.

Back at his apartment, Spence seated himself across the room from her. "Are you ready for the next secret?"

"What next secret?"

"I'll understand if you won't forgive me."

"Forgive you, Spence? What in the world are you talking about?"

"I was married before."

She was so boggled she couldn't speak. A raft of pigeons settled on the balcony, gaping at her. Finally, she said, "Did your wife die?"

No, Spence said, his ex-wife was alive and well. At least she had been the last time he'd heard from her.

"Who is she?"

"She's a whole lot of things." She'd been a Barnard student when he met her. A late-stage undergraduate: she'd been on the six-year plan. But even six years hadn't been enough for Linda. She'd dropped out of college short of her degree, though she continued to beach herself on campus, where, for the purposes of the antiwar movement, she was always front and center, shackling herself to some building when she wasn't shackling herself to some man. For a time Spence had been that man—long enough to get married, but how long did that take? You just needed an hour to get to City Hall.

Pru just sat there, taking this all in, while outside she heard a siren go off, then the sound of a car backfiring.

"That's not all of it."

What now? she thought. Was there a second ex-wife? A whole harem?

"There was a son," he said. "Pru, I'm a father."

The room canted on its axis; she was being tilt-a-whirled through space. "Where is this son?" Nothing would have surprised her. If Spence had told her his son was in the next room, that he'd been there for the last five months, an exceedingly quiet child, she'd have believed that too.

"I wish I knew where he was."

"You're telling me you don't know where your own son is?"

"Last I heard, he was in Maine." He sent monthly checks, so he knew where Linda and Arlo had been last month, but where they were one month had little bearing on where they'd be the next month. He'd proposed splitting custody, but Linda wasn't having it.

"So your son could just show up at your door?"

"My bigger fear is I'll never see him." Arlo had been a baby when Spence and Linda had split up; he was still only a toddler. "What I said before, how Enid is the great sadness of my life? Well, Arlo's really the great sadness."

Pru was making little knitting motions with her hands. This called for resources beyond her.

"If you need some time alone…"

She did need time alone, enough of it and sufficiently soon that she stood up all at once and left his apartment.

She didn't see him the next day, or the next. The phone rang, but she didn't pick up. The next time she saw him he might have a new girlfriend. Perhaps a new baby too.

She saw him one day on College Walk, eating lunch with a colleague. She headed in the other direction, fast. Afterward she thought, *He's still eating.* It was more than she could say for herself.

She came downstairs one afternoon and found him on her steps. His hair was uncombed, and he had several days of stubble. She didn't think it was possible, but he seemed to have lost weight.

"I want you to know how sorry I am."

She just stared at him.

"If you don't want to see me again, just say it. Give me the word and I'll go."

"How long were you two married?"

"Less than a year."

"Why did you get divorced?"

"Linda was sleeping with someone else. The only reason I married her was she got pregnant by accident."

"Did you drive her around on your moped?"

"Pru, come on."

"Did you?"

"Yes."

"What about your son? Describe him to me."

Back at his apartment, Spence removed an album from his bedside drawer. The word *Arlo* was printed across the front. On the first page was a photo of Spence holding a newborn. On the next page, the baby appeared to be two months old.

"How old is he now?"

"Two years, three months, and eleven days."

She looked up.

"You think I don't miss him?"

"So what does this make me?" Pru said. "The evil stepmother?"

"I'll be the evil one, I promise you."

Already she could feel herself starting to break, the tectonic plates shifting within her.

"I was scared of losing you," he said. "I know it's no excuse, but I was."

He was still tentative beside her, and even in bed there was a hesitancy to him. The night-side lamp dimpled his back, and from out the window came the last prodigal rays of sunlight. "Okay," he said. "Let's start over." He got down on one knee. "Pru Steiner, will you marry me?"

The first thing she did when she moved into his apartment was kosher their kitchen. She contacted Go Kosher—it sounded to her like a football cheer—and the next day, two men in beards and black coats arrived with blowtorches, and then they were running the dishwasher and dunking Spence's silverware in boiling water and turning the burners on high.

Afterward, lying in bed, she said, "How do you like that? We have a kosher kitchen." It wasn't lost on her that Spence was doing for her what her mother had done for her father. And when she told him that her mother had continued to eat non-kosher outside the home, she was giving him license.

On Saturday mornings, they would climb the hill to campus, Spence off to the library, Pru headed to shul. She would return from Kiddush with a piece of kichel, the driest, most tasteless biscuit in the world, but Spence liked kichel. She would hand him the kichel, swaddled in a napkin, and they would spend the next hour wandering around campus until it was time for him to return to the library.

When did she start to slip? Was it simply that Spence let her do what she wanted, that if she'd had more opposition she'd have remained steadfast? Was it that her father died, and she was waking up early to say Kaddish for him? Day after day, Kaddish after Kaddish: before long, she was all Kaddished out.

Now, in restaurants, she would order the onion soup without asking about the ingredients, though onion soup was almost always made with beef stock. She would start Shabbat half an hour late. One Saturday, when Spence had already left for the library, she turned the bathroom light on. She wasn't about to pee in the dark, and she certainly wasn't about to shower in the dark, though she'd done both those things countless times in college.

She told herself it was because of her father. It was for him that the house in Columbus had been kosher, for him that they'd had Shabbat dinner and said Kiddush and sung zemirot.

Now she would accompany Spence to the library instead of going to shul. Other times, she would head to the gym, where she would shower and blow-dry her hair (more electricity), then buy a drink from the soda machine (spending money: another violation). It wasn't long before she was eating traif—first just outside the house, then inside it also.

It scared her, this giving up of things, but it was exhilarating too, and over dinner one night at a midtown bistro, the bouillabaisse seeming to egg her on, she told Spence she'd decided to do what she hadn't realized she'd decided to do until she told him she was doing it: she was dropping out of graduate school. "It's your field," she said.

"I don't have a monopoly on it."

But she felt as if he did. He'd won a Guggenheim, and he'd signed on with Knopf to do a book: *Who Really Wrote Shakespeare?* She was doing good work herself; her professors thought she might make it in the field. But did she have the necessary passion? Even if she did, people would say she'd succeeded because of Spence, the youngest English professor ever to receive tenure at Columbia. Spence, the golden boy: even his hair shone like ore in the sun. She was the girl he'd plucked from class, and it made her feel plucked just to think about it, like a dandelion ripped from the ground.

"Choose a different century," he said. "Or a different continent. I'll give you Asia and Africa."

He made it sound like a game of Risk. She felt as if he might take over the world; he had that quiet way of overpowering you.

"Or stick with Europe and become a modernist."

Shakespeare, the Elizabethans: it was where she'd done her work. And, sure, she could switch, and maybe she would turn out to love her new field, but she would always know she'd chosen it to get out of his way.

Also—she hadn't told anyone this—she was pregnant.

4

She must have started a trend, because three of her classmates, Marie, Claire, and Theresa, dropped out, too. The M-R-S-es, the female graduate students were called. Get your master's in literature, marry, have children, then set up a nice home.

"But that's not what we're doing," Claire said. They were simply pursuing different careers. Claire was applying to medical school; Theresa was joining her family's real estate business; Marie had lined up an art gallery job.

But what about Pru?

"Pru doesn't have to do anything," Theresa said. "She's a star-fucker."

"I'm not a star-fucker," Pru said. "I married him."

"I assume that also involves fucking him."

Pru said, "How much money do you think an English professor makes?"

"It's not about the money," Marie said. "It's about the acclaim."

Claire said, "If I had a husband like Spence, I wouldn't have to worry about anything."

Pru didn't know what Claire was talking about. She loved Spence—she was thrilled to be married to him—but that didn't mean she didn't have to worry.

They started to meet every few weeks, rotating from one woman's living room to the next. Networking, Theresa called it, though mostly they sat on love seats and drank coffee and ate éclairs.

Marie said, "I could get you a job at an art gallery."

Pru didn't want to offend Marie, but she wasn't interested in the art business. She was married to Spence, the red-diaper baby, and his disdain for commerce had rubbed off on her.

One day, they met at Pru and Spence's apartment, and Pru baked a pineapple upside-down cake and a banana cream pie.

"These are amazing," Marie said. "You should become a pastry chef."

Pru did like to bake. But she could just as easily have become a paleontologist: she liked fossils too. She was good at a lot of things, but she wasn't outstanding at any one thing, and she feared she didn't have the drive to be outstanding. That was one of the things she liked about Spence. His own drive and single-mindedness made her feel ambitious vicariously.

One day, Marie pointed at Pru's stomach and said, "What's that bump I see?"

Claire said, "We've been talking about this, Pru, and we know you're not supposed to ask a girl if she's pregnant, but we're going out on a limb here."

"Yes!" Pru said. "I am!" She was relieved, finally, to be rid of her secret.

Everyone hugged her and made toasts, though they wouldn't let her drink, of course.

"Look at Mrs. Spence Robin," Theresa said, "standing before us with child!"

"My last name's not Robin," Pru said. "I kept my maiden name."

Claire said, "If I were married to Spence I'd be taking his name in an instant."

"I'm my own person," Pru said.

"Of course you are," Theresa said. "We're just saying."

As Pru's stomach grew, there was a chariness around her, almost an embarrassment, when the rest of them talked about their careers. When Claire would complain about organic chemistry, when Theresa would discuss real estate commissions, when Marie would describe a painting she'd sold, someone would ask Pru about her Lamaze class, and someone else would ask for her opinion on breast-feeding, and someone else still would ask whether she thought the baby was a boy or a girl, and before she could answer them, Marie was saying, "I think it's a boy," and Claire was saying, "It's definitely a girl," and Theresa was saying, "Which one is it, a boy if you carry low or a boy if you carry high?" and Pru said, "Can we stop talking about my pregnancy already?"

"What else should we talk about?" Theresa said, as if there could possibly be anything else.

"Don't patronize me," Pru said. "I still have a brain."

"Of course you do," Claire said.

"You're the smartest of all of us," Theresa said, and now they were patronizing her in a different way, reminding her of a seminar paper she'd written that the professor had said was publishable, and Claire mentioned Pru's GRE scores, which somehow had gotten out.

The delivery was by C-section, the recovery difficult and slow. Sarah didn't nurse well; she bit Pru's breast, and Pru would scream out in pain. Spence would kiss Sarah on the forehead, would coo, "Please don't bite Mommy," and then he'd hand her back to Pru to be bitten again.

Sarah didn't sleep well, either. She cried a lot.

"It's probably colic," the pediatrician said, and Pru said, "What do you mean, *probably*?" and the pediatrician had to admit that colic was speculative: who knew why babies did what they did?

Sarah became a toddler and she learned to sleep, but there was still daytime to worry about.

Pru, meanwhile, was studying French. Between the cost of the baby-sitter and the cost of the class, these were the most expensive French lessons on the planet. But she needed to learn French because Spence had a sabbatical coming up, and they were going to spend it in Bordeaux.

She started to do community theater, and she joined productions of *The Bald Soprano* and *Six Characters in Search of an Author*. On opening night Spence was in the front row, holding a bouquet of flowers. But the productions weren't good, certainly compared with the plays she used to act in. Community theater was democratic: the director cast whoever came along. Though who was she to be a snob? She was the faculty wife, with her Ionesco and her Pirandello, fancying herself as part of the avant-garde. It was a vanity project, and afterward, when she saw the photos Spence had taken, she was forced to look away.

Still, she loved spending time with Sarah, the trips in the morning to the Hungarian Pastry Shop for hot chocolate and brioche. Afterward, they would go to Spence's office for lunch, and Spence would dandle Sarah on his lap, a bib for her, a napkin for him, his necktie slung over his shoulder.

They spent Augusts in Vermont, where in the morning Pru would read a novel and Sarah would play in the pool with the neighbors' kids. One year, Pru proposed that Arlo come visit, but when Spence suggested it to Linda, she refused. July was Spence's month; the rest of the year Arlo was with her, except for Christmas and spring break.

Pru didn't care: she was happy for it to be just the three of them. In the afternoon, she would drink iced tea and Sarah would drink lemonade, and they would wait for Spence to come home from the library. Then the evening's activities could begin, Sarah's wet bathing suit draped over the clothesline, Pru having showered and put on some lipstick, looking lovely in her yellow sundress. "We have wheels, we can go anywhere," Spence said. Into town for dinner: fish and chips or pizza, Sarah's choice. Tuesday nights with the Singing Lady, Sarah installed on the pavement outside the old fire station singing along to "This Land Is Your Land" and "Blowin' in the Wind" while Pru and Spence stood in back, singing, too. Afterward, they would head to Double Dip, where their hot fudge made a frozen coat around their ice cream. Those August weeks, when time stretched out, supple as a rubber band: the days unspooling and unspooling and still there were more.

———

Eventually, though, Sarah started school, and Pru took a job in Barnard development. The work was tolerable, the hours good, and her salary, while low, was still a salary. And being at Barnard, Columbia's sister school, allowed Spence's burnish to rub off on her. She would cross College Walk and hear people whispering.

During lunch, she would stop by Sarah's nursery school and watch her eating with her new friends, the people who had replaced her. Sometimes Spence would join her, and they'd stand with their noses pressed to the glass. "Oh, Spence, our daughter's growing up."

She thought she'd stay in development for a few years, then try something else. She'd planned on being a professor, and now she was a supplicant, going to donors with her hat in her hand. She told herself she was supporting Barnard, supporting the free flow of ideas, but the pitch letter she'd written, the prospective donor she'd taken to lunch: it all made her feel vaguely ashamed.

Meanwhile, Spence won a Mellon, and another Guggenheim. One day, the MacArthur Foundation called.

"It seems I've won a MacArthur."

"Darling, we have to celebrate!"

But Spence didn't like to celebrate his accomplishments. He hated calling attention to himself.

"How much money is it?"

"I have no idea."

The next day, he looked in the *Times*. "Three hundred thousand dollars! Good God!"

"We could buy an apartment with that money."

"Why in the world?" Spence had grown up on the Lower East Side, where everyone hated the landlords. Now his wife was telling him to become one?

But he relented in the end, and they bought a two-bedroom apartment off Central Park West. Years later, when Spence got sick, that apartment was the only thing keeping them out of the poorhouse. *Who Really Wrote Shakespeare?* had spent a few weeks on the bestseller list, but by the time Spence got sick the royalties were gone, as was the money from his MacArthur. Sarah had gone to private school, then to Reed, and for years they'd been sending money to Linda to help take care of Arlo.

Now, though, Pru wanted to celebrate.

"You should throw him a MacArthur party," Camille said.

"He won't let me."

"Make it a surprise."

Camille lived a few blocks from Pru, and she took care of the shopping—the food, the alcohol, the flowers—while Pru sent out the invitations.

On the day of the party, Pru brought Spence into the apartment, and several dozen guests materialized from behind the furniture, everyone shouting, "Surprise!" Someone started to sing, "For he's a jolly good fellow," and Spence turned pink.

"Speech!" someone called out.

"I'm feeling shy," Spence said. "Would you mind if I didn't?"

"The man who lectures every day to all those rapt undergraduates?"

"Pru can speak for me."

But Pru, standing beside the piano, holding her glass of champagne, didn't know what to say.

"Cat steal your tongue?" someone said, and Camille said, "That's right, let's hear from the other half of the power couple!"

Finally, Pru raised her glass. "To Spence Robin, my old Shakespeare professor, not to mention my husband. For winning a genius grant!" She reached into the piano bench and removed a framed copy of the *Times* article with Spence's name highlighted.

But afterward, once everyone had left, Spence walked about the apartment, looking subdued. Someone's cigarette bobbed in a beer bottle. He turned on the water in the sink. "It was nice of you to throw that party."

"But you wish I didn't."

"It's just…"

"What?"

"You didn't have to announce it to everyone."

"Announce your MacArthur, darling? It was in the newspapers. Besides, they're our friends."

"And why did you call it a genius grant?"

"It's what everyone calls it."

"I'm not a genius. I'm just a smart enough guy who's gotten some lucky breaks."

"You're not giving yourself enough credit." She apologized for having thrown the party, and he apologized, too. If she wanted to be proud of him, she should be proud. He certainly was proud of her.

But she was *too* proud of him. She was thirty-five when he won his MacArthur, already settled into her life, but even at twenty-five, a few months removed from graduate school, she could see what she was becoming. She would sit around the living room with Theresa, Claire, and Marie, poking fun at the M-R-S-es. But she was an M-R-S herself. Spence's success was her success too. There was no separating them.

Part II

5

In the months after Sarah left for medical school, Pru recalled Mark Twain's words, *The coldest winter I ever saw was the summer I spent in San Francisco,* and she thought, What about New York in 2005? Spence got cold much more easily now. He would walk around the apartment with a sweater on; at night he needed an extra blanket.

He said, "I bet it's the coldest October on record."

But the temperature was about average for October. Maybe it was just Spence, who needed more insulation than he used to. There was a reason old people moved to Florida.

Though whom was she kidding? She was fifty-one and Spence was fifty-seven; they were squarely middle-aged.

Then why did Spence seem less alert? Why did he need eight hours of sleep a night when he used to need only five? He would nod off reading *The New York Review of Books.*

She came home one day and said, "I'm thinking of getting us a sunlamp."

"Why in the world?"

"Because they raise people's spirits. It's been documented."

"There's a document out there that can prove almost anything."

She felt defeated by his resistance. It was folly, besides, because she couldn't get him to sit in the actual sun, much less under a sunlamp. "Well, you may not be depressed, but I am."

"Why?"

"Because Sarah's flown off to UCLA." It was as if saying these words allowed her to feel them, and the depth of her isolation was cast in bright light.

———

They'd been invited to a New Year's Eve party, at the home of Spence's colleague, but Spence just sat there, refusing to get dressed. "I hate the Upper East Side."

"Come on, darling. No one's asking you to move there."

"You know what else I hate? Tuxedos."

And she hated evening gowns. But the invitation had said formal attire. She put on a long dress and a pair of slingback pumps, and she found Spence's tuxedo secreted in the closet.

"I look ridiculous," he said, seeing himself in his red bow tie. But his black bow tie was nowhere to be found, and this was what he'd unearthed from his tuxedo box.

Spence's colleague's building was made of glass, and as they ascended in the elevator they could see the sparkle of the East River, the Pepsi-Cola sign blinking at them. The planes were descending to LaGuardia, casting their shadows across Queens.

Outside the apartment, people were taking off their shoes. "Doesn't it defeat the purpose," Pru said, "everyone in their tuxedos and evening gowns walking around in stockinged feet?"

Outside in the cold, Spence had appeared sprightly and alert, but in the warmth of the building he had grown lugubrious. His face was flushed, and he was tugging on his bow tie, like a horse struggling with his bit.

"Let's get some food into you," Pru said. "Let's get some nourishment into us both."

At the entrance to the apartment, they ran into a colleague of Spence's. "And who might you be?" the man said. "Fred Astaire and Ginger Rogers?"

"We're Spence Robin and Pru Steiner," Spence said.

"Well, yes," said the colleague, who knew Spence well: they had offices down the hall from each other. "I meant for tonight."

A woman had on knee socks and pink barrettes; her husband had spray-painted his hair green. Still others were decked out as actual people. There was an Elvis Presley, and a Dorothy from *The Wizard of Oz.* A man was dressed as Vice President Cheney and another man was dressed as Alan Greenspan.

"Blast from the past?" a woman said to Spence, pointing at a couple dressed as the Captain & Tennille. But it wasn't a blast from *Spence's* past: he had no idea who the Captain & Tennille were.

"I don't get it," Pru said. "Is this New Year's Eve or Halloween?"

"You said it was formal attire," Spence said.

"No, Spence, *you* said it was formal attire. I didn't even see the invitation."

Spence searched for the invitation in his jacket pockets. Now his pockets hung at his sides, like donkey ears.

Pru removed the envelope from his breast pocket. "Well, that explains it." At the top of the invitation were the words *Come costumed in your most festive attire.* "Spence, we were invited to a costume party!"

"Give me that," Spence said. He held a club soda in one hand, the invitation in the other, and he was reading the words over and over again. "I can't believe I misread it."

"That's okay, darling. For you, a tuxedo *is* a costume."

Spence just stood there, and now he'd placed his club soda on the floor and was examining the invitation even more closely. "This is so embarrassing."

She tried to object.

"Don't tell me it's not embarrassing if I think it is."

She pointed to the words on the invitation, which Spence was parsing with such care. *Festive* and *formal:* it was easy to get them confused. And the phrase *come costumed* was ambiguous. They were all costumed just by being dressed.

But Spence wouldn't be consoled. "We might as well have come naked for all that we stick out."

"Darling, it's New Year's Eve. Let's just have a good time."

"I can't have a good time." And he spent the next hour moving listlessly among the guests, lagging several steps behind her.

"At least eat something," she said. "The food's outstanding."

He bit into a carrot stick and said, "You're right, it's an outstanding carrot stick. It's the most delectable carrot stick I've ever tasted." He deposited the half-eaten carrot stick onto the table.

He announced that he wanted to leave.

"It's only ten-thirty."

"I don't care."

"Fine," she said. "You want to leave, we'll leave." She didn't know why she was making such a fuss about this; this was his party, not hers. She hated New Year's Eve, with its forced merriment, everyone insisting you whoop it up.

She tucked him into bed when they got home, and with nothing else to do, she turned on the TV; she couldn't remember the last time she'd watched the ball drop. It was 11:40, and she didn't think she could stomach another twenty minutes of this.

In the early-morning hours of 2006, she listened to the revelers on the street, to the residual fireworks going off, and, beside her, to Spence's quiet breathing. Why had he ruined the party for her? Why had he ruined it for them both? Formal wear, festive wear: what difference did it make? She could have made that mistake herself.

One night, she saw a rat outside their building, wading through the garbage. "I hate rats," she said.

"Just be thankful it's not in our apartment."

He must have jinxed them because the following week she saw not a rat, but its close cousin, a mouse, scuttling down the hallway.

"How did it get here?" Spence said.

"The way mice always get places. They squeeze through holes."

"Well, we need a plan."

"The plan will be to call Felix." It was one of the benefits of a full-service building. The superintendent killed your mice for you.

But Spence insisted on killing the mouse himself.

"You want to lay traps?"

"I'm going to catch it with my own two hands."

She thought he was joking, but the next day, she found him opening drawers and cabinets, looking in the utility closet, burrowing into nooks. He kept the broom at his side, as if he were hoping to impale the mouse.

The next night, she spotted the mouse again, coming out of the linen closet, and she screamed.

Soon Spence was in the closet himself, swatting at the pillows and blankets.

"That's not how you catch a mouse."

"Screaming's not how you catch a mouse either." He was clutching the broom, moving from one end of the apartment to the other, lurching like a drunkard.

In the middle of the night, he shot up from bed.

"What's wrong?"

"I thought I saw the mouse."

"You didn't see the mouse. Go back to sleep, please."

But he had the light on and was searching about the room.

The following day, he saw the mouse several more times. He kept lunging at it—with his hands, with the broom, one time with a letter opener. The mouse appalled Pru—she walked around expecting to see it, which made her feel as if she were seeing it—but more distressing was what it was doing to Spence. She wanted to catch the mouse just so he would stop giving chase. "This can't go on. I'm calling Felix."

"Give me one more week. If I haven't caught it by then, you can call in reinforcements."

But when a week passed and the mouse was still alive, and when Spence, despite his promises, said they should leave Felix out of this, she went to the store and bought mousetraps. She baited two with peanut butter and two with cheese and spread them strategically about the apartment.

"It's not going to work," Spence said.

"You act as if you don't want it to work." Pru herself wasn't sure she wanted it to work; if it did work, she'd have to dispose of the body.

The next night, she heard a snap in the kitchen. She knew what had happened, but just to be sure, she spent the next hour rereading the same page of her book.

Finally, she went into the kitchen.

She put on a pair of dish gloves, and with her eyes closed, her breath held, she dropped the dead mouse into a garbage bag. Then she placed the gloves into the garbage bag, too. Finally, she placed the garbage bag inside another garbage bag.

When she got to the lobby, she moved quickly and deposited the mouse in the dumpster across the street.

Back upstairs, she had a thought. She wouldn't tell Spence what had happened. He would be upset to know her plan had worked. The mouse would simply stop showing up, and before long he would put the broom away. She bought another trap and replaced the discarded one.

Over the next few days, Spence became lethargic. It was as if, without a mouse to chase, he'd lost his resolve.

They went out to dinner at a local Italian place, but he just picked at his food. "Don't think you can fool me."

"What?"

"I know you trapped that mouse."

She started to speak, but he wouldn't let her. "Mice don't just disappear."

"Spence…"

"The trap was missing when I woke up the other day. You went out and bought a new one."

"I didn't want to…"

"What?" he said. "Show me up?"

"Come on, darling. Do you really think I care if you can catch a mouse?"

He lowered his head to the table. "You're right. I don't know what got into me."

"Honey…"

"The whole thing was lunatic."

"The mouse is gone. That's the only thing that matters."

Dessert had come—cannoli and tiramisu—and Spence's appetite had returned; he ate his own dessert and half of hers. His spirits had lifted; the color had returned to his face. Things were going to get better, she was sure of it. She paid the check, and they went out onto the street.

6

Rosh Hashanah came, and Pru proposed that they make New Year's resolutions. "I resolve to be a more patient person," she said. "And I resolve to start exercising." She thought if she exercised, maybe Spence would exercise, too. He needed to get the endorphins coursing through him.

"Here's my New Year's resolution," Spence said. "I'm going to make headway on that book I've been writing."

Pru was relieved to hear this. Spence had signed a contract with his publisher for a new annotated Shakespeare. They needed the money, living on Spence's modest salary and her own even more meager one, siphoning off funds to whatever supplicant came their way: to Enid, to Linda, for years to Arlo. When his agent had sent him the contract, Pru nearly forced him to sign it, and the ink hadn't even dried before he was ruing what he'd done. "It's a book for general readers," he'd said. "It's not real scholarship."

"Real scholarship doesn't pay the bills."

Now he went straight to his study, and not a sound came from inside until lunchtime, when she knocked on the door.

"Leave me alone," he said. "I need to concentrate."

But his computer had gone to sleep, and he looked sleepy himself. His cheek was imprinted with the pattern of the desk. His face had been lying against it.

The next day she said, "How's it going?"

"You're asking about my book?"

She was. But she was trying to do it unobtrusively and, once again, she was failing. When Spence signed the contract, he'd gotten a quarter of his advance, but that had been almost two years ago. "When's your next deadline?"

"Sometime soon, I think."

"You don't know?"

She found the contract in his files, and slowly the information settled on her. He was three months late on his next installment! If he didn't make progress soon, she worried his publisher would take back his advance.

His hands fell onto the keyboard, and on some unnamed document he hadn't begun there appeared a row of Ms, Ls, Ws, and Zs: a hieroglyph of resignation. "There," he said. "That's what I think of this book."

She simply stared at him.

"Don't look at me that way. I don't see you writing any books."

"That's because I didn't agree to write one."

He picked up the phone.

"What are you doing?"

"I'm calling my agent. I'm asking for more time."

But a few seconds later, he hung up. "You don't know me."

"Of course I know you." There was no one in the world she knew better. And there was no one he knew better than her.

"Then you should understand I'm not suited for this. It's taking me away from my scholarship."

One afternoon, Pru saw Phillip, Spence's teaching assistant, walking along Broadway.

"Is everything okay with Professor Robin?"

"I think so," she said. "Why?"

"Something seems off about him." He had bags under his eyes, Phillip said; he looked depleted. Sometimes, when Spence was talking to Phillip and the other TAs, he would lose his train of thought. It had started to happen in class too. "It's bizarre," he said. "It's like he's having, I don't know, an episode."

"That *is* bizarre."

"He's probably just tired."

She was several strides away when he called out again. "I don't know if I should mention this, but his class evaluations have gotten worse."

"How much worse?"

Over the last couple of years, Phillip said, there had been a steady decline. But with the most recent evaluations, the drop had been so steep he thought he was looking at the wrong evaluations.

In the TAs' office, Pru stood behind Phillip while he scrolled through the computer. The phrase came to her, *The numbers don't lie.* She didn't know whose words those were; they certainly weren't hers or Spence's. They'd been trained in the humanities; they believed the numbers always lied.

But these numbers were deflating. There was a drop followed by another drop followed by a plummet, like a man falling off a cliff. "Spence has been going through a rough spell. It's been a hard few months." She shook Phillip's hand, and this time she walked quickly out of the office before he could call her back.

She told Camille what had been happening, and Camille said, "You should take him to the doctor."

"Spence hates doctors."

"They don't have to be friends."

The next night, standing in her nightgown as she brushed her teeth, she said, "I want you to go to the doctor."

"What's a doctor going to tell me?"

"If I knew, I'd be a doctor myself."

Months later, she would wonder why she hadn't realized what she should have, and why, once she did realize, she continued to pretend.

When had she first noticed something? When she'd turned fifty and Spence called her a youthful forty? When he woke up one night at four in the morning and put on his clothes to go to work? At the time she thought nothing of it: people got confused in the middle of the night. How, she wondered now, brushing her teeth, could there be something wrong with a man who so resisted going to the doctor? His very opposition was the proof.

———

One night, she found a letter from Spence's agent left out on his desk. He was a year late on the next installment of his book. If he didn't get the pages in soon, the publisher was threatening to cancel his contract.

"What's this?" she said.

He didn't answer her.

"That's a lot of money we'll be forced to return. Money we don't have."

The next day, she called Spence's agent. "He could use an extra six months."

The agent hesitated. "Every year that passes, that's thousands more students who go untapped."

"I understand."

"The publishing industry has become less forgiving."

"Will you at least try?"

A couple of days later, the agent called back. She had gotten Spence an extra year.

"How about thanking me?" Pru said to Spence.

But he just went into his study and closed the door.

A few months passed, and she realized the extension wouldn't make a difference. "Level with me," she said. "Can you write this book?"

"I make no promises." Again he mentioned his values, the mercenary nature of writing a general-interest book. But it was all a fig leaf, as far as she was concerned. "Can you see this happening?" she said. And from the way he looked at her, staring into the great beyond, she had her answer.

"Okay," she said. "I'll help you write the book."

"You're not qualified."

"I went to graduate school."

He laughed at her, cruelly.

"At least tell me your thoughts."

"I don't have any thoughts."

"Come on, darling, of course you do. What's the next chapter supposed to be about?"

"The tragedies."

"Are you organizing them chronologically?"

He didn't respond.

"Okay," she said, "chronologically it is." On a yellow legal pad she wrote the words *Shakespeare's Early Tragedies*. *Titus Andronicus*, she wrote beneath the heading, then *Romeo and Juliet*, followed by *Julius Caesar*, followed by *Coriolanus*. Was *Coriolanus* an early tragedy or a later one? It had been half a lifetime since she'd been in graduate school.

"I can't do it," he said. The other week, he'd paused during lecture and hadn't said anything for a full minute. There had been a stirring, then a silence, and one of the TAs had to escort him from the room, and another TA took over the class, saying he'd come down with the flu. "I wish it were the flu," he said now. "Something's wrong with me."

This was what she'd wanted—for him to stop pretending, so she could stop pretending, too.

But now that he'd done it, she was stricken.

She stayed up late surfing the web, typing symptoms into search engines, moving from website to website, a rat caroming through a maze, until it was six in the morning and she fell asleep with the computer still on, her head pitched against the desk.

The next day, she wrote a check to Spence's agent for $65,000. She expected him to fight her, but he simply hung his head. On the way to work, she dropped the check in the mail.

7

Sarah's flight was late, so Pru sat armored in her Zipcar in a game of predator and prey with the airport police, idling outside Arrivals until she was told to leave, at which point she circled around to Departures, where she was allowed to tarry for a few minutes until the game started up once more. She spent an hour moving from terminal to terminal and along the Grand Central and the Van Wyck, revolving like the earth around the sun.

Sarah, breezing through the New York night, cantering out the terminal doors and between the SuperShuttle vans and the limo drivers holding up their cards, looked tall as a beanpole, Pru thought. She'd always been tall, but she looked more elongated in her ankle-tight jeans and open-collared shirt, with only the flimsiest of scarves covering her. "Oh, Mom, I wish you'd called ahead. Didn't you know my flight was late?"

Pru shrugged. "It'll be good practice for when you're a doctor. You'll be keeping people waiting for the rest of your life."

As they maneuvered into traffic, a pocket of silence settled over them. "How's the patient?"

"It depends when you catch him. Nighttime's worse."

Spence was asleep when they got home, but he must have sensed Sarah's arrival, because he tilted his head back.

"Daddy, I'm home."

Then he was asleep again, and Pru settled herself in Sarah's old bedroom, with the Pearl Jam and Soundgarden stickers plastered to the desk, carbon-dating her back to high school.

"He looks terrible," Sarah said. "I wasn't expecting..." But she didn't know what she'd been expecting. He had become drawn, the hollows of his cheeks like the scooped-out peel of an avocado. "What's the point of studying medicine if the patient's living in New York?" Out at UCLA, her professor would point at the screen—at the liver, the pancreas—and she would think, *Can't you just get to the brain?*

"He'll be better in the morning," Pru said.

He *was* better in the morning—ruddier, haler—and on the subway up to the hospital he was holding forth on the day's news. He seemed like his old self until, just as suddenly, he didn't, saying, "Why are we going uptown?" and it was only when Pru reminded him that New York–Presbyterian *was* uptown that he recovered himself sufficiently to pretend he hadn't asked the question in the first place.

In the waiting room, Pru sat with her hands pressed to her pocket-book, as if it were a pet she were trying to keep still. Spence was down the hall, in the bathroom.

"Dad, are you okay in there?" Sarah said. "Your appointment's soon."

"Go away," he said. "I'm not coming out."

But he emerged a minute later, looking agreeable, the smell of soap on him. "Okay," he said, "where do I go to humor your mother?"

They were brought into an office, where a physician assistant directed them to sit. She would be taking Spence's medical history and giving him the mini–mental state exam. "It won't be stressful," she said, but her words produced the very stress they were intended to prevent. It reminded Sarah of the phrase *It's nothing personal,* which was always followed by something highly personal and was made more so by the disclaimer.

Sarah's mother described Sarah's father's medical history. Sarah had seen this in attending rounds; the wives knew more about their husbands' health than the husbands themselves did. Now her mother was telling the physician assistant that Spence's parents had had heart disease and cancer, though Spence himself had neither heart disease nor cancer.

"Is there any history of dementia?"

"None that I know of." Spence's parents had died in their mid-fifties, a few years younger than Spence was now. They'd been too young to have dementia. But then Spence was too young to have dementia, too.

"Anxiety or depression?"

Pru hesitated. Spence's mood wasn't the same; neither was his energy. "I don't know if I'd call it depression. My husband gets cold easily, even when it's warm out."

"I'm not depressed," Spence said.

"But you do get cold all the time."

"I'm not depressed," he repeated, but he sank deeper into himself, as if she hadn't diagnosed him as much as decreed it. "I'll tell you what I find depressing. That you're talking about me like I'm not in the room."

Sarah agreed: she found it depressing, too.

It was noon, and her father looked sleepy. He woke up feeling robust, but as the day wore on he deflated.

Now it was time for the mini-mental exam.

"Do you mind if I get him a snack?" Pru said. "His blood sugar is low."

She returned from the vending machines with a granola bar and a can of Coke. But Spence placed the granola bar on the floor, and the can of Coke just rested on his lap until Sarah opened the tab for him.

"Professor Robin, do you know why you're here?"

"My wife..."

"She brought you?"

"And also." He was looking at Sarah.

The physician assistant asked Spence to recite the words *apple*, *penny*, and *table* and commit them to memory.

He repeated the words.

"Professor Robin, can you tell me the month, the date, and the year?"

Spence didn't respond.

"Do you know what the season is, Professor Robin?"

He raked his hands through his hair. "It depends on the hemisphere. When it's winter in the top hemisphere..."

"But in the hemisphere you're in, Professor Robin. In New York City, where you live."

"It's spring, more or less."

It *was* spring, more or less, Pru thought: it was March 3. But the physician assistant just sat there, writing something down.

"Professor Robin, can you tell me the name of the president of the United States?"

With his fists pressed against his chin, Spence had the bunched-up aspect of a Shar-Pei. He lowered his head to the desk. "All I know is I don't like him."

"His father was president, too," the physician assistant said, and Pru's heart went out to her: she was giving Spence a hint. Of course Spence knew who the president was. Just last week, they'd been talking about tax cuts, and Spence had said, *Bush, that bastard.* Now, though, he was stumped, and when the physician assistant asked him to recall those three words, he couldn't remember any of them.

The physician assistant asked Spence to count backward by sevens from one hundred.

"One hundred," Spence said, and then he said it again. "One hundred."

"Keep going," the physician assistant said.

"Ninety-three," Spence said, and Pru was so agitated she didn't realize he was right. But then he said, "Eighty-three, seventy-three, sixty-three," and all the while the physician assistant was nodding, just the sound of her pen marking something down.

Sweat appeared on Spence's forehead, and Pru took a tissue and dabbed it away.

The physician assistant showed Spence a wristwatch and a pencil and asked him to name them. She asked him to repeat the phrase *No ifs, ands, or buts.* She gave him a piece of paper and told him to take it in his right hand, fold it, and place it on the floor. She wrote something on a pad and said, "Please read this and do what it says." She gave him a picture of two pentagons intersecting at a right angle and asked him to copy the drawing.

Pru couldn't watch any of this. He was doing badly at these tasks, and she had to look away.

The first thing she noticed when the neurologist entered the room was how much he resembled Spence. They had the same auburn hair right down to the cowlick, the same green eyes. "Let's take a look," the doctor said, and he examined Spence's reflexes, then shone a light in his eyes and ears. He nudged him lightly, then harder, to test his balance.

He was looking over the results of the mini–mental exam. "He's pretty far along."

"Far along in what?" Sarah said. Pru had introduced her as a medical school student, and the doctor was directing the conversation to her. "He's young for Alzheimer's," Sarah said. "He's fifty-nine."

"He's younger than most," the neurologist agreed. "But five percent of cases…" He looked up at them. "I've seen it in the early fifties, occasionally even the forties."

"Doesn't education protect you?" Pru said. "My husband's a professor."

"If you look at the overall population, it does, on average, seem to delay onset." But they were getting ahead of themselves, the doctor said. If Spence had been seventy-five, he would have said with near certainty it was Alzheimer's, or if not Alzheimer's, then something just as bad. But at fifty-nine, there were other possibilities they would need to rule out first.

Pru tried to include Spence in the conversation, but he wouldn't be drawn in.

"There are other types of dementia," the doctor said. There was Lewy body dementia and frontotemporal dementia, but Spence's symptoms made those unlikely; vascular dementia was unlikely, too. "A brain tumor isn't out of the question."

"A malignant one?" Pru said.

"Possibly. Though depending on where it's located, a benign tumor can wreak havoc, too. The happier news," the doctor said, "would be something reversible." Thyroid problems could cause memory loss, as could low levels of B_{12}. Even NPH was potentially reversible.

"What's NPH?" Pru said.

"Normal pressure hydrocephalus," Sarah said.

"But let's not play guessing games," the doctor said. "We'll do some blood work. I'd recommend some scans too, and an assessment by a neuropsychologist." He lifted himself out of the chair as if from the force of his decision.

———

Pru was silent on the way home, blaming herself for what she'd sub-jected Spence to, blaming Spence for having done so badly. As they entered the apartment Spence said, "I hated that place. I'm never going back there."

Ridiculously, she said, "You don't have to," though she'd already scheduled his next appointment.

There was no consultation with the physician assistant the next time around, just the neurologist, who entered the room with brisk effi-ciency. Sarah had gone back to California; she couldn't miss any more school. "It's pretty much what I expected."

Pru didn't know what the doctor expected, having let her own expectations take over. "How were the blood tests?"

"Unremarkable."

"Is there a vitamin deficiency?"

"His levels are fine." The doctor dimmed the lights, and Spence, who had been wearing an abstract look, snapped to. He was staring at the images from his MRI displayed across the screen. It showed some shrinkage in the brain, but otherwise, the doctor said, it looked normal.

"Normal's good," Pru said.

"Good for some purposes, less good for others. The brain shrink-age, especially in these regions"—the doctor touched his pen to the screen—"that's consistent with Alzheimer's."

Pru tried to see Spence's reaction, but he just sat there, not absorb-ing the words. She said, "So it's definite?"

"You can't know for certain, but given the symptoms, blood work, and scans, I'd be shocked if it was anything else."

Pru tucked her skirt beneath her, trying to recompose herself stitch by stitch. "Spence, my husband—he's not even sixty years old."

The doctor nodded.

"Do you know what an exceptional man he is?" She allowed herself to think this was punishment. But for what? For Spence's success? For his being exceptional?

"Unfortunately, early onset tends to be the most aggressive kind."

"So what do I do now?"

"You try to give him the best care possible. There are a couple of drugs on the market. The problem is, they aren't any good."

She stared at him unblinkingly. "Is there no hope?"

"Over the long run, I think we'll beat this disease—certainly contain it if we don't beat it outright."

"And in the short run?"

"You could enroll him in a drug trial. But at a certain point, too much damage has been done. The brain has been incinerated."

With what little strength she had left, she said, "But he's still teaching."

The doctor looked startled. "That's not possible."

"It's not only possible, it's true." Except it wasn't true, not really. Spence still went to class, but in the last few months alone his decline had been so great, his TAs had to take over for him.

"Your husband has to retire," the doctor said. "Letting him teach is unethical."

"That's for me to decide." Pru took hold of Spence's hand, and then they were plummeting down the nine flights, as if the elevator had been loosed from its cables.

As soon as she got home, Pru called Sarah. "Dad has Alzheimer's," she said. "We need to tell Arlo."

Part III

8

Arlo Zackheim always got wind of things. He didn't have ESP, exactly; he was simply more intuitive than other people. This helped him, he believed, in business and in life. He liked to have the maximum information about others while revealing the minimum information about himself. He listed his phone numbers as anonymous so that people wouldn't know who was calling. Sometimes, just for the kick of it, he would leave an automated email message. *I don't feel like checking email today. I'll get back to you when the urge overtakes me.* But all the while, he was secretly checking.

"You hate surprise," his mother told him once. Who could blame him? His own childhood had been so replete with surprise, the only constant was the surprise itself, starting with his parents' divorce, when he was only eight months old. He was convinced he could remember his parents together, but his father told him that was impossible.

Arlo didn't care what his father said; he'd spent his whole life trying to forget his father even as he yearned for him from afar, and he considered the word *impossible* a challenge. Impossible to hold your breath for as long as he'd held his as a baby, holding it until he turned blue. People spoke about iron wills, but scientists had yet to discover a will as strong as his. He had run two marathons forty-eight hours apart. Two hundred push-ups, fasting for days, lying in a hyperbaric chamber, extreme caving, tantric sex, dry orgasm. He didn't care what his father said. He remembered his parents together, recalled his father saying, "Well, good goddamn," his father, who never cursed, who referred to it as cussing, who called dog shit dog *dirt*. "I hate my father."

"Of course you do," his mother said, good at encouraging that hatred while pretending not to. "Who wouldn't hate someone who abandoned him?"

"That's not what happened." But Arlo didn't know what had happened; he just knew it was more complicated than his mother let on.

"Things are always more complicated," his mother said, "and at the same time they're really quite simple." Which was how his mother spoke, in koans, her meaning as obscure as her gaze.

By the time he turned ten, Arlo had lived in so many places, he had trouble remembering them all. His mother had once told him she wanted to poop in all fifty states. In this way, she was following in the footsteps of her father, a kosher butcher, who had moved the family from state to state, always in search of an underserved Jewish community. If Arlo had been older and more sophisticated, he would have realized his mother was visiting upon him what her father had visited upon her. He would have recalled the words of the prophet Jeremiah. *The fathers have eaten sour grapes and the children's teeth have been set on edge.* But Arlo hadn't read the Bible at that point—or much else, for that matter.

One day, Arlo picked up the receiver and heard his parents on the phone. "What about his schooling?" his father said. "It's required by law."

"The law!" Why, Arlo's mother wanted to know, should she follow the law when the cops were pigs and the district attorney was, too, when every lawyer was corrupt from the lowest ambulance chaser all the way up to the attorney general? Had Arlo's father forgotten about Vietnam? Had he forgotten about the Gulf of Tonkin and the Pentagon Papers and My Lai?

No, Arlo's father sighed, he hadn't. But it was beside the point: a red herring. He was talking about their son's education, and what kind of education was Arlo getting when Linda was moving him from place to place?

"Is that all you care about? Education?"

"Listen, Linda." Arlo father's voice was as steady as his mother's was deranged. His father's very calmness set his mother off. The more placid he became, the more ill tempered it made her.

"I *am* listening," she said. "What else is there for me to do but listen to you? He's getting an education. I'm homeschooling him."

Arlo stifled a laugh. He'd been in and out of a dozen schools, never staying long enough to gain traction. "You have a native intelligence," his mother said. "Now you just have to go out and cultivate it." That it was her responsibility to help him cultivate it never occurred to her. He did have a native intelligence, but he read poorly, which shamed him, and his classmates mocked him for his reading, which shamed him even more.

Soon he started to skip school. His mother, busy at the café or bookstore or arts supplier, at whatever job she'd secured that month, was too tired to fight him. "If you want to play hooky, it's your loss." But secretly she was grateful for his company. So when he said, "You could homeschool me," she said, "I don't see why not."

She would take him to the library, and she would become mesmerized by the rows of books, the little round stickers of the Dewey decimal system lined up like shirt buttons on their spines. "I'm like a child in a candy store," his mother said, but a child who looked at the candy without buying any, because they would leave the library without having borrowed any books.

At the local diner, Arlo's mother would flip through *USA Today* to the micro-flash of news from each of the fifty states. "Okay, I'm going to homeschool you. Tell me which state this is from." But Arlo wasn't good at geography, and he couldn't possibly have known whether the home fire that killed a grandmother and her two grandchildren had been set in Minnesota or Vermont, or whether Arkansas was where the power had gone out, and so he was just guessing.

"Here," his mother said, "explain to me about ERAs," and Arlo, who liked baseball and was good at math, wrote the figures on a napkin.

But Arlo's mother wasn't good at math, and Arlo had to repeat the process, so if anyone was being homeschooled, it was her.

Arlo's father said, "You're homeschooling him, Linda? I'm not sure what qualifies you to do that."

"You know how I feel about the American education system."

"I'm not talking about the American education system. I'm talking about our son. What are you teaching him?"

"Math, geography, social studies, physics."

"Physics?" he said. "You're teaching Arlo *physics*?"

This, Arlo thought, was typical of his mother. She would get caught in the bramble of her deceit, and soon she'd be sounding ridiculous. Maybe it was those very words, *geography* and *physics,* that magnified her lie, but hearing her say them made him cough.

Now his parents realized he was on the phone, and his mother was saying, "Arlo, you can't go snooping around like that," but his father said, "Wait a second, Linda. Arlo, can I have a word with you?"

The phone felt heavier in Arlo's hand, and in the midday sun that pulsed through the blinds he started to sweat.

"How are you, Arlo?"

"I'm okay," he said, but whenever he spoke to his father he realized he was less okay than he'd thought. "I have to go," he said, and as he hung up he heard his father say, "I love you, Arlo," the sound percussing as he walked out of the apartment and down the road, past the gas station and the laundromat and the check-cashing store, the pawn shops flashing even in daytime. If his father loved him, why didn't he come get him? Why did they only spend July together, and a week over Christmas, and a week over spring break? Secretly, Arlo slept with his father's shirt, which he'd filched on a visit to New York. His father would have given him that shirt, but the filching had been important, just as the secrecy of sleeping with it was important, knowing he was betraying his mother by sleeping with his father's shirt.

When he was twelve, Arlo moved with his mother to a commune in Delaware. "Oh, Arlo, all this time we were meant to live here, and I just didn't realize it."

Arlo himself wasn't nearly so sure they were meant to live here. But he adjusted to the commune's routine, to morning meetings and the dividing up of tasks, to long days picking beets and radishes. He enjoyed sitting with the other children in the mess hall, the soccer and kickball games, nights in the gazebo beneath the stars.

No animal products were allowed on the commune, and no sugar.

Some of the commune members were on food stamps and disability. For a time Arlo's mother was on disability herself, though Arlo was never sure what her disability was. Something about a bum ankle, but then it was a bad back; often she used the word *sciatica*.

Soon Arlo's mother was studying to become a midwife. "I'm getting my midwifery degree." She laughed when she said this, perhaps because she hadn't been good at getting degrees—she still had six credits to go at Barnard—perhaps because the commune didn't confer degrees. "It's on-the-job training. Though don't go saying that to the pregnant girls. They might get nervous."

Afternoons Arlo would hitchhike into town, where he would take out his ukulele and busk. "Hey, there, little man," someone said. "Take a look at the little man with his little instrument." Arlo didn't like being called a little man, and he thought his instrument was big enough, but he was happy to have a few dollars dropped into his case, so he didn't say anything.

He wore a New York City subway token around his neck, as a reminder of where his father lived and that he could leave whenever he wanted to. But leaving wasn't easy. There were schedules to coordinate, and his mother needed him.

Soon his mother started to deliver babies. Even now, as an adult, Arlo could still recall the afterbirth, everyone gathering for a celebratory meal, starting with placenta soup. Seitan and soy cheese: he could still taste those, though now he refused to eat them. The commune members grew herbs: echinacea and ginseng and kava and Saint-John's-wort. Men wore dashikis. The word *namaste* was used. There was the smell of beeswax. People walked around naked because it was warm out and the body came in all shapes and sizes and all shapes and sizes were beautiful. The commune generator sometimes didn't work, so there were blackouts, like the one in New York City in 1977, when Arlo's mother had been on a picnic, the lampposts and streetlights extinguished, mayonnaise oozing through her sandwich bag while on the streets the looting had started. But on the commune there was no looting. Years later, Arlo would think there was nothing to loot—they were piss poor, all of them—but at the time he thought what his mother thought: that no one looted because it was all for one and one for all and everyone loved everyone. "I'm happy here," he told his mother.

"Oh, darling, I'm so glad to hear that."

But he'd just said those words because they made his mother brighten, as if a candle had been lit inside her. His mother, with her far-off gazes, cloudy as sea glass, saying, *I need some alone time, darling.* Or: *Darling, I'm doing something for my solitary self.* Or: *It's just going to be the three of us now, darling, me, myself, and I.* Always that *darling* attached like a charm to the strand of her words, allowing her to pretend she wasn't saying what she was saying.

Sometimes Arlo would find his mother not, as she'd claimed, keeping her own company, but keeping company with a man. She'd be sitting by the campfire, her skirt bunched between her thighs, the sounds of the guitar rising with the marijuana smoke.

"I thought you were taking a walk."

"I *was* taking a walk, and look what I found while I was walking. Danny, this is my son Arlo."

"Hello, Arlo," Danny said, and he laughed, and Arlo's mother did, too, and so did the man sitting next to Danny, and the woman sitting next to that man, so the laughter was going around the campfire, like the bong.

"I named him after Arlo Guthrie," Arlo's mother said.

"Well, hello, Arlo Guthrie," Danny said, and now the man on the guitar was playing "Ukulele Lady," and Arlo's mother said, "That's funny, because Arlo plays the ukulele, don't you, darling?" and Arlo had to admit he did.

The year he was thirteen, on his annual Christmas visit, Arlo brought the map he'd drawn with all the states he'd lived in. His sister, Sarah, was only ten, but she was precocious and quick-witted, and she had a copy of the world map puttied to her wall. She had long auburn hair, curls catapulting this way and that, which Arlo detested; he kept finding clumps of hair in the sink. "Can't you clean up after yourself?"

But Sarah didn't deign to respond. She just did what she always did, leaving her hair wherever she saw fit, playing Geography with her mother and GHOST with her father, and before she went to sleep, she practiced her violin and ate a snack of three marshmallows and a handful of Wise potato chips.

Arlo was dizzied by the marshmallows and potato chips, by the cans of Fresca that lined his father's fridge.

"You can bring that food home with you," his mother said. "We'll get you a pouch. Or three extra stomachs, like a cow has."

"But the commune doesn't allow junk food."

"True enough. I guess you'll have to do with your single stomach."

When Pru served pasta for dinner, Arlo would compete with Sarah, whom he thought of as half his age and half his size so she should get half as much food. It was dumb luck that he'd ended up where he was; just as easily he could have had the potato chips and the marsh-mallows and the nice home, the bedroom that smelled of lemon, the washcloths in the bathroom hanging like flags. Life was unfair, but in his father's apartment he would make up for it. If Sarah had two portions of fettuccini, he would have three; if she had three portions, he would have four. He ate as fast as he could because to the fastest eater went the spoils. So when his father said, "Arlo, have you taken up speed-eating?" Arlo just stared back at him uncomprehendingly, thinking, What other kind of eating is there?

Now, as an adult, Arlo could have eaten as much pasta as he liked, but he studiously avoided refined carbohydrates. At six feet tall, he weighed 138 pounds. He did two hundred crunches every morning, followed by two hundred push-ups. His composition of body fat was 8 percent, which put him ahead of most professional athletes. He had become like his father, who had once said that if only he didn't have to eat and sleep, he would get so much more done. Arlo himself got by on four hours of sleep a night. And he was on a restricted-calorie diet. He ate little and he ate fast—little because he was hoping to achieve immortality (mice and chimpanzees kept on a restricted-calorie diet lived 50 percent longer, and he was out to prove it would work for humans too); fast because, though his will was unassailable, he'd never been able to break the habit born from those visits to his father, when, if he ate faster than his sister, he would get extra food.

It was on that trip to his father's when he was thirteen that the full extent of his deprivation settled on Arlo. One night, he showed Sarah the map he'd drawn. He'd lived in nine states and Sarah had lived in only one. "My mother has pooped in thirty-nine states. How many states has your mother pooped in?"

Sarah had no idea how many states her mother had pooped in, and she didn't care. "Here," she said, grabbing the map. "You drew this all wrong. You've got Maine over here where California's supposed to be, and Illinois might as well be in Europe. And Delaware, where you live? You've placed it in the middle of the country, practically in Mountain Time."

Delaware *was* in the middle of the country, Arlo wanted to say, because the commune was the center of everything.

That night, Arlo overheard Sarah saying to Pru, "He's thirteen years old and I'm smarter than him."

"There are different kinds of knowledge, darling. Different ways of being smart. He hasn't had the same opportunities as you."

Lying in bed, Arlo seethed. But he didn't seethe at Sarah, or at Pru. He seethed at his mother, who had moved him like a chess piece around the country. What good was living in so many places if you put Illinois where Europe was supposed to be, and what kind of mother were you if you claimed to love your son but you didn't teach him anything?

On the bus back home, Arlo unwrapped the egg salad sandwich Pru had made for him. She'd given him a second sandwich, too, tucked into a pouch, and he thought of the pouch his mother had talked about, of the cow with its three extra stomachs. Pru had also given him a palmier. "They're French," she said, "though in English they're called elephant ears." Their size aside—they were, in fact, enormous— Arlo thought they looked nothing like elephants' ears, but then he realized he didn't know what elephants' ears looked like. It was just another thing he didn't know, and as the bus passed from New Jersey into Pennsylvania, his hatred for his mother grew and grew and he hoped she wouldn't be there to greet him.

But when he got to the station, she was at the front of the line, such eagerness across her face he thought she might asphyxiate him. "Arlo!"

He hated hearing his name like that, hated being named after Arlo Guthrie. At Barnard, his mother would leave class early to stand in line at the Bitter End. That was why she'd dropped out of college, to follow Arlo Guthrie, the way people were starting to follow the Grateful Dead. She was the original Deadhead, his mother liked to say, though what she really was was an Arlo-Guthrie-head. What a strange, improbable couple his parents had been. He'd once asked his mother how she and his father had ended up together, and she said, "How does anyone end up together? You're young and you fall in love. I'll tell you one thing, though. Don't go marrying your college sweetheart. It's like driving while impaired."

One day, when Arlo was fifteen, his mother said, "We're leaving the commune. It's time to move on."

"Why?" When he'd first gotten to the commune he'd been unhappy, but now that he'd lived there for three years, it was home to him.

A few days later, Arlo heard a rumor that his mother was being kicked out. Something had gone wrong at a commune member's birth. An umbilical cord noosed around a baby's throat: oxygen loss, a heart rate plummeting. Brain damage, people were saying: the child would be debilitated for life. "Did something happen to a baby you delivered?"

"Oh, Arlo, that's just awful. Why in the world would you say that?"

"Did it?"

"Do you know how many babies I've delivered? I did the best I could with the training I had."

"So it's true." But there were tears in his mother's eyes, and he knew he had to stop talking.

When he spoke again he said, "I want to go live with my father."

"What makes you think your father wants to live with you?"

"I just do."

Arlo was right. The timing was good, his father said. It was June, and this way, Arlo could get settled in New York before the school year started.

"Can I give you some advice?" his mother said. "Don't go burning bridges."

As he watched his mother put her clothes in a suitcase, Arlo thought he was destined to live out his life this way, standing there once more while his mother packed her bags, poised between comprehension and incomprehension.

9

The day he moved in, Arlo's father and stepmother took him straight to Macy's, where he was allowed to lie down on whatever bed he chose. The beds were covered with quilts, and there was something called a bed skirt and something called a dust ruffle. *Should it be this one?* Arlo thought, lying down on a bed. *Should it be that one?* He'd never chosen a bed before, and in moving into his father's apartment, he was being revealed as a fraud, and this was just the first example of his fraudulence.

"We don't have all day," Sarah said.

"We have as long as Arlo needs," their father said.

Finally, Arlo chose the bed he was lying on. He was just happy the test was over.

"Okay," Pru told the clerk, "wrap it up," and for an instant Arlo thought they'd be carrying the bed home, before realizing that, of course, it would be put on a truck.

Arlo's new bedroom had been his father's study, but all that remained were the computer and printer. Pru would knock when she needed to print, but Sarah would enter unannounced, until Pru said, "Sarah, honey, you have to knock," and there emerged from Sarah the faintest of snorts, and Arlo allowed himself to think she was simply breathing heavily. "I don't care if she knocks. Privacy isn't important to me." He'd been living on the commune, where no one knocked, mostly because there was nowhere to knock.

Used to sleeping in the gazebo, Arlo slept with his door open, listening for the sounds of his new family and the noises that came through the open window: a taxi honking on 73rd Street, a woman yodeling in

Central Park. But as the weeks passed, he started to close his door at night. Maybe he liked privacy, after all.

July 4th came, and he watched the fireworks from the roof of his new building. One afternoon, Pru took him to Coney Island, where he got a Nathan's hot dog and went on the rides. He tried to convince her to join him on the Cyclone, but she said, "Not on your life, Arlo. You go get nauseated for both of us." So he rode the roller coaster on his own, and what remained of his hot dog flew off during the ride, and the rest of his hot dog, already in his stomach, nearly catapulted out of him.

The next day, he took the subway to the East Village, and though he was underage, he sneaked into a club. The day after that, he went to the Statue of Liberty, and on the morning of July 14 his father said, "Happy Bastille Day, Arlo," and Arlo, having no idea what Bastille Day was, said, "Yes, okay, sounds good to me," before he finally said, "You too."

One morning, Arlo said, "Do you know what Mom told me when I said I was moving here? She said, 'What makes you think your father wants to live with you?'"

"Oh, Arlo, of course I want you to live with me."

"Then why didn't you ask me sooner?"

His father hesitated.

"Is it because of Pru?" Arlo's mother was always saying that Pru had stolen his father from her.

"Actually, it was Pru who suggested it."

"Then what took you so long?"

Arlo's father didn't know what to say. After he and Linda divorced, she would write him with requests for money. Money wasn't worth fighting over; nothing was less important in the world. But Linda's requests were for much more than child support, and it was money he didn't have. "It's pure spite," Pru said once. "She just wants to bleed us." One time, in a fit of pique, Pru said, "Sometimes I wish Arlo hadn't been born. At least then we wouldn't have to deal with Linda."

She immediately apologized, but Spence remembered her words. Not counting those first eight months, he'd spent less than two years total with Arlo. How did you take care of a fifteen-year-old? *Did* you take care of a fifteen-year-old? Less than two years out of fifteen: he didn't know his own son.

Arlo called his mother in Chicago, where she was sleeping on a friend's couch. She'd been having a hankering for a bigger city; she thought the anonymity would do her good. "Oh, Arlo, it's so wonderful to hear from you. I haven't been this happy in months."

"Then why didn't you call me?" Arlo thought he could hear voices through the phone, the sound of something banging. "How's Chicago?"

"Not as windy as advertised, but then it's only July."

"And the anonymity?"

"Too much anonymity and a person gets lost."

Arlo knew what she meant. He'd never appreciated the phrase *packed like sardines,* but when he took the ferry to the Statue of Liberty, he'd had a boaty, nauseated feeling, as if he were being fished out of New York Harbor. When he got back to the city, he took the subway to Penn Station, where he stood in front of the information booth, then did the same at Grand Central, where, at five o'clock, the terminal was as busy as a wasp hive. He thought if he went to all the busy places at once, New York would come to seem more manageable. But if anything, he felt the opposite, that Grand Central and Penn Station were all New York was and movement was the city's resting point. Standing in Grand Central, he thought he could park himself there for months at a time and not see anyone he knew. As he took the subway back uptown, he grew convinced that his father and step-mother had disappeared. Even as he stepped into the elevator, he worried that someone had changed the locks and the only people he would know would be the Hansons from across the hall, and the doorman, Maurice, who stood sentinel in front of the building, as immobile as a guard outside an embassy. So when he found Pru in the kitchen, his father in the living room reading a book, he was so relieved he had to stop himself from saying, *Thank God you're still here.*

"I went to a Cubs game yesterday," his mother said.

"I didn't know you liked baseball." That morning at the diner, when his mother had asked him about ERAs, her mind had veered off a minute into their lesson.

"Oh, Arlo, I wasn't going to tell you this."

"Is something wrong?" Arlo was suddenly convinced his mother was sick—she was dying—and that was why she hadn't called him.

"Actually, it's the most wonderful news. I've met someone."

"A man?"

"His name is Oliver and he's from London. We've been spending all our time together."

"That's nice," Arlo said, but he could hear his own insincerity.

"I think I'm in love with him."

What did that mean? Love was something that enveloped you, and if you had to think about it, the feeling was counterfeit.

"And the sad thing is he's going back to London in a few weeks."

"That's too bad," Arlo said, but again he sounded dishonest. The men came and the men went, and as soon as he'd accommodated to one, it was time to accommodate to the next one.

"And do you want to know the happy thing? Oliver asked me to come with him." Oliver was an attorney, his mother said, and he had a son, Victor, who was Arlo's age, and a daughter, Penelope, who was two years younger.

"You've just met him," Arlo said, "and you're already moving to London with him? You're moving all the way across the world with someone I don't know?"

"You'll get to know him," his mother said. "And London isn't all the way across the world. I could be in London right now, and you wouldn't even realize it."

Maybe his mother *was* in London right now and this was the next news she would lower on him. "You really work fast."

"Oh, Arlo, that's a terrible thing to say. I had a feeling you wouldn't take this well."

"How would you like me to take it?"

"You could be happy for me. I always try to be happy for you." She was quiet for a moment. "You set things in motion, Arlo. You couldn't have expected me to wait around."

So his mother was moving to London because he'd chosen his father.

———

Those first few weeks, Arlo's father would come into Arlo's bedroom at night and watch him sleep.

One night Arlo said, "Why do you sit there in the dark?"

"Because I'm amazed you're here. I used to watch you sleep when you were a baby."

The next day his father said, "It's so bare in your room. Why don't you decorate the walls?"

Maybe it was because he believed he was a squatter, and so it was best not to leave a mark.

His father took him to a print shop, and a week later the prints arrived, one of Ernie Banks—Arlo thought of his mother watching the Cubs—the other of the Sex Pistols.

"Ernie Banks I know, but who are the Sex Pistols?"

Arlo was surprised his father even knew Ernie Banks; no one knew less about popular culture than his father. "The Sex Pistols are a punk rock band."

"I see," his father said, though he didn't seem to.

The next night, Sarah heard a commotion in Arlo's room. Their father was by the dresser, lining up bowls of ice cream. "We're having a party," he said. "Arlo and I are making up for lost time."

The night after that, Sarah heard noises: the percussing of objects, the pounding of walls. "What's going on in there?"

"Dad and I are having a pillow fight."

"Oh, I bet."

But the next day, when she asked him about this, her father said, "Of course we were having a pillow fight. I've never had so much fun in my life."

One morning, Arlo's father produced a pair of handball gloves and set them down on Arlo's plate. "I used to play handball when I was a kid. I could probably still teach you a thing or two."

They walked up to Columbia, where Arlo's father did an hour's work, then changed into a T-shirt and medical scrubs.

"You look like you're ready to do surgery."

"Surgery on you," his father said, and he rapped the handball against Arlo's chin.

They went down to the Interchurch Center, with its wide exterior flat as sheet metal. Staring at the traffic on Riverside Drive, Arlo said, "If I miss the ball, it'll go into the street."

"Incentive, in that case, not to miss the ball."

The learning curve for handball wasn't steep: when the ball came at you, you just whacked it. One time, when Arlo lost the point and it was his turn to give chase, a bus knocked the ball toward Grant's Tomb, and when he returned, his father was out of breath, bent over his sneakers. "I'm just lulling you into complacency," his father said.

His father must have been right, because he was up 8–3, then 10–4, and then the game was over.

But in the second game, Arlo was the one making his father run back and forth, sending him into the park to retrieve his winners.

"Rubber game?" his father said, but he was spent, and Arlo won the third game easily.

When they got home, Sarah said, "Why don't you ever play handball with me?"

"I'd be happy to," her father said.

"Then why don't you?"

That night Pru said, "I'm glad you have your son back. Just don't forget about your daughter."

"Forget about her? She's the apple of my eye." But now that Arlo had moved in, he was all Spence could think about.

Arlo was enrolled at his sister's progressive private school, but everyone agreed he would need time to adjust, so on the first day Pru said, "Go easy on yourself, Arlo. You should cut yourself some slack."

But Arlo would need a lot more than slack. He would need reading skills, the rudiments of world and American history, the basics of biology and geography, the fundamentals of writing. The rest of the students were studying a second language and he was still stuck on his first. Even math was proving difficult because the math he'd excelled at was arithmetic, and his classmates were studying trigonometry; some had already moved on to precalculus.

When his father was a child, he'd been skipped two grades ahead. Now, as if in payback, Arlo started the day in tenth grade and by lunchtime he'd been demoted to ninth. By the end of the day he was in a classroom a floor below, seated among the eighth graders.

"Where will they send him next?" Sarah asked her mother. "Preschool?"

Arlo knew where they would send him next: to seventh grade, his sister's class.

One day Sarah's friend said, "How did he even get into this school?"

"Because I go here," Sarah said ruefully.

"Sibling's prerogative," someone else said. "Once the first sibling gets in, the rest of the octuplets get to go, too. It's good for fund-raising."

"His problem is reading," Sarah said.

"You should buy him *Reading for Dummies.*"

"The problem is, he'd have to read it."

Three weeks after he started at his sister's school, Arlo's father and stepmother removed him from it. They took him to a private reading specialist in a room covered with posters of books, and the results were abundantly clear. "He's dyslexic," the specialist said. "I'm surprised no one discovered it sooner."

Arlo was sent to a new school, for students with learning disabilities, and sometimes he would see Sarah on the bus ride home, and they would nod at each other like vague familiars. "Go talk to your brother," her friend said.

"I have the rest of the night to talk to him. I have the rest of my life, unfortunately."

"So you flunked out of school," she said to him that night.

"I didn't flunk out." But that was only technically true. He'd been told he would do better somewhere else, so his father and stepmother removed him from school. It was like a politician offering to resign: once you excavated a little deeper, not many resignations were voluntary.

———

Every day, Arlo's father would come home with vocabulary words, and Arlo was forced to look them up. "It's different for you," he said. "You don't have dyslexia."

"That shouldn't stop you from looking things up." It was 1992, and Columbia had an Office of Disability Services, which everyone called ODS, but Arlo's father liked to blend the letters into a single word: *odious*. In another decade, Arlo's father would see a true mushrooming of students with learning disabilities, kids who arrived at college with a diagnosis and a doctor's note, who required extra time to take their tests and a quiet room of their own in which to be examined. Arlo's father wasn't a particularly good roller skater, but he wasn't allowed to skate on a special rink. Yet all his students felt entitled to their own rink. Now some hapless teaching assistant was always coming to him with a student who couldn't hand in his paper. *My medicine ate my homework*, Arlo's father called these excuses.

With Arlo's diagnosis of dyslexia, his father might have become more sympathetic to learning disabilities, and in certain respects he did. But another part of him remained dubious. What if Arlo simply wasn't smart? How was that possible? He was Spence Robin, number one in his class at Stuyvesant High School and then again at Cornell, on to Princeton for graduate school, where he finished his doctorate in four years. The youngest English professor ever to receive tenure at Columbia. Intelligence was the answer, and when intelligence left you short, you relied on pluck. With the right teacher anything could be taught and with the right student anything could be learned, and he was the right teacher and his children were the right students. All Arlo had to do was ask Sarah, who would have told him that when she'd gone to the pediatrician for her six-month checkup, her father had asked the doctor if he, Sarah's father, could teach her to sit up. "I'd like to speed up the process," he'd said.

To speed up the process. That had been Arlo's father's attitude toward Sarah, and it would be his attitude toward Arlo too. The difference was, Sarah had an aptitude for school and she'd lived her whole life under her father's roof. With Arlo, there were years of bad influence to overcome.

So Arlo's father set to making repairs. Arlo, at his new school, was back in tenth grade; in a year and a half, his father said, he would be taking the SAT. If his father had mentioned this to Arlo's teachers, they would have said, *Well, hold your horses there, Professor Robin. We'll have to see what comes to pass.* But Arlo's father didn't like to hold his horses, and he didn't believe in waiting for what came to pass. He would *make* things come to pass. So he returned from work with vocabulary words for Arlo. Some were long and hard to pronounce and others were short and easy to pronounce, but Arlo believed they had one thing in common: they had never appeared on the SAT and they would never appear on the SAT, and what in the world kind of books was his father reading that he came across these words? *Quondam*, for instance, which meant *erstwhile*, which meant *former*, and which Arlo would never encounter, on the SAT or off it.

In his father's dining room, so many books lined the shelves it could have been mistaken for a library with some food in the middle. Many of his father's words Sarah didn't know either. She didn't know *recondite* or *hortatory* or *perspicacious* or *louche*. But when their father picked up a flashcard and said *"Adhere,"* she said, *"Adhere* is easy."

Arlo tried to define *adhere*, but all he could say was, "You know, adhere."

His father said, "You don't know a word if you can't define it." In the bathroom, he removed a package of Band-Aids; the word *adhesive* was printed across the front. "They're bandages," he said. "They stick to you."

And the meaning of *adhere* stuck to Arlo. It stuck to him the next day when he went to school, and in the cafeteria at lunch.

But that night, when Sarah found him alone, she said, "You didn't know *adhere*, you moron."

"It means *stick to*, you little cunt!"

"You've been tough on Arlo," Pru said one night. "How about going easier on the vocabulary lessons?"

Spence wanted to go easier; he just didn't know how. All his life, he'd made a virtue of self-reliance. When he was a boy, his father worked long hours at the shoe factory, his mother at the grocery checkout; the rest of the time they were leafleting for the Party, going to meetings, helping the workers rise up. "You take care of yourself," his mother told him one day. She was going out for just an hour, but those might as well have been the last words she ever said to him, the proclamation she left him with for the rest of his life.

He woke up one day with a subnormal temperature, and he put the thermometer on the radiator so his temperature would rise. It did rise: the thermometer exploded. His parents were furious, but he would have done anything not to miss school. After Enid's accident it was even worse, and the dark halls of Stuyvesant were his only refuge.

Now, when he looked at Arlo, he was reminded of Enid: the same bullheadedness, the same impetuousness, the same waywardness, the same rage. Arlo sneaked out one night and slept in Central Park.

"Do you know how dangerous that was?"

"I'm not afraid of anything."

But this only made Spence more afraid, just as he was afraid when Arlo struggled at school, the very thing he'd been good at.

There were advantages, Arlo thought, to being at his new school. He was back in tenth grade, back among fifteen-year-olds. And he was at the top of his class. But there were disadvantages too. He'd been diagnosed—branded was how he thought of it—and when he saw THE QUINCY SCHOOL FOR THE SPECIAL CHILD above the entrance, he knew *special* was a euphemism, just as *jolly* meant fat and *sweet* meant unattractive and *articulate* meant surprisingly so.

In class, he read sounds in isolation, then combined sounds into syllables and syllables into words. The lessons were as organized as meals at a mess hall. Vowels and consonants, diphthongs and digraphs: only once he'd learned those did he advance to roots, prefixes, and suffixes. His teacher would show him the letter *A,* and he would name the letter, say its sound, and write it in the air. She would write *handkerchief,* then pass him a handkerchief, and he would say *handkerchief* and spell it and hold it and even smell it, and the word would get lodged in him. He had an excellent memory, and when he set his mind to something, no one worked harder than he did. He thought of his mother's words, *You have a native intelligence.* In the nethermost regions of his mind, he allowed himself to believe he was smart.

But when his father came home with his vocabulary words, Arlo thought he was just fooling himself. Even now, as an adult, Arlo dreamed about his father quizzing him on vocabulary, would wake up in his townhouse in Georgetown to his father saying, *"Contentious, dilate, phrenology, concupiscent, peremptory, scintillate, temerity, wherewithal,"* the sound of these words, whose meanings he now knew—he'd made sure of it—scrolling across his mind, the sound of them and the sight of them following one after the other like sheep jumping over a fence while he tried to count them.

Sometimes after school, Arlo would stop by his father's office. Those were the happiest times, when he had his father to himself. "Butchy!" his father said, and Arlo would sit there, doing his homework.

"I have an idea," his father said one day. He was teaching an evening class that semester; Arlo could do his homework in the back of the auditorium while his father lectured up front.

One night his father said, "Hold on, class. I have an announcement to make. Arlo, would you please stand up?"

Arlo was so startled he dropped his homework on the floor.

"Everybody, this is my son, Arlo Zackheim. He'll be sitting in on class this term."

One of the students started to clap, and another student followed. Soon the applause spread across the room.

"Oh, God," Arlo said as they left the auditorium. "That was so embarrassing." But he wasn't embarrassed, not really, and when his father said, "I wanted my students to know who you are," he swelled.

But on the subway home, he felt as if the air had been squeezed out of him.

That night he said, "Why do you call me *Butchy*?"

"It's what my father called me when I was growing up."

"Why?"

"I have no idea. I lived with him for years, but I never got to know him."

"What was his name?"

"In Yiddish it was Shmulik, but people called him Sam. I wanted to name you after him, but your mother insisted on Arlo."

The next day, Arlo called his mother in London and told her he was changing his name to Sam. He expected her to be hurt, but she said, "That's fine with me, darling. A person gets to choose how he wants to be called."

"I want to change my name legally."

"Then have Dad take you to City Hall."

He felt defeated by her willingness. Changing his name wouldn't change anything, just as living with his father wouldn't change anything. His father had said they were making up for lost time, but that wasn't possible.

One night, when Pru asked him to clear the table, Arlo said, "Well, that's a pain in the ass."

"*Neck* would be fine," his father said.

Ass, neck: what difference did it make? He would speak the way he wanted to. At sixteen, he would fart in front of his father, which his father didn't call *farting* but *passing gas,* and he would walk around the apartment naked, as if he were still on the commune. He liked to curse, and to use words that, while not technically curses, were, in his father's parlance, *off-color.* Words like *jizm, blunt, spliff, spunk, leak, dump,* and *hurl. Épater le bourgeois,* Arlo might have said, but he didn't know French; he was having enough trouble with English. As an adult, he still didn't know French, but his knowledge ranged wide and deep—he'd spent his whole life compensating—and he certainly knew *bourgeois,* which, like it or not, his father was. You could call yourself a Communist, but you weren't a Communist when you had tenure at Columbia and you owned an apartment on the Upper West Side.

Jizm, blunt, spliff, spunk, leak, dump, and *hurl.* To Arlo's surprise, his father didn't make rules about language, didn't say, *Arlo, please stop farting,* didn't say, *You can't walk around naked in the house.* His father was made so uncomfortable by his language and his nakedness that he was rendered mute. The most he could say was *Neck would be fine,* forced to turn away in embarrassment.

Tuesdays and Thursdays, Arlo had soccer after school, so the family went back to how it used to be. Sarah and her parents would go out for dinner; at the end of the meal she would delay, ordering coffee and dessert. Sometimes Camille would come along, too. It didn't bother Sarah that Camille was there: just as long as Arlo wasn't with them. But once she got home he was back, his cleats scattered across the floor, spreading his stench throughout the apartment.

Her parents had inherited a car from her grandmother, and her father moved it every night, in deference to alternate-side-of-the-street parking. Now that Arlo had moved in, it was her time alone with her father. She enjoyed being his copilot, enjoyed seeing who could find the first parking spot. "Down Columbus," she would say. "Over on Seventy-fourth." And there it would be, as if waiting for them to claim it.

One night, the car got sideswiped on Central Park West and ended up accordioned to a park bench; thankfully, no one was hurt. The crash was a blessing in the end: her parents collected the insurance and her father didn't have to move the car at night. But she missed their trips together. Her father must have missed them, too, because a few weeks later, with the car decaying in some heap, he said, "How about we take the car for a stroll," and they went out, taking the route they'd always taken, only on foot this time, her father asking which way they should turn, Sarah saying, "I'm thinking Seventy-fourth Street, I have a feeling it's Seventy-fourth Street tonight."

But when they got home Arlo was there, and her mother was helping him with his grammar homework.

"Do you even know I'm alive?" Sarah said.

"Sweetie, come on."

"He's not even your son, and you act like he's your child and I'm not. I hate him! I wish he hadn't been born!"

———

Secretly, though, Sarah was starting to like Arlo. He was good at math, and when she wasn't fighting with him, she was asking him for help with her math homework. A friend of hers said, "I think your brother might be a secret genius."

Their father was good at math, too, but he was contemptuous of money. "You mean you can go to school for that?" he'd once asked the dean of the Business School. Arlo, on the other hand, had saved the commune several thousand dollars by having them buy dairy whole-sale, and on football Saturdays he'd rented parking spaces at the local college and leased them out to visiting fans. Now, in New York, he bought boxes of doughnuts and sold them individually to his class-mates. He knocked on the doors of the neighbors' brownstones, offer-ing to shovel their snow. Then he hired his friends to do the job and skimmed a fee off the top. "You could make money, too," he told Sarah.

"How? By selling lemonade?"

It was winter, he said, so hot chocolate would be better. And cookies. He returned from the store with Pepperidge Farm Mint Milanos and laid them out on napkins with the words CELEBRATE THE SOLSTICE printed across the front. "Tell me something. Where are the good refu-gees these days?"

"Bosnia," she said.

He came back downstairs with a piece of cardboard that read 20 PERCENT OF PROCEEDS GO TO BOSNIAN REFUGEES, and two hours later they'd cleared $150.

One night Arlo said, "I wish this whole family wasn't dead."

"Who's dead?" said Sarah.

"My grandparents." Arlo's father's parents had been Communists, which made them seem like exotic figures, as if they hadn't existed at all. His maternal grandparents were dead, too, and his mother was an only child. He was bereft of cousins, cut off from his past, and how could he get to know his father if he didn't know where his father came from? Even Enid was shrouded in mystery. Every other Sunday, his father would visit her on the Lower East Side. "Why don't you go with him?" Arlo asked Sarah.

"I did one time, and I had nightmares for months." It was the smell of the nursing home, Sarah said—the smell of Enid herself: ammonia and pickles, as if she'd been brined. Now Sarah had a phobia. She was terrified to go to a nursing home.

But Arlo wasn't terrified. "Why don't you take me there?" he asked his father.

"Maybe I will sometime."

If Arlo was a genius, then why was he being sent to a special school? And why was his stepmother reading a book about him? The book was about gifted children, and Pru covered the book up whenever Arlo walked in, like a teenager covering up pornography.

Sarah said, "You're the only person in the world who gets called gifted and thinks it's an insult."

So that was another problem of his: he was too sensitive.

When he and Sarah played Mastermind, he didn't need the little clue pegs. Sarah would give him the clues orally, and he would remember them from turn to turn.

"You play Mastermind in your head?" Sarah said. "You're not just a genius, you're a savant."

"Would you stop it with the genius already?" What difference did it make if he was good at Mastermind? If you couldn't make money at what you did, it wasn't worth anything. He might as well have been swallowing swords.

This was why Arlo cared about money: he had so little of it. Back on the commune, he would go into town to play his ukulele, but whatever money he earned his mother took away. Every month, his father sent his mother a check. Arlo would rifle through her drawers and find those checks, determined to pay his father back.

Now, when school let out, he installed himself on the subway platform and played his mother's music from around the campfire: "Hey Hey, My My" and "Out on the Weekend" by Neil Young; "Teach Your Children" by Crosby, Stills, Nash & Young; "Broken Arrow" by Buffalo

Springfield; "The Circle Game" by Joni Mitchell; and "It's Too Late" by Carole King. He played "Knockin' on Heaven's Door" and "Tangled Up in Blue" and "It Ain't Me Babe" and "Lay, Lady, Lay," which was his favorite, because when his father heard him play that song he said, "It should be *lie, lady, lie,* Arlo—you don't lay on a bed, you lie on it."

Now, as the subway came into the station and the crowds swelled around him, Arlo belted out the words *lay, lady, lay* with particular enthusiasm, giving the big fuck-you to his father.

Sometimes a dollar bill would get dropped into his ukulele case, occasionally a little more. Mostly, though, it was just quarters, good for pinball. But the quarters added up, and in his first week of busking Arlo made $91.67. His second week he made $57.50, and his third week, thanks to two people who tossed in twenty-dollar bills, he crossed the three-figure threshold: $112 even.

But when his father got word that he was busking, he said, "You need to be doing your homework, Arlo."

"I'm already doing my homework."

"Then do it some more. I'll tell you what," he said. "I'll find you a real job. Something you can do on weekends."

But nothing came of his father's offer. So Arlo went back to busking—he did it secretly now—selling doughnuts at school, sweeping the snow off people's stoops, and gathering his money at the end of the week and hiding it under his mattress.

10

Spring break came, and Sarah was away visiting a friend, and Pru was traveling for work, so Arlo had his father to himself. They walked around the reservoir one afternoon, just the two of them with their gaits in alignment, just their steady breathing. Arlo watched the skateboarders and Rollerbladers, a man on stilts, and a unicyclist behind him: everyone with their tricks. Beyond the trees, he could make out the West Side and, to the south, the lofty buildings presiding over Columbus Circle. "I wonder how many people are in the park today."

"Thousands, I'm betting. Thousands of people and millions of gallons of water. Thank goodness for rain."

"Is that where our water comes from? This reservoir?"

"The truth is, I don't know." It was just as possible, his father said, that the city's water was shipped to Pennsylvania and Pennsylvania's water was shipped right back; with everything, there were inefficiencies. "I wish I knew more about these things."

"About reservoirs?"

His father nodded. "Other things, too." Electric currents, oil heat, elevators. He kept a book in his office called *The Way Things Work.* You opened to one page and there was a picture of a cockpit with all its parts. You opened to another page and there was a picture of a car engine.

Dusk was descending; a firefly landed on Arlo's father's shoulder. "We all have our struggles," his father said, and Arlo wondered if he was still talking about the way things worked or about some other kind of struggle. He had come to rely on his father's calm regard; it made him feel all was right in the world. His mother had taken her allotment of high drama and made it enough for them both. "Do you think about me when you write down your vocabulary words?"

"I think about you all the time," his father said.

"But especially then?"

"Yes," his father said. "Especially then."

"I'm glad about that," Arlo said, though sometimes he didn't want to be thought about. It could be burdensome knowing you were on someone's mind. "Do you think about Mom?"

"About Linda?" his father said, and he gave a sudden, mirthless laugh.

Two men jogged by holding hands, and Arlo realized one of them was blind and the other one was guiding him. "Do you think Mom's beautiful?"

"I suppose," his father said. "Mom's always been a handsome woman."

Handsome, Arlo thought: what a strange word to use for a woman, but then his father often spoke with a lilting formality. Arlo pictured his mother in a tuxedo jacket and bow tie, her hair clipped short. She'd have been beautiful that way, just as she was beautiful now, with her long hair dark as squid ink. "What about Pru? Do you think she's beautiful?"

"All these questions."

"Do you?"

"Absolutely," his father said. "But that's not why I married her. Or what made me marry her is what makes me think she's beautiful."

"I think Pru's beautiful," Arlo said, but then he regretted having said that.

"What about you?" his father said. "Is there anyone in your class you think is beautiful?"

There was: a girl named Katie, whom Arlo would make out with next to school. On the commune, a girl used to kiss him late at night in the open fields, and one time she stuck her hand down his jeans, and in mere seconds he ejaculated. But that wasn't any of his father's business. He felt as if it weren't any of his business either, as if simply to think about it were to violate a trust. He wondered if that girl still thought about him the way his father thought about him when he wrote down his vocabulary words. "I wonder what would have happened if Sarah hadn't been born. If you'd only had me, maybe you'd have fought Mom harder."

"Fought Mom harder for what?"

For me, he wanted to say, but he couldn't get the words out.

"How about we try this?" his father said, and all at once he was off, running along the path in his work shoes. He was twenty yards ahead, thirty yards now, while Arlo stood riveted to the ground. Finally, he went into a trot himself, and it wasn't until the top of the path that he finally caught up with his father. "Since when are you such an athlete?"

"I ran track at Cornell," his father said.

Arlo looked at him dubiously.

"I got practice in the old neighborhood. The Italians and the Irish would beat each other up, and then they'd join forces against the Jews."

They were out of the park now, poised by the horses carriaged on 72nd Street. The ices man was closing up shop. A Labrador retriever, hoping to get some scraps, pulled toward the pretzel cart.

"We should go upstairs," Arlo's father said. "Pru will be waiting for us."

"No, she won't," Arlo said. "She's in California."

"Of course," his father said. "Silly me."

Years later, Arlo would wonder whether this was an early sign. At the time, though, he thought nothing of it. His father was forty-five years old. He was a genius.

They stepped onto the balcony when they got upstairs. Below them, on Central Park West, the trees glowed blue-black. It was eight in the evening, but the traffic was heavy, the cars lined up stern to prow. "You're in pretty good shape for someone who hasn't run in twenty-five years."

"I make sure to stay fit," his father said.

"How?"

"I do these arm raises every night." He placed one hand on each shoulder and lifted them straight above his head.

Arlo did a few arm raises himself. He wondered how he looked to the rest of the city, lifting his arms in the air.

It had started to rain. Below them, a jogger made his way along the street in a yellow track suit.

"He reminds me of your mother," Arlo's father said. "Too cool to feel cold."

"Was she too cool for you?"

"Everyone was too cool for me, but that was the least of our problems."

What was the most of your problems? Arlo wanted to say. He'd asked his mother this many times, but she always gave him the brush-off.

"She'd go out in twenty degrees in just a T-shirt," his father said. "Nose down, blinders on. I have some of that myself, but it comes out differently."

"Was she a good runner?"

His father nodded. "We're both athletes of a sort."

"Do you see Mom in me?"

"Sometimes," his father said. "Maybe. I don't know."

The wind had picked up, the trees bending in supplication. The cars moved along the street, gleaming in the rain like brass.

The next morning, Arlo's father took him to a bookstore. "How would you like to work here?"

"At this store?"

"I told you I'd find you a job."

"Don't I need to know how to read?"

"You know how to read."

He was getting better, true, but he was a plodder—the tortoise—and though in the story the tortoise won, in real life the hare was the winner.

"You like books, don't you?"

Arlo loved books. It was less the reading than the books themselves—the feel of them, the smell of them, even the taste of them: he had half a mind to lick their pages. Late at night, he would run his hand along the spines of the books on the built-in bookshelves in his father's living room.

They found Paul, the bookstore manager, seated in the stockroom.

He was thirtyish and low-slung, with a shaved head, little round spectacles, and the vaguest hint of a blond beard.

"So you're looking for a weekend job," Paul said.

"Yes, sir," Arlo said.

"He lives under my roof," Arlo's father said, "so I can vouch for him. And I can vouch for Paul," he told Arlo. "He stocks all the books for my courses."

"Do I have to take a test?" Arlo said. There was nothing that terrified him more than tests.

Paul pointed to a box of books. "Can you lift that?"

Arlo hefted the box, easily.

Paul placed another box on top of the first one. "How about that?"

Arlo hefted that too.

"Congratulations, Arlo, you passed the test. We'll put you over in Weight Lifting. The books are shelved alphabetically by author. I trust you know the alphabet."

"I do," Arlo said. Fatuously, he began to recite it. Fearing he would forget under the pressure of Paul's gaze, he started to sing the letters. He sang the alphabet song because he was musical, and because he remembered things better when he put them to a tune. He was known to sing passages from his social studies textbook.

"Bravo!" Paul said. "We'll put you in Weight Lifting and Music. And Children's. Pretty soon, Arlo, you'll be running the whole store."

A tabby appeared in the doorway. "That's Crenshaw," Paul said. "You're not allergic to cats, are you?"

"No," Arlo said. He was, in fact, allergic to cats, but he wasn't about to lose his job before he'd even started it.

The next day, Arlo's father took him down to the Lower East Side. At Columbus Circle, they stood on the staircase between the two platforms, waiting to see which train would come first. "I used to do this as a boy," his father said. "Always perched between two levels."

"Better than perched between two cars."

"I did some of that too."

The conductor announced the next stop, and Arlo's father, pretending to be a conductor, cupped his hands over his mouth and said, "Seventh Avenue, Rockefeller Center, Forty-second Street, Thirty-fourth Street, West Fourth Street, Broadway-Lafayette, Grand Street."

When they got off the subway, Arlo's father said, "Rumor has it this neighborhood is where people go to hear a band."

Arlo smiled: he, after all, was the purveyor of these rumors. He'd started to spend time outside CBGB and other clubs. He'd become a devotee of hardcore—and a practitioner of sorts, though it was difficult to play hardcore on the ukulele.

"Needless to say, when I was growing up, I didn't know about bands." His father said these words with self-mockery, but also with pride. For people like his father, Arlo was beginning to realize, what you didn't know could be as much a source of pride as what you did know.

They stopped at a Jewish deli on Essex Street. When Arlo's father was growing up, the Lower East Side had been lined with delis, but now most of them were gone, and the ones that remained were kosher-style, not kosher.

"What's kosher-style?"

"It's ersatz kosher," Arlo's father said, but that didn't clarify anything.

His father, pointing at the tubes of salami that hung like billy clubs from hooks and the dishes of smoked meat behind the glass, said, "It's not kosher, but it's still corned beef."

"What's corned beef?"

"And you call yourself a Jew?"

Arlo didn't call himself a Jew, not really. He was simply himself: he was Arlo. But one time he'd heard the phrase *wandering Jew,* and he thought if wandering was what made someone Jewish, then he was a Jew a thousand times over.

"In that case," his father said, "welcome to New York."

And there Arlo had been, thinking Jewish food was the dumplings at the Szechuan place on 74th Street. "Pork blessed by a rabbi," Sarah had called it, but Arlo was at such a far cultural remove, there were layers upon layers he didn't understand.

He ordered a corned beef on rye and his father ordered a pastrami.

"You're eating that sandwich in two bites," his father said.

"I'm the world's fastest eater," Arlo said, unsure whether to be embarrassed or proud.

They entered a building, the lobby of which was so bright it could have been the headquarters of a sleep experiment. Above the bank of elevators hung the words SCHOENFELD REHABILITATION CENTER. "Rehabilitation," his father snorted. "That's a euphemism if I ever heard one."

"Where are we?" Arlo said. "Is this a nursing home?"

"You said you wanted to meet Enid."

When they emerged from the elevator Arlo's father whispered, "Get ready for FBI clearance." They were asked to show ID, then put through a metal detector and ushered down the hall, where their names were looked up on a list. "Here she comes," his father said.

Arlo was too stunned to speak. Enid looked old enough to be his grandmother. Her arms were like tubes of flesh—they reminded him of those salamis at the deli—but her cheeks were hollowed out. Then he remembered: the car crash. She was just feet away from him, and he smelled her, salty as herring. She just looked at him and looked at him.

"Baby," Enid said. Forty-five years later, she still called Arlo's father that.

"I've brought someone to meet you," Arlo's father said. "Enid, this is my son, Arlo."

Enid seemed confused.

"Not from Pru," his father said. "From Linda, my first wife. This is Arlo," he repeated. "I've told you about him."

Arlo wondered whether this was true.

His sister was afraid of nursing homes, but Arlo wasn't afraid. He was overcome, instead, by a quiet awe. This is my aunt, he thought. Except for his father, mother, and sister, he'd never met a blood relative in his life.

Enid was clutching a small implement. "That's Enid's transistor radio," the attendant said, and Arlo thought of his own transistor radio, which he'd listened to with his mother in Maine, the Red Sox announcer doing the play-by-play.

But it was music, not sports, Enid listened to. A Yiddish broadcast came on, and a calm settled over Enid, and she started to sing. She had a lovely voice, which startled Arlo. Then he felt embarrassed for being startled, for thinking that if you were mentally impaired you couldn't sing.

"Sing with me, baby brother," Enid said, and Arlo's father, who wasn't musical, did his best to sing along. Seated between Enid and his father, Arlo felt as if he were stuck between two radio stations and he was being delivered both the music and the news.

The attendant asked if he wanted some lemonade.

"I'd like some lemonade," Enid said, but the attendant wouldn't give her any because sugar made her agitated and didn't interact well with her medications.

"Where do you live?" Enid asked him.

"In New York City," Arlo said. He felt as if he were being asked this by someone who didn't herself live in New York City, and he had to explain what New York City was.

Now the attendant was asking him what he wanted to be when he grew up.

"Rich," he said.

The attendant laughed. "Who doesn't?"

The difference was, the attendant was working in a nursing home, and he wasn't going to work in a nursing home. Living with his father, he had his own bedroom with a lock on the door, and he was being given a small allowance and he was starting a part-time job. But that just made things worse. He'd gotten a taste of the good life, and now he wanted more of it.

"You have a wonderful voice," the attendant said.

"Thank you," Arlo said, though he'd only been humming.

A Yiddish polka came on, and Enid took his hand. She wanted to dance the polka with him.

Arlo didn't know the Yiddish polka. He didn't know the polka in any language. He didn't even know what a polka was. He wasn't a good dancer; he moved most effectively with a ball in his hands. But the only thing in his hands was Enid, his lumpish, blundering aunt, and he was afraid she would collapse beneath him. The polka was supposed to be fast, probably like the fox trot, though he didn't know that either. The only thing he knew was the waltz, which he'd seen danced in old black-and-white movies and which his mother had taught him, saying, "Go ahead, darling, you're the man, you take the lead."

Arlo led Enid around in a haphazard box step while the Yiddish music galloped past them.

"Bravo!" the attendant called out, and Arlo's father said, "Bravo!"

Enid bent over and kissed Arlo's hand. He started at the touch of her lips, brittle as onion skin.

He stood in the hallway while his father kissed Enid goodbye. A visitor had arrived for someone else, and Arlo heard the words *authorized guest*. Enid must have had authorized guests, too. But then he realized it was just his father, the only guest Enid ever had, his father who arrived every other Sunday with the solemn duty of a churchgoer.

On the subway home, Arlo's father was silent. Grand Street to Broadway-Lafayette to West 4th Street to 34th Street to 42nd Street to Rockefeller Center to 7th Avenue to Columbus Circle. It was the route Arlo's father had taken out of the Lower East Side.

"I'm just thinking about Enid," his father said. "And my parents. It makes me sad every time I go back."

Arlo thought of something Pru had once said, how his father was more fragile than he let on.

"Do you think I should visit her more often? Is every other week enough?"

Arlo shrugged: he didn't know how often was enough.

"I could go every week. I could go every day if it made a difference."

The conductor's voice sputtered through the feedback. A deaf man, handing out business cards, trundled down the aisle.

"I'm always saying that before the accident Enid and I were close."

"Were you?"

His father shook his head. "A lot of siblings fought more than we did, but we were on different paths. My parents used to say about me, *Enough naches for two*."

"Tell me about the car accident," Arlo said.

"What's there to say? The lesson to be learned is don't drive drunk."

"Was Enid drinking?"

"She might have been, for all I know. She did a lot of things earlier than she should have, but that wasn't the problem that night." His cousin Stanley had been the one at the wheel, but the other driver had been the one drinking.

"Who's Stanley?" Arlo said.

"My mother's sister's son."

"Where is he now?"

"In New Jersey. I haven't seen him in years. What happened that night tore up two families. Three, probably, if you count the drunk driver, but it's hard to care about him."

11

A family reunion? When Arlo mentioned the idea, Sarah said, "There's nobody to have a reunion with."

"What about Stanley?"

"Who?"

"Dad's cousin." Which made him Arlo's cousin, too. They were headed now to Fort Lee, where Stanley and his wife Karen lived.

"This is crazy," Karen said when Arlo's father got out of the car. "I don't think we've seen you since our wedding."

In the foyer, a dachshund rubbed against Arlo's leg, but Arlo was too distracted to notice. He was focused on Stanley, who had the same tuft of auburn hair as his father, the same lean body, the same long, straight nose as if it had been cut with a plane. Arlo had expected a small gathering, but there must have been forty people in the dining room, milling about in the chandelier light. "Are all these people our cousins?"

"If they are," Sarah said, "they're distant cousins."

It was strange seeing Stanley talk to his father. Maybe it was the dachshund, which Stanley picked up and handed to his father, and now Arlo's father wore a startled look. Or maybe it was the tetherball set on the lawn, or the large-screen TV, so different from the TV in Arlo's father's apartment, which was black-and-white and kept in the closet, and which his father called the boob tube.

Sarah returned with a glass of ginger ale. "Some of them do appear to be our cousins."

"And the others?"

"They're probably people's cousins, just not ours." Several of the guests were from Karen's side of the family. The next-door neighbors were there, too. If it had been just their relatives, there would have been no reunion to speak of. It was like a VIP event where the tickets went unclaimed, so it was opened to the public.

Stanley tapped his fork against a glass. "I'd like to introduce my cousin, Arlo Zackheim. Arlo, would you please stand up?"

Arlo was already standing up. He stepped forward.

"It was Arlo's idea to hold this event. I want to thank you for making this happen."

"You're welcome," Arlo said.

"Would you like to say a few words?"

Arlo stepped forward again. If he kept on going, he'd walk clear across the room. He thought of the playground game Red Rover. *Red rover, red rover, let Arlo come over.* "Well, all right," he said. "Thank you. Thank you for coming. I didn't know I had so many cousins. It's good to meet you all." He sat down on the chair that was closest to him.

"To cousins!" someone called out, and someone else called out, "Blood is thicker than water!"

His pulse abuzz, Arlo stepped out into the yard. The tetherball pole stood like a denuded tree, and Arlo, in his loafers and necktie, hit the ball and it snapped back at him.

"Aren't you cold?" someone said. It was Stanley. Arlo thought of his father's words about his mother. *Too cool to feel cold.* Was the same thing true of him?

Stanley returned with a down vest. He threaded Arlo's hands through the holes, like someone helping his date with a coat.

"Do you like tetherball?"

Arlo shrugged. He'd never played much, but he was as happy as the next person to swat at a ball.

"I used to play with my sons," Stanley said. He was in just his tie and blazer; he was probably cold himself.

"How many sons do you have?"

"Twin boys," Stanley said. "They're sophomores at Rutgers. We were hoping they'd be here today, but they have midterms coming up."

Stanley hit the tetherball, and Arlo hit it back. "I'm sorry I asked you to speak. I didn't mean to embarrass you."

"That's okay," Arlo said. He explained to Stanley about his dyslexia, but it was clear he didn't understand.

Someone came out on the porch. "We're the only two people wearing ties," Arlo said.

Stanley nodded. "Karen says she wouldn't be surprised if I wore a tie to sleep."

"My father sometimes wears a tie to work, but never on weekends."

"Yet you wear one on weekends too."

Actually, Arlo hardly ever wore a tie. But today was a special day, though he was embarrassed to admit this to Stanley. "What was my father like when he was young?"

"He was smart," Stanley said, "but that probably won't surprise you. We used to call him Professor."

"Everyone calls him that."

"But back then, he was only twelve."

"My father's famous," Arlo said, but now he felt foolish, because his father was famous in only the smallest of circles.

"When he was a kid, your father was king of the handball courts."

"I beat my father at handball." Why was he saying this? He was sixteen and his father was forty-five; it would have been embarrassing not to beat his father at handball.

"I used to have this chinning bar," Stanley said, "and my friends and I would see who could hang from it longer. When your father showed up, he wouldn't let us win. We were older and stronger, but he was stronger up here." Stanley pointed to his head.

"I used to hold my breath until I turned blue."

"Well, that wasn't very smart."

"I was only a baby," Arlo said. Was he trying to show off?

The wind picked up, and Arlo's tie got wrapped around the tetherball pole. Someone had turned on the porch lights, and he noticed for the first time a tiny scar above Stanley's right eye. Maybe it was from the car crash. "Tell me about my aunt."

"Who?"

"Enid."

For a moment, Stanley appeared startled. "Enid was a wild one," he said. "She ran before she walked, she flew before she jumped. She scared all of us, your father especially."

Arlo wanted to know about the car crash. Though he didn't know what he wanted to know. The car crash had happened decades ago; he was rubbernecking thirty years after the fact.

"After the accident," Stanley said, "your father started to act out."

"How?"

"You promise you won't tell?"

Arlo nodded.

"He broke into someone's house and wrote graffiti on the wall. The police showed up and arrested him. For a few weeks there, the professor became a juvenile delinquent."

"Did he go to jail?"

Stanley shook his head. "Getting arrested scared him straight. Ever since then, he's been a model citizen."

Arlo was quiet on the car ride home.

"It was a nice afternoon," his father said. "I'm glad you thought of this."

But Arlo had fallen into a funk. He'd wanted to understand his father: why, sometimes, he was overcome by gloom, why he retreated into work. But he didn't think he would ever understand him. What could Stanley tell him—Stanley, who hadn't seen his father in twenty-five years, not since his own wedding? Arlo should have made Stanley tell him about Enid, but Stanley would have wanted to know why he cared about Enid, a brain-damaged woman he'd met only once, whom he couldn't even have a conversation with. "What did that person mean, 'Blood is thicker than water'?"

His father said, "It means blood relations are the most important ones."

Then why hadn't Arlo met Stanley before? Why hadn't his father seen him in twenty-five years? He wanted to ask his father about having been arrested, but he'd promised Stanley he wouldn't tell.

12

At the bookstore, most of the other employees were graduate students, and they congregated outside during lunch, eating their takeout from paper bags. To save money, Arlo brought his lunch from home, which he ate in the stockroom, hunched over his food like a gigantic rodent. Sometimes Crenshaw would join him, and he would rest his paws on Arlo's lap, and Arlo would grow congested.

A couple of times Arlo mentioned the Yankees, thinking everyone could talk about baseball, but his coworkers weren't interested in talking about the Yankees, at least not with him. Once, when they returned from the Chinese place on 116th, he asked how the food was, and when one of them said, "It's edible, it serves the purposes," he said, "Do they have moo shu pancakes?"

Someone handed him the menu, but the pressure of people watching him made him illiterate once more. He ran his finger down the page—he acted as if the menu were in Braille—and he said, "Yup, they have moo shu pancakes," though he didn't know if they did.

"We can pick you up an order," someone said, and Arlo was forced to say he would like that, though he brought his lunch from home, and also, he didn't like moo shu pancakes.

One time, a couple of his coworkers were shelving books in Literature, and he said, "My father's an English professor."

"So I heard," one of them said, and the other one said, "Getting a head start on things, are you, there, Arlo?"

He found one of his coworkers, lithe and attractive, trying to place a book high on a shelf. As she stood on tiptoe, her T-shirt rode up her stomach, and he caught a glimpse of her midriff, and of her silver bellybutton ring, which shone like a nickel in the light. "I'll help you," he said, and someone else said, "Easy does it, Arlo. You'll get to grad school in due course."

After that, he spent even more time alone. He came to work when he was supposed to and he didn't leave early, but he wasn't as efficient as he'd have liked. One time, seeing him stare down at a box of books, Paul said, "Perseverating over the wares, Arlo?" and Arlo, who didn't know what *perseverating* meant, simply said, "You bet." Another time a coworker said, "Slow and steady wins the race," and someone else, seeing him line up the books just so, said, "Perfect is the enemy of good. Just ask Voltaire." His coworkers ribbed him good-naturedly, but when they weren't doing that they were keeping their distance, which made him wonder whether the ribbing was as good-natured as he'd thought. He avoided the customers because his job was to stock, and because, when they asked him about books, the answers drained through him as if from a sieve.

"At least I'm working with books," he told Sarah, whom he would find at home in front of the TV, and who, sprawled out in an exaggeration of repose, seemed to be taunting him; even her hair seemed to be taunting him, slung casually across the couch. The problem was, he didn't love books the way he thought he did. He liked treading down the hall to his father's living room, but at the bookstore it was all bustle and commerce and the breaking down of boxes; it wasn't like his father's living room at all. And the money he'd been promised was just that—a solemn pledge—because he got paid only every other week, so he would come home most days without anything to show for it.

"At least you're learning something," his father said, but Arlo didn't know what he was learning besides the indignities of a menial job. "You're supporting independent bookstores," his father said, but that, too, was meager consolation. He was sacrificing his own independence for the store's independence, which made him feel like a fool.

One day, his father stopped in to the store.

"Arlo's our star worker," Paul said. "He keeps it up, and we're going to have to name him employee of the month."

As far as Arlo knew, there was no employee of the month, so he took Paul to be mocking him.

"Arlo's told me none of this," his father said.

"That's because he's too modest."

Arlo's pretty coworker walked by, carrying a coffee-table book. Jennifer—Arlo had learned her name—held the book in one hand, and Arlo could see the tendons in her forearm.

Paul said, "I was going to ask Arlo if he wanted to stick around for the summer. I was thinking we could bump up his hours. There would, of course, be a corresponding bump in pay."

"Would you like extra hours?" Arlo's father said, and Arlo, relieved to be a party to these negotiations, said, "Yes, sir."

"I can't tell you how happy I am," Paul said, but again he was talking to Arlo's father.

"I think this is an excellent plan," Arlo's father was saying.

It wasn't that Arlo regretted his decision. It was, rather, that his increase in hours was like his hiring itself: a force greater than he was. His father had wanted him to work in a bookstore, so he was working in a bookstore. His father had told him it was one of the best bookstores in the country, and what Arlo heard was that he, Arlo, was one of the best *people* in the country. His father called someone he respected an *able fellow*, and now Arlo was an able fellow, too.

School was off for the summer, and the weather, which the previous week had been unseasonably mild, was now unseasonably hot. Someone suggested the air-conditioning be turned up, but Paul was concerned about electricity bills. It was a tough go, they understood, working at an independent bookstore. You had to contribute to the cause, so Arlo contributed to it by sweating through his shirt.

His hourly wage had increased from $6.50 to $6.75. This was a nearly 4 percent raise, but to Arlo it was a measly quarter, which his mother used to place under his pillow—his mother, the tooth fairy, who would put on a pair of wings and flutter about the room before depositing the coin in its resting spot.

He'd moved from hauling and opening boxes to shelving books, and soon books were being discovered in the wrong sections of the store.

Someone said, "What's *The Catcher in the Rye* doing in Sports?"

"That's Arlo's section."

Arlo denied having shelved *The Catcher in the Rye* in Sports.

Over the next two weeks, Virginia Woolf's *A Room of One's Own* was found in Home Furnishing, Graham Greene's *The Quiet American* in Spirituality and Meditation, Harper Lee's *To Kill a Mockingbird* in Nature, Henry Miller's *Tropic of Cancer* in Science and Medicine, and William Burroughs's *Naked Lunch* in Cookbooks. "What's *A Farewell to Arms* doing in Military History?" someone said. Soon there were more sightings: Jean Rhys's *Wide Sargasso Sea* in Marine Biology, William Faulkner's *As I Lay Dying* in Death and Mourning, John Irving's *A Prayer for Owen Meany* in Religion and Spirituality, and George Orwell's *Animal Farm* in Gardening. Evelyn Waugh's *Brideshead Revisited* wasn't with the books at all but was shelved instead with the bridal magazines.

The mis-shelvings were Arlo's doing, but whether they were mistakes would have been hard for him to say. Some were oversights; others came closer to acts of sabotage.

Then one of his coworkers, who had been quietly trailing him, caught him shelving Paul Bowles's *The Sheltering Sky* in Astronomy. "Aha!" he said. "We caught him red-handed! *In flagrante delicto,* indeed!"

"I'm sorry," Arlo said. "It was a mistake."

Word must have gotten out, because the next morning he overheard someone say, "Frank Lloyd Wright, the famous midwestern archaeologist," and someone else said, "Rembrandt van Rijn, the acclaimed Dutch botanist," and someone else said, "Émile Durkheim, the great German chef," everyone kicking the words around like a Hacky Sack, not caring if Arlo heard.

Now, whenever anything went wrong on the floor, people assumed he was responsible. "Whoa, dude," someone said, "you pulled a Zackheim," and someone else said, "I Zackheimed up."

If Arlo could have retreated any further, he would have. He was out on the floor as little as possible. The rest of the time he withdrew to the stockroom, where even Crenshaw kept his distance.

One afternoon, he had a pile of books at his feet and a cup of coffee on the chair beside him. It was intentional, even as he also believed it was unintentional, his bumping into the chair as he went to shelve a book. The chair was jostled, the cup got toppled, the coffee spilled onto the books.

And there was Paul, immediately on top of him. "Jesus Christ, Arlo!" He wiped off the coffee with a paper towel, but there was no point: the books were ruined. "That's almost three hundred dollars in damages. I should dock your pay."

Arlo thought he'd feel satisfied, but the next few days he was jittery.

One time, he saw Jennifer outside the store. "Hey, you," she said. "Don't look so glum."

"I'm not glum," he said, but he wasn't good at hiding his feelings.

"Why should you know as much as they do? When I was your age I was hanging out at the mall."

"My father got me this job," Arlo said. "That's the only reason I'm here."

"Well, good for him," Jennifer said. "Good for you both." She was crouched above the sidewalk, and Arlo reflexively crouched down, too. He could see the customers walking in and out, their legs moving like chopsticks.

"Paul shouldn't allow people to treat you like that."

"Paul's in on it, too." Arlo told Jennifer how Paul had berated him.

"Then Paul's as bad as everyone else."

Arlo agreed: sometimes he thought Paul was the worst of them.

"Arlo, you're sweet, you know that?" Jennifer stood up. "Don't let what people are saying bother you. Someday you'll look back and laugh at us."

"I won't laugh at you," Arlo said, but Jennifer had already gone back into the store.

The next day, Arlo saw someone who looked like Jennifer walking on the street, holding a man's hand. He quickened his pace until he was only a few yards behind them. The woman swiveled her head. It was Jennifer. She went to kiss the man, and as the man turned toward her, Arlo was startled to discover it was Paul.

———

He was paid overtime to work on July 4th, but he didn't care about overtime. He would call in sick and rollerblade through Central Park, go downtown and catch a band. He'd stick it to Paul the way Paul had stuck it to him, the way Jennifer had stuck it to him, too.

He didn't even bother to call in sick; he simply didn't show up. And when he came to work the next day, hungover from the fireworks and the beer, Paul was in the stockroom, waiting for him. "You have a lot of explaining to do." He'd had July 4th plans himself, Paul said, and he'd had to cancel them.

Paul's plans had probably been with Jennifer: Arlo was glad to have ruined the holiday for them both.

The next week, he arrived late for a staff meeting. Soon he was showing up late every day—fifteen minutes, half an hour, sometimes more.

Finally, Paul called him into his office. "If the circumstances were different, I'd have put an end to this sooner."

"What circumstances? If I wasn't my father's son? I could be scooping ice cream for the pay I'm making here."

"And you're welcome to do that. Häagen-Dazs is right down the block, Arlo. Just make sure to get to work on time. And don't confuse the flavors."

He was angry at everyone now—at Paul, at Jennifer—but mostly he was angry at his father for having gotten him the job in the first place. His father had done it for his own vanity; he enjoyed wielding his influence.

One day Sarah said, "Doesn't your school give you summer homework?"

"It's none of your business," Arlo said. "Do you think anyone cares that you're going to get a PhD?"

"Who says I'm going to get a PhD? I want to be a doctor."

"Since when?"

"Since right now. I'm good at science, and I want to save people's lives." A thought seemed to alight on her. "Hey, Arlo, maybe you can be a doctor, too."

Arlo laughed.

"Come on. We can go into practice together."

"What makes you think I'd be a good doctor?"

"You're excellent at math, and your handwriting is terrible."

Now Arlo knew she was taunting him.

But Sarah insisted she was serious. They could be a brother-and-sister medical practice. Arlo could be in charge of the business side of things. She certainly needed help with that.

Fall came and Arlo had new teachers, who forced him to repeat what he'd learned last year. He hated the repetition, hated the sounding out of words. He thought of that word *mnemonic,* which his father had written on one of his flashcards. He needed a mnemonic to remember the word *mnemonic,* and what was the point of that?

For thousands of years humans had done fine without reading, and during the fall of his junior year Arlo resolved to do fine without reading, too. As the semester wore on and he continued to disappoint himself, he thought of another word his father had taught him, *abdicate,* and he started to see school, to see his whole time in New York, as a well-meaning but failed experiment.

Then it was Christmas, which he'd always celebrated—not in church, of course, but with eggnog and presents under the tree, in the church of consumerism, as his father liked to call it, but Pru wouldn't have countenanced celebrating Christmas, even in its watered-down consumerist form. So Arlo was left to celebrate Chanukah, which had dreidels, latkes, and jelly doughnuts, but he felt that the holiday wasn't really his, that he was witnessing a foreign ritual that wasn't supposed to be foreign, as if he were poaching on his own land.

Christmas Eve came without eggnog or a tree, though Sarah, as if to toss him a bone, left presents at the foot of his bed: a pair of his own blue jeans and a couple of his T-shirts, which she'd pilfered from his dresser and wrapped for him.

"How's your mother doing?" Pru asked him one night.

"Why would you care?" Arlo said. "You've always hated her."

"Arlo, come on."

"At least my mother knows how to give people space."

"What's that supposed to mean?"

"Sarah's thirteen, and you still make her lunch for her. One time, you cut off the crusts on her sandwich."

"It was for old times' sake. I used to do that when she was little."

"Maybe if you liked your work more, you'd hover less."

"I like my work just fine."

"You raise money so my dad can teach. You might as well be making *his* sandwiches. You gave up your career for him."

She started to deny it, but there was no point. Everyone made their choices.

"You still pretend you're an actor."

"Are you kidding me? I haven't acted in years."

"What about that community theater you do?"

"It's a hobby."

"But my dad sits in front like he's proud of you."

"Maybe he *is* proud of me."

"Yet you look down on my mother because she doesn't have a career."

"When have I ever said anything about your mother's career?"

"Say what you want, but my mother never gave up her dreams for a man."

"Oh, really? Your mother moved to London for a man she barely knew."

And she'd moved to other places for other men. But fundamentally she followed her own compass. Which was more than he could say for Pru.

———

The next morning Sarah said, "I heard my mother crying last night."

"Well, boo-hoo," Arlo said.

"You made my mother cry, Arlo. I've never done that in my life."

"Do you know how many people have made me cry in my life?"

"My mother doesn't owe you anything. You're only here out of the goodness of her heart."

"What goodness? Your mother broke up my parents' marriage."

"You've got to be kidding." Sarah called her mother inside. "Tell my mother what you just said."

"You stole my father from my mother."

"That's the most ridiculous thing I've ever heard."

"So you just happened to come along and my father just happened to leave my mother?"

"No one happened to do anything. I was barely out of college when your parents got divorced. It was months before your father told me about your mother. I didn't know about her, or about you."

Arlo just stared at her.

"The only reason your father married your mother was she got pregnant."

"What are you talking about?"

"You were a mistake."

"That's a lie."

"It's not."

"I'll go ask my father."

"Be my guest."

"I'll go ask my mother."

"By all means."

As Arlo dialed his mother's number, his pulse thrummed in his throat.

"Arlo?" she said. He heard a strange echo through the phone, as if she weren't across the Atlantic but beneath it.

"Did Pru steal Dad from you?"

"Oh, Arlo, it was ages ago. How can I possibly remember?"

"Was I a mistake?"

"You, darling? You're the most important person in my life."

"But was I an accident?"

"Everything's an accident, darling. Millions of sperm, thousands of eggs. What are the odds that any of us is alive?"

At first he was decimated, but soon it was clarifying, cool and clear as a brook. His careless, wayward mother paying him no heed. And his father: all those years keeping him at bay. Now it was so obvious, it was laughable: he hadn't been wanted. It was sad, but it was true. And with the truth came liberation. He could leave now and never see them again. He could murder all of them.

After midnight, he entered Sarah's bedroom and saw her lying there, her head lifted as if she'd been taxidermied. And the words came to him: the sleep of the dead. Her hair was in a braid, lying like a snake across the pillow. There were scissors on her desk, just two feet away. He grabbed them. How long did it take to do the deed? Three seconds? Only two? A single snip and the braid was off, the snake's body severed. Just as quietly as he'd entered the room, he left it.

In the morning, he heard Sarah scream. He locked his bedroom door. Then he changed his mind: he would meet what was coming at him head-on.

He went into the kitchen, where Sarah was eating breakfast. She didn't even look up.

Then his father came inside and saw her. "Good God."

Pru came in, too. "My lord, Sarah, what have you done?"

Sarah glanced at him for such a sliver of a second he wasn't sure she'd looked at him at all. "I cut my hair," she said equably. "I've always wanted it short." Then she grabbed her backpack and left for school.

He'd been waiting for his punishment, but instead there was this: no rebuke, no drama, nothing at all. He could have amputated her leg and she wouldn't have said anything. Maybe she was scared of him. She *should* have been scared of him: he was scared of himself.

He'd done a hack job on her hair, so she went to the beauty salon and had the ends evened out. She even got a streak of purple running through it.

At home, she did a pirouette in front of the mirror. This creeped him out. She was only thirteen, but she already seemed like a young woman in a way he didn't feel like a young man. *You're fucking with me*, he wanted to say. *Stop fucking with me.*

Secretly, though, Sarah had told her mother.

"This can't go on," Pru said to Spence. Arlo could call her a deferring wife, he could call her a bad mother, but if she let him chop off her daughter's hair, then she would really be a bad mother. "I'm at the end of my rope. He keeps this up, and I don't know how much longer he can live with us."

13

"I want to go to a club," Sarah told him one night. "Take me to see a band you like."

"You're only thirteen," Arlo reminded her.

"I'll be fourteen next month." Sarah's music taste had evolved and was starting to resemble his. With her hair cut short and that streak down the middle like a zebra stripe, she was looking hardcore herself.

A few days later, he tossed an ID card onto her bed. "I made you legal."

She glanced down at the card. "Oh, Arlo, this isn't going to work. I don't look twenty-one. And what are we going to tell Mom and Dad?"

"That I'm taking you out for your birthday dinner."

On the appointed night, they said goodbye to their parents and took the subway downtown.

"What's the band called?" Sarah said.

"Bad Brains."

A velvet rope lined the sidewalk. The bouncer, a pale-skinned man of about thirty, paced back and forth like an enormous cat. His head was shaved, and he stared at the crowd with barely concealed venom.

"Just look confident," Arlo said.

Then they were in—the bouncer barely glanced at their IDs—and Arlo nodded tersely at his own accomplishment.

He walked up front to listen, but the music was so loud it hurt Sarah's ears, so she circled the bar, away from the amps.

"Are you thirsty?" he asked her between songs. He removed a twenty-dollar bill. "Go get us some beers."

"Now?"

"Why?" he said. "Is there a waiting period?"

She had taken a few sips of beer once, enough to determine she didn't like it. She returned to Arlo with two cups of beer.

"Happy birthday, kid." They clinked cups, and the beer sloshed around and nearly spilled on her.

"I'm starting to get drunk."

"You've taken, what, two sips? You can't get drunk just from smelling the stuff."

"I'm not just smelling it." But she did smell it, too, and the stench repulsed her.

Arlo returned with two more beers.

"I haven't even finished my first one."

"Then you better drink up."

She balanced herself on her high heels, feeling as if she were on ice skates.

"Well, look who's here," Arlo said. "It's Henry and Max." He was already past her, conferring with two boys his age. "This is Sarah," he said. "My kid sister."

Henry was dressed in blue jeans and a black T-shirt. Max, taller and thinner than Henry, wore khakis and a white shirt with a red necktie like a strip of bacon. "We go to school with Arlo," Henry said.

Arlo said, "Max and Henry can't read any better than I can, but you don't need to read to like hardcore."

"In fact," Max said, "it's a disadvantage."

"I can read the word *Molson*," Henry said.

"I didn't know your friends would be here," Sarah said.

"Well, *I* didn't know *you'd* be here," Max said.

Henry said, "We didn't even know Arlo had a kid sister."

"It's not something I advertise," Arlo said. "Boys, it's Sarah's birthday. She turned twenty-one today."

Max raised a dubious eyebrow. "Would that be in dog years?"

"Show them your ID," Arlo said.

Sarah handed her ID to Henry, who handed it to Max.

"Zackheim," Max said, "you're an expert counterfeiter."

"Well, happy birthday to Sarah," Henry said. "May she be legal for many years to come."

As the band played on, Sarah instinctively lifted her cup to her mouth. She felt as if she were playing a drinking game called Drink for Your Brother, and now she was really getting drunk. "Jesus Christ," she said, grabbing Arlo's arm. "It's eight-forty-five!"

"The main act never comes on before ten."

"We told Mom and Dad we'd be home by nine."

"It's hard to see that happening. Unless we find ourselves a helicopter pad. Even then, I'd say the odds are poor."

"They're going to kill us."

"Relax," he said. "They'll be fine."

But when she persisted, he agreed to give them a call. He went out onto the street to find a pay phone.

When he returned, he bounced across the floor to the residual sounds of the music. "They said we could stay out as late as we like."

"I don't believe you."

"Believe what you want."

Woozy and wobbly-footed, Sarah was discovering at fourteen what she would discover afresh at college, when she would like beer only slightly more than she did now, and she would stand at parties, surrounded by strangers, unable to get herself to leave. "You were supposed to take me out to dinner."

"I was supposed to take you out to this club. You've been begging me to go, and now, guess what, you're here."

"That doesn't mean I have to skip dinner. I'm hungry."

"Well, luck is with you." Arlo grabbed her by the wrist.

Outside, Max and Henry had bivouacked themselves on an SUV. It had started to rain, and Max had purchased an umbrella, which he held ceremoniously over Sarah's head while Henry harpooned candles into a cake.

"It's freezing out," she said.

"Embrace the cold," Arlo said. "Make a wish."

She wished the owner of the SUV wouldn't show up. She wished he wouldn't have them arrested.

"Don't accuse my friends of not being gentlemen."

They *were* being gentlemen, but the way they were being gentlemen was so exaggerated they seemed to be ridiculing her.

"It's a Brooklyn Blackout," Henry said.

"Manhattan imports its cakes from Brooklyn," Arlo said. "What has the world come to?"

How jaded her brother was, when two years ago he couldn't have even named the five boroughs.

"Jesus, kid, will you blow out the candles before the wind does it for you?"

Then they were gone, and she was left with chocolate crumbs spread across the SUV.

Back in the club, she scanned the room for an EXIT sign. "I want to go home," she told Arlo.

He laughed.

"I'm fourteen," she reminded him. "I have school tomorrow. I hate hardcore."

"It's an acquired taste."

"Well, I haven't acquired it."

He led her roughly back onto the street. "It wasn't easy making you that ID. It took talent and time, and you haven't even thanked me for it."

"Thank you," she said churlishly.

"Your attitude is shitty, you know that?"

"Fine," she said, and she went back inside and drank her beer as quickly as she could, then drank another one. She would embrace this, she thought, do whatever was required of her. How many beers did she drink? More, certainly, than she'd drunk in her whole life, but that wasn't hard.

It was one in the morning when the last set was over. She barely made it outside before she threw up.

"Up and out of there," Arlo said, holding her hair away from her face. "Clear out the passageways."

"Happy birthday, Sarah," Max said, and Henry, cupping his hands over his mouth, said, "Watch Arlo's little sister hurl!"

"Jesus," Arlo said, "you're a real mess."

She was a mess because of him, but she couldn't even get the words out.

It was two in the morning when they got home. She'd thought her parents would be asleep, but all the lights were on in the apartment. Her parents sat beside each other on the couch.

Her father said, "I hope you know we called the police."

"You what?"

"You were supposed to be home five hours ago."

"Arlo told you we'd be late."

"He most certainly didn't," her mother said.

"Not that we'd have allowed it even if he did."

Sarah started to speak, but Arlo interrupted her. "Would you please just shut up?"

In the morning, she felt too ill to go to school. Arlo felt ill, too, but he knew better than to stick around, so he put on his clothes and left the apartment.

At home, they secluded themselves in their respective bedrooms, knowing they might be pitted against each other.

Sarah was grounded for the rest of the year. Arlo remained scarce, seeming to think that if he didn't meet his fate, it wouldn't meet him in return. But he really just wanted to be left alone, so he ate dinner in his bedroom and slipped out early every day.

One night, Arlo overheard his father through the bedroom wall, talking to Pru.

"I'm sorry," Pru said, "but I can't do this anymore."

"What do you suggest we do? Put him on the street?"

"Send him to London, for all I care."

"His mother won't take him."

"Then send him to one of those military schools."

"What he needs is our love," his father said. "And our patience."

The next day, Arlo called his mother in London. He started to cry.

"Arlo, darling, what's wrong?"

"The things they're doing to me."

"What are they doing?"

"I don't care if I have to live on the streets. I'll run away if you don't come get me."

On the day he left, Arlo woke Sarah up at six in the morning. He'd put a tag on each of his two suitcases, with his name, Arlo Zackheim, written across them; they were his only possessions in the world.

"You're really leaving."

He nodded.

"You can still turn back." She stood before him in her pajamas; the lights flickered overhead. "Mom and Dad said you should wake them."

He knew they had, but he refused to do it. He couldn't endure another goodbye.

"When does your mother come?"

"In fifteen minutes."

"Where's she taking you?"

"I'll know when I'm in the cab."

She took him by the sleeve. "I'll go downstairs with you."

"No, Sarah, please."

Standing beside the elevator, he hugged her. "I'm sorry for taking you to that club."

"I wanted to go to that club. I couldn't admit it, but I had a good time."

"I was a jerk," he said.

"No," she said, "*I* was."

The elevator door opened, and he stepped inside. She hesitated for a second, thinking she might follow him—for an instant she contemplated running away herself—but then the door closed and he plunged out of sight.

Downstairs, Arlo saw his mother for the first time, two years older, a little grayer, calling to him from the open window of a cab. "Darling," she said, "I missed you so." She was still a Joni Mitchell fan, always with a folk song at the ready: she had her head out the window and was singing "Big Yellow Taxi" through the dawn mist.

Arlo could smell her, talcum and lemon and clove. Now the taxi was wending its way through the city, ferrying him through the streets for the last time. Morning was rising, the cityscape was barnacled with light, and Arlo, staving off tears, sat quietly in the cab, waiting to see where his mother would take him, watching the streets recede in the mirror, terrified of what would come next.

Part IV

14

Pru lined them up like hens: a friend's housekeeper who had worked in eldercare, a nanny who cared for triplets, a retired nurse. She wanted someone strong enough for the job, but the first woman, Ginny, was wearing layers—a peacoat over a cardigan—so she couldn't assess her build. "Please," she said. "Sit down." She didn't know what to look for on Ginny's résumé, so Pru made a purposeful show of reading it, even as she felt no purpose at all.

Ginny was in her mid-forties. Her hair was cut in a short Afro, and she had on large, dark-framed glasses; on her forehead was a tiny birthmark like a smudge of clay. She wore post earrings and a dab of burgundy lipstick. Pru was wearing pressed pants and she'd put on lipstick, too.

"Is this the first time you've hired someone?"

"Yes," Pru said. "It was my daughter's idea." But she didn't like the way that sounded, so she said, "But I agreed, of course."

But she hadn't agreed, at least not at first. A stranger in the apartment: it was too close to communal living. And she couldn't afford to hire someone. Sarah had suggested she take out a loan ("Follow my example"), but the difference was, Sarah would be a doctor someday.

Ginny was from Jamaica originally. She'd moved to the States with her husband and young son and settled in North Carolina, where her mother lived. But things didn't work out between Ginny and her husband, and she thought the North would be better for Rafe. So they moved to Brooklyn, to East New York. That was ten years ago, and now Rafe was fourteen, starting high school in the fall.

The job Ginny had quit was with a retired opera singer, a woman sufficiently well known that Pru had heard of her, and Pru didn't know much about opera. A diva, Pru had heard, on the stage and off. Was that why Ginny had quit? If it was, she wasn't saying. She spoke carefully, maintaining a circumspect, reticent air, as if husbanding her own dignity. Her employer, Ginny said, had multiple sclerosis. She lived in Connecticut and Ginny didn't have a car; even with a car, it was too long a drive to Westport. As it was, she had to take the subway to Grand Central and board the Metro-North, and it was ten at night before she got home. "I'm willing to commute, but there are limits."

"It's a commute here," Pru said. "We don't live in East New York either."

"At least it's New York," Ginny said. "Everyone has to commute to work."

"Some of us get to walk." Pru was thinking of when the weather was good and she would hike the couple of miles to campus.

"Oh, I walk," Ginny said. "If I end up working for you, I can take the 2 instead of the C, and then I'll walk from Broadway."

"So you have it all mapped out."

Ginny looked at her strangely, as if to say who in the world interviewed for a job without mapping it out first?

Ginny had once thought to become a nurse. Actually, she'd more than thought of it: she'd studied nursing in North Carolina. "Night classes," she said. "I was a good student and I was enrolled part-time, but even part-time I couldn't make it work. It's hard to hold a job and study."

"And be a parent," Pru said.

"And be a parent." Ginny touched her glasses. "I'm surprised I even made it halfway through the program. I would nod off in class."

"I've fallen asleep in my fair share of classes."

"But did you do it when you were sitting in the front row? And did the professor drop the textbook onto your desk to startle you?"

No, Pru admitted, that hadn't happened.

"Anyway, my nursing classes were years ago. Nursing changes, just like everything else. With Rafe, I was just starting to understand the new math when it became the new-new math. But I do know first aid. And I was recertified in CPR last year." It was good timing, Ginny said, because a week after she was recertified, a man had a heart attack on the subway.

"You gave CPR on the subway?" Pru felt nauseated, but Ginny herself didn't appear nauseated. She spoke matter-of-factly, as if to say this was simply what had happened on her subway ride. "A long time ago I wanted to be a nurse, and now Rafe wants to be a doctor."

"My daughter's in medical school," Pru said.

"The difference is, your daughter's already in medical school and my son's in the eighth grade. He hasn't gotten a single A in high school yet."

"Or a single C, presumably. Listen," Pru said, "I don't know much about multiple sclerosis, but does it affect a person's thinking? Because my husband..."

"The professor?" Ginny said. "Is he not here?"

Now Pru understood why Ginny had appeared uncertain when she entered the room: she'd been looking for Spence. Was it possible Pru was keeping Spence from Ginny, fearing that, if she met him, she wouldn't want the job? "My husband's resting," she said. "But when he gets up, I'd like you to meet him."

"Does your husband have Alzheimer's?"

Pru thought of the neurologist's words. *You can't know for certain.* Then she thought of his other words. *Given the symptoms, blood work, and scans, I'd be shocked if it was anything else.* "Yes," she said, "my husband has Alzheimer's." She hadn't said these words to anyone but Sarah, and to her surprise, she felt relief.

A rumbling came from across the apartment. Spence used to move with such grace; now he lurched like a drunkard.

"Darling," she said, "you're up." She was glad it was morning, when he was most alert. Get the job, she thought, as if he, not Ginny, were the one applying for it.

"How are you this morning, Professor?"

Spence regarded her appraisingly.

"Ginny came for an interview," Pru said. "I'm going to hire someone in case help is needed."

"Why would she need my help? She looks able to me."

"I'm able enough, Professor, but there are lots of things I don't know. You'll have to be patient with me."

"Patience is my forte," Spence said, pronouncing the word like *fort,* which, he would have told Ginny, was the correct way to pronounce it. Pru wasn't so convinced patience was Spence's forte. He'd never demonstrated much patience when, for instance, people mispronounced *forte* or any number of other words they continued to mispronounce and he continued to pronounce correctly. "Do you play cards?"

"Do I play cards? I tell my son he spends too much time on the computer, and he tells me I spend too much time on bridge."

"I don't play bridge," Spence said. He spoke as if this were a matter of principle, but then everything was a matter of principle with him. He was always saying *De gustibus non est disputandum,* but nothing was a matter of taste to Spence, including the uttering of that phrase, which, he believed, should be uttered in Latin.

He was staring at the cross around Ginny's neck. "Darling," Pru said, trying to distract him. "Spence is an atheist," she explained.

"I've met a few of those."

"The Christians are all right," Spence said. "They made some great works of art." He told Ginny about Michelangelo and El Greco, about Rembrandt's famous paintings of biblical scenes from the New Testament and the Old.

"So you see?" Ginny said. "The Bible's good for something." And when Spence didn't respond she said, "The professor can have his beliefs, and I can have mine."

Spence excused himself. He had tasks to attend to, work to do.

"So that was the professor."

"You met him in the morning," Pru said. "As the day wears on, he becomes less alert."

"I know all about sundowning."

Pru hated that term. Though really what she hated was the fact itself, the light in Spence's face diminishing with the day's sunlight. A bad day from six months ago was a good day now, and how he behaved in the evening would, in another six months, be how he would act in the light of day.

"Does he need help using the toilet?"

"Sometimes." She had to remind him to go to the bathroom. He was starting to urinate in his pants. "Is that a problem?"

"It's embarrassing for him, I assume."

"Yes." If things went the way they inevitably would, he would grow less embarrassed. Embarrassment served no purpose, but it also made Spence who he was—modest, fastidious, always taking good care—and now it was fading. He still hadn't soiled himself, still hadn't defecated in his pants, but that would come, too, she understood. "I'm just saying he won't always be so easy."

"I don't expect him to be. But I liked him. He said what he thought. He's a direct man."

"Sometimes too direct."

"He has a sense of humor. And he likes to play cards."

"He likes to *win* at cards."

"I'm the same way." When she was a girl, Ginny said, she would cry when she lost at board games. And she could never admit when she made a mistake; she would trip and fall and say she'd done it on purpose. "Rafe has some of that in him, too. Too much pride, is what I say. He's inherited all my worst qualities."

Pru stood up. Another candidate was coming soon. "I have one last question for you."

Ginny waited.

"Are you strong?"

"Why do you ask?"

Because Spence would need a cane soon. And after that, he would need a wheelchair. Because his caregiver would have to push him over curbs and potholes and up and down ramps.

"I grew up with three older sisters," Ginny said.

So what, Pru thought. She had grown up with an older brother, and it hadn't made her strong.

"We fought all the time," Ginny said. "We scratched and bit. I don't suppose you have a shot put."

Pru just looked at her.

"Even if you did, I couldn't make any promises. It's been a long time."

"You did the shot put?"

"Back in high school, I was an average shot-putter on a below-average team." Ginny stood up. "Okay," she said, "I'm going to show you I'm still strong." She told Pru to get down on the floor.

Pru hesitated for a moment. Then she lowered herself to the floor. She lay facedown like a dead person, and she could smell the rug, feel the fibers pressed to her lips.

Ginny lifted her in the air. She was carrying her around the living room, holding her like a sack of grain. How long was Pru suspended there? Five seconds? Maybe ten? Looking back, she felt as if she'd been held aloft the whole interview.

Then Ginny was gone, and when Pru opened the door for the next candidate, she said, "I'm sorry, but I've already given the job to someone else."

15

Three days a week, Ginny would come in the morning and stand outside the bathroom while Spence was getting dressed. "Do you need help, Professor?"

"No one's helping me get dressed." Through the door came the clanking of his belt and the clomping of his shoes like the sound of horse hooves.

"Well, I'm around, in case you need me."

"I know you're around. I can hear you right through the door. Can't you see I'm in the bathroom?"

Most of the time, Spence would come out properly dressed, but sometimes his shirt would be unbuttoned or his shoelaces untied, and Ginny would say, "Here, Professor, let me make some adjustments." He tried to appear resentful, but Pru could tell it was just a show, and Ginny, too, seemed to enjoy the air of amicable combat.

Spence wasn't really teaching anymore, but so far, the department was allowing him to keep up pretenses. He would stand at the lectern as a sage presence while his TAs did the teaching for him.

In the foyer lay his emergency alert. Pru hated that emergency alert, the sight of Spence with a chain around his neck, like a criminal, or a cow.

"Okay, Professor, on with your ball and chain." Ginny was good at mimicking Spence's exasperation and taking it on as her own. Most of the time he didn't seem bothered by the alert, but when a colleague would visit he'd button his shirt, like a man with a comb-over patting his hair down.

A couple of hours in the morning, a couple of hours in the late afternoon: the rest of the day Spence was alone. But Pru was going to lose

Ginny if she didn't give her more hours, so she hired her full-time, five days a week.

A few times, Spence convinced Ginny to join him for lunch at the Faculty Club, but Ginny was uncomfortable at the Faculty Club, a black woman from Jamaica among the white professors. "It's meant for faculty," she told Pru, and when Pru said, "It's meant for faculty and their guests," Ginny made clear she preferred to eat elsewhere.

One time, seeing Ginny stationed outside Spence's office, a secretary said, "You should go inside," but Ginny just smiled and said, "I'm fine out here." Another time, Spence himself invited her in, but Ginny said, "I don't want to cramp your style, Professor. People will be coming by for your office hours." Once, when Spence suggested she come inside, Ginny said, "How about you teach me some Shakespeare, Professor," but Spence just stared down at the book in front of him, a book, it turned out, he'd written himself, and didn't know what to say.

"Tell me about Rafe," Pru said to Ginny one day.

"What's there to tell you?" At the moment, Ginny said, Rafe was doing his homework. At least, she hoped he was. If Rafe wanted to go to medical school, he would have to work harder.

"He'll have time to work harder," Pru said. "He's only a child."

"If he's only a child, then why is he talking about curing hemophilia?" Rafe wanted to cure hemophilia because he had hemophilia himself. Born a decade earlier, he might have died of AIDS. Now the blood supply was clean. But there was still danger: a trip, a fall, a shard of glass. Paradoxically, hemophilia had served Rafe well: it had made him more cautious. "Rafe wants to cure hemophilia so he can get a tattoo."

"If he cures hemophilia, he deserves one."

"Not if you ask me."

But that was the point: no one was going to ask Ginny, certainly not Rafe. "So when do I get to meet this son of yours?"

"You'll meet him when you meet him," Ginny said, which made Pru think it wouldn't happen soon.

———

But the next day, a buzz came from downstairs. A teenager, rangy and handsome, stamped his feet against the floor. "Rafe's a mud magnet," Ginny said. "Remove your shoes, young man."

"It's nice to meet you," Rafe said. He was narrower-faced than Ginny—he was narrower in general—though his feet were tremendous; they reminded Pru of puppies' paws. His eyes were hazel, lighter than Ginny's, and his chin tapered to a point. But he looked like his mother, the way he held himself gently spooled, that air of self-containment.

"Rafe came to meet me," Ginny said. "I want him seeing other parts of the city."

"Mom," Rafe said, "do you have to talk about me so much?"

"Would you rather I *didn't* talk about you?"

"Probably." A frozen-yogurt card stuck out of Rafe's shirt pocket.

"There's someone I want to introduce you to," Ginny said. She took Rafe into the kitchen. "Professor, this is my son, Rafe. He's come all the way from Brooklyn to meet you."

"I'm pleased to meet you," Rafe said, and there it was again, that lilting formality Rafe shared with his mother, the formality that reminded Pru of Spence.

"I owe you an apology," Ginny said the next morning. "I can't just invite a stranger into your home."

"Rafe's not a stranger."

"In that case," Ginny said, "might he be able to come in the morning too?" Summer was beginning soon, and Rafe would be at a chess camp on the Upper West Side. The camp didn't start until ten, and Ginny didn't want Rafe wandering alone around the neighborhood.

"What about after camp?" Pru said. "He shouldn't be wandering alone around the neighborhood then either." It would be nice, she said, for Spence to get to know Rafe. She had a feeling they would like each other.

———

Now, when Pru returned from work, Rafe would be reading a book in the living room while Ginny was in the bedroom with Spence.

"Is that a chess book you're reading?"

Rafe looked up at her.

"Isn't that what you're doing this summer? Learning how to play chess?"

"I don't read about chess," Rafe said. "I play it." He took out a folding chessboard and removed the embedded pieces from the green felt. "My mother wants me to get a chess scholarship to college."

"Would you turn it down?"

"I'm not even sure there are chess scholarships."

"Maybe your mother's kidding you."

"Then you don't know my mother." Half the time Rafe thought his mother was kidding him she wasn't kidding him at all.

"Tell me something," Pru said. "Don't you like chess?"

Rafe shrugged. "It's kind of beautiful." He examined the chess pieces in his hand. He reminded Pru of a gemologist, those Hasidim in the Diamond District with their precious stones. She said, "Do you think the pieces are beautiful?"

"They're beautiful enough. I meant more what they can do." Rafe grabbed a rook between his thumb and forefinger. "My chess teacher thinks chess is elegance in motion."

"What do *you* think?"

"I think ice hockey is elegance in motion." Rafe had a friend at chess camp who played ice hockey, and now Rafe wanted to play ice hockey, too. In fact, he seemed to want to play ice hockey right now, because he rose from his chair and slid across the floor on his socked feet.

"Have you asked your mother whether you can play ice hockey?"

"What's the point? She thinks I have hemophilia."

"You don't?"

"Oh, I have it, all right. I just don't see why it makes a difference."

"Hockey's a violent sport," Pru said, recalling for Rafe that old joke: *I went to a fight and a hockey game broke out.*

"I wonder if there's ever been a chess fight." Rafe had a knight and a bishop squaring off on the board, one on a light square, the other on a dark square, assessing each other like action figures.

"So your ice-hockey-playing friend—does he also have a mother who makes him go to chess camp?"

"Everyone has a mother who makes them go to chess camp. If there weren't mothers making their kids go to chess camp, there wouldn't be any chess camps." Rafe paused. "The problem is, I think I like chess."

"Don't worry," Pru said. "I won't tell your mother."

"Tell her what you want. She finds out everything anyway."

"And that book," Pru said, pointing at Rafe's lap. "Are you reading it for high school?"

Rafe laughed. "Now I know why my mother likes you. All you two think about is high school."

"Actually, it's been ages since I thought about high school. The day my daughter graduated, I stopped thinking about it."

Rafe held up the book. "The professor gave it to me. It's by some guy named Wittgenstein."

Pru said, "Oy."

"I'm not sure the professor understands him anymore. I know I don't."

"If it's any consolation, I never understood him. Come on, Rafe, school's out. Your mother won't like me saying this, but you don't need to be reading Wittgenstein on your summer break. Teach me some chess strategy. Help me impress my friends."

Rafe told her about pawn structure, how to use a pawn to pry open a locked position, how to array pawns as a duo, side by side. The player who controlled the most space was the player who controlled the game. E4, e5, d4, and d5: those were the most important spaces. There were cramping moves and freeing moves. A cramping move restricted your opponent's space, and a freeing move opened up space for you. "Don't lock in your bishops behind your pawns." A bishop stuck behind one of its own pawns was worth less than an unobstructed knight. A knight was worth three pawns, as was a bishop, but a rook was worth five pawns, a queen nine.

"How about you give me an extra queen?" Pru said. "And a couple of extra bishops while you're at it." When Sarah was a girl, they'd allowed her to play Scrabble with ten letters while they played with only seven.

"You'll have the same number of queens as I have. How else will you learn?"

Spence and Ginny came down the hall.

"Professor," Rafe said, "do you want to play?"

There was a competitive gleam in Spence's eye. Boggle, Probe, checkers, Casino: he always played to win. And he'd passed down that competitiveness to his children. When Arlo was five, he sat down to the chessboard on one of his visits, and after a few turns, he swept his hand across the board and knocked over all of his father's pieces. "I won!" he said. "Beginner's luck!"

"Here, I'll help you," Rafe said. He moved Spence's bishop, saying, "Look there, Professor, you've gained a tempo."

Spence nodded as if to say he knew as much.

Rafe explained what the Center Counter was. Beginning chess players were always giving check, but check wasn't important; only checkmate was. There was a saying he'd learned at chess camp. *Monkey sees a check, monkey gives a check.* "Don't be a monkey," Rafe said.

"The professor doesn't understand you," Ginny said. "*I* don't understand you. A good teacher doesn't show off."

But Rafe was too busy talking about pawn structure to care what his mother said. He was extolling the virtues of passed pawns and noting the dangers of isolated pawns. There were backward pawns and hanging pawns and doubled pawns and pawn chains, and Spence, perched above Rafe on a chair, was wearing a look of contemplation, saying, "Sounds good to me."

Now Rafe was using terms like *shrinking the square* and *skewer* and *fork* and *absolute pin* and *bishop sacrifice.* "Your turn, Professor. Show me your best move."

But Spence was becoming tired, so Rafe lifted him from his chair.

"It would be nice to have Rafe here all the time," Pru said. Watching Rafe accompany Spence to the bedroom, a step behind him, a step to the side, his arms out to catch him if he fell, Pru wasn't worried he would fall and, if he did fall, Rafe would catch him. And with that realization came another one: she was worried about Spence all the time. Ginny was strong, but Rafe was even stronger. What if Spence fell when Ginny wasn't there? Would she be able to lift him?

The next afternoon, Pru took Ginny and Rafe up to Columbia's campus. Spence came along, too, and as they approached Philosophy Hall, he seemed to inflate. "Here we are," Pru said. "The house that Spence built."

A few teenagers were playing Hacky Sack in the grass.

"I like this college," Rafe said.

"You and the rest of the world," said Ginny.

"Seriously, is this what people do in college? Play games in the grass? I'm into this place."

"In order to be into this place, you'll have to get into this place."

"How hard is that?"

"Harder than you can imagine. And once you get in—*if* you get in— that's when things really get hard."

"Why?"

"The homework, for one. And the tuition. Do you have any idea how much a college like this costs?"

"How much?"

Ginny turned to Pru. "You tell him."

"It's ridiculous," Pru said, though she didn't name a figure.

"Come on," Ginny said. "Tell him how much."

"I have no idea," Pru said, though she did. But it shamed her to say the number aloud.

"Do professors' children get a discount?"

"I imagine," Pru said, though she didn't need to imagine it. Professors' kids got to go for free. But if she told Ginny this, she'd have to explain why Sarah had turned down Columbia to go to Reed.

Finally, she was forced to come clean, and she explained that Columbia was two miles from home and Sarah had wanted to go away for college. And Ginny nodded as if to say she understood.

But a minute later Ginny said, "Seriously, how much is tuition?"

"Tens of thousands of dollars."

Rafe whistled in horror.

"That's per year," Ginny told him.

Actually, Pru thought, that's per semester.

"That's what I've been trying to tell you, Rafe. There's a big world out there, and you have no idea about it."

"I'll take out loans," he said cheerfully.

"Don't go worrying about loans before there's any need to borrow."

"Maybe the professor could adopt me. Couldn't you, Professor Robin?" Rafe tugged on Spence's sleeve.

"We'd adopt him if we could," Pru said.

"Well, I wouldn't let you." Ginny's face tightened.

"Come on," Pru said. "I was just kidding."

"I'll adopt you," Spence said. He searched through his pockets for a pen, as if hoping to sign the paperwork.

Ginny said, "It's an excellent college, Rafe, but if there's one thing I've learned, it's if someone doesn't want you, they're not worth it."

"Who says Columbia doesn't want him?" Hadn't that been the point of this trip? To take Rafe to see a real college campus? To encourage him to set his sights on things? But seeing Ginny, terse and tightly wound, Pru could tell the visit had backfired. She shouldn't have admitted that Sarah went away for college. She shouldn't have made that joke about adopting Rafe.

Pru came home from work one day to find Ginny on the phone.

"That was Barbara," Ginny said when she got off. "My old employer."

A few days later, Barbara called again, and this time Ginny spoke to her for ten minutes.

"What was that about?" Pru said. "Not that it's any of my business."

Ginny said, "If Barbara didn't want it to be your business, she shouldn't have called me on your phone. She just misses me, that's all."

"Of course she misses you. I miss you when you're not here and I see you every day."

Ginny turned red.

"Now you're blushing."

"Well, I don't like compliments. You know that."

Pru understood. She didn't like compliments either, especially when they were issued too forcefully. But she hadn't intended to be aggressive with Ginny: she was just telling the truth.

"Barbara's feeling sorry for herself."

"Well, she does have a disease." Pru wondered why she was sticking up for Barbara, this woman she didn't even know.

"Barbara came into the world feeling sorry for herself. It has nothing to do with a disease."

"Has she found another aide?"

"She's found several."

Pru looked up.

"She goes through people quickly."

"So she wants you to recommend someone else?"

"She wants me to recommend myself."

"I don't understand."

"She wants me back, Pru."

"And what did you tell her?"

"That I'm not available."

"So that was it? End of discussion?"

Ginny laughed. With Barbara, it was never the end of the discussion. Bring me a softer pillow, Barbara would say. Get me that paper lantern I saw in the gift shop. Buy me that brand of seltzer at Whole Foods, then pick up that brand of gin at the liquor store and make me a Tom Collins.

"So Barbara wants you to come back and make Tom Collinses for her?"

"She said she'd hire a car to drive me to Connecticut. And she told me she'd double my pay."

"And what did you say to that?"

"I told you," Ginny said. "I've made a commitment to you. You and the professor—you're the people I work for."

"Well, I'm glad to hear that. Because as much as I'd like to, I can't get into a bidding war for you."

———

But words, once uttered, couldn't be reeled in, and Ginny started to speak about what they'd been resisting speaking about. So as not to speak about Barbara, they spoke about little else. Barbara with her Tom Collinses and her fuzzy slippers, Barbara whose sheets needed to be folded back just so. Everything in Barbara's house was hidden behind wood. The TV looked like an armoire. Even the refrigerator had a wood exterior, as if it, too, needed to be hidden. "Barbara's a strange bird," Ginny said. She even imitated Barbara's singing, which was unlike her—to mock someone so directly, or to sing. Ginny referred to Barbara as Barbra Streisand, and Pru referred to her as Barbara Walters, and Ginny referred to her as Barbara Bush, the two of them trying to outdo each other. But it had the counterfeit air of a performance, and in their professed fealty, their ardor for each other, Pru found a fraying, as if something that hadn't been called into question needed to be shored up.

As she was leaving work the next day, Ginny said, "I've gotten another job offer, and the pay starts at twenty dollars an hour."

"Is it with Barbara?"

"It's with someone else."

Pru couldn't afford twenty dollars an hour. She paid Ginny fifteen, and she couldn't afford that. "Okay," she said, "here's what I can do. I'll raise your pay to seventeen dollars an hour."

Slowly, without fully realizing it, she started to throw in perks. An old chess set she'd found in the closet. Her pass to MoMA and the Met. Tickets to Lincoln Center: she and Spence had a subscription, but now that he couldn't go, she didn't want to go either. Crassly, she let it be known how much these tickets cost. Divide that cost over a period of months and she was paying Ginny more than seventeen dollars an hour.

She took the clothes she didn't wear anymore and loaded them into shopping bags. She gave Ginny an old bread machine, a toaster oven, and a VCR.

Ginny took the VCR just as she took Pru's clothes, with a nod of the head, a pantomime of gratitude. And maybe it wasn't a pantomime: maybe she really wanted these things. But Pru saw in Ginny's eyes a clot of resentment, as if she were saying she didn't need Pru's castaways, even as she trundled them out the door.

16

Pru was at work when she got the call from campus, Ginny's voice pulled tight as a lanyard. "The professor's stuck," she said, and the image Pru had was of Winnie-the-Pooh stuck in the honey jar. "He's in the bathroom," Ginny said, "and he won't come out."

Ginny had taken Spence to the men's room, and half an hour later, he was still inside. She called to him through the bathroom door. "You need to come out soon, Professor. Someone will want to use the stall."

He didn't respond.

"Hello, Professor?" Tentatively, she went inside. Two urinals stood beside each other, with no partition between them: how could men urinate so openly, in public? "Professor?" she said, but he was so quiet she thought he might have passed out.

Then his feet started to move, pawing over the floor in a frenzy.

"If you don't come out, I'm going to have to eat your sandwich for you."

"Go home," he said.

"I can't go home. Your wife is paying me to be with you."

"I'll pay you to go home."

Finally, she called for help. That had been her mistake, she told Pru over the phone, because as soon as she notified a secretary, another secretary got word, and then an administrator from the chair's office, and then the chair himself. They were clustered now outside the men's room.

"I'll take care of this," Pru said when she arrived. She opened the stall door. Spence just sat there with his pants at his feet, staring up at her with a hangdog affect.

He'd soiled himself. The stink was all over his underwear and pants. She had known this would happen—she was surprised it hadn't happened yet—but her imagination had been sealed. "Come on, darling, let's go home. We'll get you into a new set of clothes. Accidents happen." She reached over to help him up.

When she got to the chair's office the next morning, he closed the door behind her and ushered her inside. Looking at him from across the vast expanse of his desk, she had the outrageous premonition that she was about to take an exam. She was back in graduate school, defending the dissertation she hadn't even written.

The chair was fair-complected, and he had a shaved head. He wore an earring, and he was dressed fashionably, in a navy silk shirt and a tie the color of beef tongue. A dandy, Spence had called him once. He'd said that word without asperity; the truth was, he thought most of his colleagues—most English professors in general—were dandies; he had a low bar when it came to such things.

The chair was in his mid-forties, and he was relatively affable. *Pleasant enough* was the term Spence had used. He did reasonable scholarship. Unspectacular, Spence had said, but then spectacular was reserved for the chosen. He'd been a competent chair, and Spence was grateful that he made the trains run on time and that he ensured that Spence himself would never have to be chair.

The chair and his wife had had Pru and Spence over for dinner once, and Pru and Spence had reciprocated. Noises had been made about further socializing. The chair had a house in the country, and there had been talk of a weekend visit, but nothing came of it. Spence and the chair had a collegial relationship, but then that was Spence's relationship with everyone in the department: there was a reason they were called colleagues. He had turned down other job offers, and one of the reasons was that if you lived in Cambridge or Madison or Berkeley or Hyde Park, your colleagues weren't just your colleagues, they were your friends. In New York, you got to wear your cloak of anonymity.

Now, though, sitting across from the chair, Pru thought they had miscalculated. They should have been more sociable with the chair and his wife. They should have invited them over for dinner more; they should have gone up to their house in the country.

Though whom was she kidding? No number of gatherings at country houses would have prevented her from sitting where she was sitting now.

The chair laid his fists on the desk: little mounds of dough, like dinner rolls. "Pru."

"Alex." What was the phrase that passenger had used, the one heard over the voice recorder on September 11? *Let's roll?*

The chair told Pru what a great scholar Spence was, and also an electrifying teacher. The chair had gone to Duke, and he invoked the Duke basketball team, outside of whose arena the students would camp out for nights at a time to secure tickets; the Cameron Crazies, the students were called. That was what it was like to have Spence in the department, the lengths students went to to get into his class. "This is very painful for me."

Pru didn't doubt it was, but then the chair twisted his hands in a gesture of pain, which turned his sincerity into something else. "Spence is a once-in-a-generation scholar."

"I know that."

"Pru, it's a terrible disease."

She knew that too.

"What happened yesterday afternoon…"

"Believe me, Spence feels terrible about it. No one feels more humiliated than he does."

"The thing is, it wasn't the first time."

"Of course it was." If it had happened before, didn't the chair think she would know about it?

"There have been other things."

"Like what?"

"He wanders through the hallway."

"That's what hallways are for. To wander through."

"It's just…"

"He has Ginny," she said.

"And by all accounts, she's doing a very good job. But she gives him—how should I put it—perhaps a longer leash than is ideal."

"It's important to have autonomy," Pru said. "Ask any doctor."

"I understand that, and if it were just Spence I had to worry about, the solution would be simple. But I have the rest of the department to contend with. Spence has wandered into colleagues' offices. He's scared people."

"Just by walking in?"

"He's begun to make noises. Sometimes he moans. It can be disorienting."

"To Spence?"

"To him, too, I imagine. It's been happening in the classroom as well. There have been complaints—more than a few, if I'm being honest. Some students have become frightened."

"Oh, come on, Alex. Spence wouldn't hurt a fly. At this point, he's not even capable."

The chair reached across the desk. Was it possible he was going to touch her? "Pru, I'm afraid the end has come. Spence can't teach for us anymore."

"But he's *not* teaching for you anymore. He just sits at the front of the classroom. His TAs are doing the teaching for him."

"And that's not fair to anyone." Spence, the chair said—the man he'd been colleagues with for fifteen years—that man wouldn't want to be placed beside the podium, perched there like a toad. "You can't convince me he'd want that."

The chair was right. If Pru had shown the old Spence what the new Spence was like, the old Spence would have been horrified. But the old Spence couldn't see the new Spence, and when Pru told the new Spence that he should retire, the new Spence refused. Because, feeble as he was, compromised as he had become, he hadn't lost his will. And was she going to ignore the wishes of the man she'd eaten breakfast with this morning, the man she would lie in bed with tonight, to respect a man who no longer existed? "I'm sorry," she said. "I can't get him to retire."

"And you shouldn't have to." In her position, the chair said, he wouldn't be able to, either. "This isn't easy," he said. "If it was, we'd have had this conversation months ago."

"So you're forcing him out?"

The chair nodded.

"Effective when?" She took out her calendar as if to write down the date, but she just left it unopened.

"The end of the semester."

"What about his salary?"

"He'll be paid until then."

"And after that?"

"He'll have his IRA."

Pru stood up.

"And another thing. He can keep his office."

"For how long?"

"For as long as he—for as long as you both want him to. His aide, the woman who helps him…"

"Ginny."

"She can bring him in whenever she'd like. Once a month, once a week, every day if she must, though I'd recommend against doing it that often."

Pru was rifling through her bag, searching for something, she didn't know what.

"Office space in this department," the chair said, "I don't have to tell you the kind of demand it's in."

And Pru didn't have to tell the chair that Spence deserved it. The things he'd done for Columbia for the past thirty-plus years. He should have been allowed to keep his office in perpetuity, to pass it down to his children and grandchildren.

Pru was halfway out the door when the chair called out. "We'll throw him a retirement party! Big or small, however you'd like it! We want it to be something that befits the occasion!"

But there was no party that befitted the occasion, and so there wouldn't be one.

17

"They made Spence retire," Pru told her mother over the phone. "They tossed him out on his ear. And I'm living with a caregiver in my home. I don't have any privacy anymore."

"I'll move to New York," her mother said. "I'll help take care of him."

"You can't do that."

"Why not? What do I have keeping me here? This old house? A handful of friends, who are growing old themselves?"

Years ago, Pru had suggested her mother move to New York. That way, she could spend more time with Sarah, and when she got older, Pru and Spence could help take care of her. But she'd refused: her life was in Columbus. And if her life had been in Columbus then, how much more so now?

"The difference is, now you need me."

That was the problem. Having her mother, at eighty-two, help take care of her husband was a reversal of the cosmic order. It was bad enough that Spence had taken over her life; she couldn't let him take over her mother's life, too.

"Then I'll fly in for a week. Dad's yahrtzeit is coming up. We'll go to shul together."

It was evening when they got to shul, and they found a few men milling about the sanctuary, and a few more studying the Talmud in back.

When the service began, Pru and her mother watched through the mechitza as the man up front recited Barchu. Soon the rest of the congregants were saying the Shema, and Pru and her mother were saying it with them.

When it came to Judaism, Pru had arrived at feminism late. She hadn't cared, growing up, that the girls didn't read the Torah or lead services; she could play hooky from synagogue, spend Saturday mornings in the bleachers of the local high school, which never would have been tolerated if she'd been a boy. She'd liked tradition: the men on one side, the women on the other, the men saying Kiddush on Friday nights, the women lighting the Shabbat candles. In her twenties, she was a member of not one but two synagogues, but she didn't go to either of them, so she canceled her memberships. It wasn't until Sarah reached school age that her interest in Judaism was rekindled and, like a plant that had long been assumed dead, she enrolled Sarah in Hebrew school so she could have a Bat Mitzvah. Friday nights they would go to services together, but the synagogue they went to was large and progressive; it wasn't the kind of synagogue her father would have liked. The synagogue she was in now, to say Kaddish for him, was small and Orthodox, like her father himself. It was where he would have wanted her to go, and she preferred the anonymity, besides, knowing she wouldn't run into anyone.

Another woman was saying Kaddish, too, but she was reciting it so softly Pru couldn't hear her.

When the service was over, the rabbi walked through the aisles, straightening up. "Are you new here?"

"No," Pru said. "Actually, yes. I mean, sort of."

"That's a lot of answers."

What could she tell him? That she was new to this synagogue but not to synagogues in general? That she wasn't even new to this synagogue, having come here a couple of times over the years? That she had grown up in a kosher home? That her father had kept kosher until the day he died? That her mother—she introduced her now to the rabbi—still kept kosher? That when she'd moved in with Spence, the first thing they'd done was kosher the kitchen, call in those men with their blowtorches and beards? That three decades later, though her kitchen was traif, she still made an annual contribution to Go Kosher? It was too much information, as people liked to say, and also not enough. So she told the rabbi the truth: she was here to say Kaddish for her father.

"We welcome newcomers," the rabbi said.

"I remember."

"You've been here before?"

She nodded. She recalled a Rosh Hashanah service and a random Shabbat when she'd woken up overcome by a long-dormant spiritual longing. She thought of synagogue worship like punctuated equilibrium, bursts of attendance followed by long periods of lying fallow.

"Welcoming but forgetful," the rabbi said.

"It was years ago," she assured him.

"I'm not good with faces. It's not the best quality in a rabbi." He pulled on his jacket sleeves. He didn't have a beard, but there was something rabbinic-seeming about him nonetheless—the yarmulke, of course, and the dark jacket, the close-cropped hair, an open manner that she could only call pastoral. He was about her age. She wondered if he was married. For an instant she imagined being his wife, going to shul every Shabbat, living a different life entirely.

"When you were saying Kaddish before? That's the way to belt it out."

"I'm Pru," she said. "Hear me roar."

"As in *pru u'rvu*," the rabbi said. "Be fruitful and multiply."

She finished the verse for him: *"Oo'meeloo et ha'aretz v'chivshuha."*

"So you have a Jewish education."

"Nine years of Torah Academy," Pru's mother said.

"Your parents taught you well," the rabbi told Pru.

"The things you remember from when you were a child."

Now it was the rabbi's turn to quote Hebrew to her. *"Ha'lomaid yeled, l'mah hoo domeh? L'dyo kitoovah al neeyar chadash. V'ha'lomaid zakain, l'mah hoo domeh? L'dyo kitoovah al neeyar machuk."*

Pru knew these verses, too. *He who learns as a child, what is that like? It's like ink written on new paper. And he who learns as an old person, what is that like? It's like ink written on erased paper.* She'd studied Pirkei Avot with her father, a chapter a week on Shabbat afternoons.

The rabbi stepped back into the sanctuary. "We're open every day!"

he called out. "We're even better than the post office! We're open Sundays and holidays too!"

Out on the street, Pru opened her bag and found an apple. She ate it down to the core, thinking of her father, who used to eat his apples down to the pits. And then he ate the pits too, leaving only the stem.

"How are you?" Camille said when Pru got to her apartment. More than thirty years later, Pru and Camille were still best friends.

"Lonely," Pru said. She was lonely without Spence and—this was worse—she was lonely with him. Spence was the person she talked to, and now she couldn't talk to him anymore.

"You can talk to me," Camille said. "I know it's not the same thing..."

It wasn't, Pru thought, but it wasn't nothing either. She had known Camille since they were eighteen.

She heard a banging. "What's that?"

"It's the next-door neighbor's boy. Retaliation for all those years when I played my music too loud."

"In my old age," Pru said, "I've developed the hearing of a bat."

"Now, don't you go pretending you're getting old, too. Whatever Spence has, it's not contagious."

Camille's cat jumped onto her lap.

"Seriously, Camille, I'm only fifty-four, but taking care of Spence makes me feel like I'm seventy-four. And look at you, fifty-four and you're out having sex."

"You're not having sex?"

"It hasn't happened in months."

"Spence doesn't want to?"

"I don't even know if he's capable anymore."

Camille was quiet.

"You'd be handling this differently if you were me."

"How would I be handling it?"

"More effortlessly. More gallantly."

Camille laughed. "I'm the least gallant companion in the world. Why do you think I live alone?" The cat stretched out on Camille's lap.

He was a new cat. There was always a new cat, just as there was always a new boyfriend. Though Camille was between boyfriends now.

"You could still get married," Pru said. "You'd have the pick of the litter."

"I already do." Camille lifted the cat and brought him into the kitchen, where she poured him a bowl of food.

18

One morning Pru said to Spence, "I don't know if you'll be teaching next term."

"Of course I'll be teaching. They'll have to bury me beneath my office before I retire."

Maybe by the time classes started he'd be so bad off he wouldn't realize he wasn't teaching. Was that what she was hoping for, a decline so steep he wouldn't understand?

"Am I going to die from this?" he asked her one night.

"I hope not."

"But will I?"

She couldn't bear to answer him.

"I apologize for getting sick."

"Oh, darling, it's not your fault."

One day, when he was more clearheaded than he'd been in weeks, he said, "I'd rather kill myself than let this disease take me."

"You don't mean that."

"To be robbed of my mind? I've never meant anything more."

He'd always insisted he would never die. Now there was this.

He took out a bread knife to cut a bagel, and she screamed, "What are you doing? Watch out!"

He just looked at her, bewildered.

"Give me that!" she said, and she took the knife and cut the bagel for him.

After that, she put away the knives and the household medications. She removed a strand of rope from the utility closet.

———

She called Sarah in L.A.

"How's he doing?"

"Some days better, some days worse. How are *you* doing?"

"Terrible. I've been going on neurology rounds. It's a lot of brain tumors and stroke victims, and who cares about that?"

"I'm sure the patients do. And their families. Seriously, darling, you're doing God's work."

"I'm in the library all night reading medical journals. Plaque, tau, ApoE4, ApoE3."

"I don't even begin to understand."

"No one does. If they did, they'd have a cure."

"At least you left me a stethoscope. And a blood pressure cuff."

Sarah laughed darkly. "My daughter went to med school and all I got was this lousy blood pressure cuff."

Pru didn't speak.

"How *is* his blood pressure?"

"It's all right."

"And his heart?"

"It's beating."

"Any problems at all, I want you to call me. Two in the morning, three in the morning, I don't care."

Pru came home one night and found him lying on the couch. "How was your day?"

"Fine."

"Now it's your turn."

"My turn to do what?"

"Your turn to ask me how my day was."

"How was your day?"

"My day was horrible. In the morning, I called donors and got hung up on. In the afternoon, I wrote pitch letter after pitch letter. I might as well have been writing to the moon."

Spence closed his eyes.

"You see? You never cared about my work. You don't think what I do is worth anything."

"What you do is worth something."

"Do you even know what I do?"

He hesitated.

"Tell me what I do when I go to work."

He didn't speak.

"The school is called Barnard, Spence. If colleges didn't raise money, professors wouldn't get paid. People sneer at development, but we're the air you breathe."

"I'm nothing without you." He started to cry.

Afterward, she said to herself, Are you crazy? Testing the memory of a demented man? Blaming him for your unpleasant job?

Spence carried a pen wherever he went, taking notes like a stenographer. "Your birthday's in November, right?"

"Yes, darling."

"When in November?"

She gave him the date.

"Tell me all the things I'm going to forget."

"With every person it's different."

"Will I forget to love you?"

"I hope not."

"Don't let me forget to love you." But now he was back to his notebook, writing something down.

Every day he would ask about her birthday, though November was ten months off.

"Professor," Ginny said, "what are you worried about? Do you want to make sure you buy Pru a gift?"

"I want to buy her a nightgown."

"You can buy her one when the date gets closer."

But he wanted to buy her one now.

So Ginny took him shopping, but when they got to the department store, he insisted on going in alone. She waited for him outside, but when he didn't come out, she went in to find him.

She spotted him in the leather department, running his hands over a pair of shoes. "Professor, if you want to buy a nightgown you have to look in lingerie."

"It's so disorganized in here."

"It's a department store, Professor."

He followed her up the escalator, but when they got to lingerie he again asked her to step aside.

She was uncomfortable standing in lingerie—uncomfortable for them both. But she was even more uncomfortable seeing him across the floor, staring vacantly at the nightgowns. His very stillness looked like lechery.

A saleswoman approached him. "It's okay!" Ginny called out. "He's with me!" She ran across the floor and took him by the arm.

Now he seemed more confused than ever. There were rows and rows of nightgowns, and he was made immobile by the choice. "It's the thought that counts, Professor. It doesn't matter which one you buy."

But it mattered to him.

"Do you know what size she is?"

He did not.

She removed a nightgown from the rack and held it up to herself. She was bigger than Pru: heftier, taller. But if she continued like this, Spence would ask her to try it on.

She pointed to a random nightgown. "What do you think of that one?"

He was exhausted now, indifferent to choice.

"Well, I like it," she said. "I'm sure Pru will, too."

When they got home, Spence handed Pru the box. "Happy birthday," he said.

"Darling, my birthday isn't for months."

"I don't know if I'll be alive on your birthday."

"Of course you'll be alive." *You could be alive for years,* she wanted to say, but would that even be a comfort?

That night, she wore the nightgown to bed, but in the morning Spence said, "What can I get you for your birthday?"

"You already got me something, darling."

"What?"

"This nightgown."

He just stared at her. "I've never seen it in my life."

She'd been having a hankering for Ethiopian food, so she made a reservation at an Ethiopian restaurant. But immediately she regretted it, because Spence had never had an adventurous palate.

When the food came, he looked down in astonishment and disarray. "Where are the utensils?"

She pointed at the injera. "You just scoop up the food with the bread."

Spence was a fastidious eater—he'd never so much as spotted his shirt—and now she was telling him to eat with his hands.

She removed a plastic fork from her pocketbook, and he sawed at the injera before giving up.

"Next time, we can go out to the movies and eat pizza."

"What if there isn't a next time?" Spence said.

She wondered: was he thinking about suicide again?

She found him one morning at the stove, dropping silverware into a pot. "Jesus, Spence, what are you doing?"

"I'm koshering our kitchen."

"Why?"

"Because when your mother visits she'll want to eat." But he just stood there, not knowing what to do, and she removed the pot from the flame.

"You should divorce me," he said.

"Why? Because I wouldn't let you kosher our kitchen?"

"Because you have to take care of me. Would you want me to have to take care of you?"

"I wouldn't want you to have to, but I know you would."

"You've always been better off without me."

"Spence, you're crazy."

He just looked at her as if she were far away.

———

She called Camille and said, "He talks about suicide, he talks about divorce. I've had to hide the knives so he won't kill himself."

"Alzheimer's patients rarely kill themselves."

"How do you know?"

"I asked a neurologist."

Why, Pru wondered, hadn't she asked a neurologist herself? Was she afraid that he might take Spence away from her, put him in an institution?

"You should have him see a therapist," Camille said.

Pru laughed. Spence? Talking about his feelings with a stranger? Talking about his feelings with anyone but her?

"It might help him."

Of course it might help him. But only if he was a willing participant. Before he'd gotten sick, he'd been the most stubborn person she knew. Now he was even more so.

"*You* should see a therapist," Camille said.

"Oh, Camille." She had neither the money nor the time for a therapist. She went to work in the morning and came home at night. She would have fallen asleep on the therapist's couch.

She googled "Alzheimer's" and "suicide" and found an article about a professor with Alzheimer's who had, in fact, killed herself.

Afterward, she found Spence lying asleep in the living room, so still he might as well have been dead. "Spence, darling?"

He didn't respond.

She touched his cheek, but he still didn't move, so she put her forefinger under his nose to make sure he was still breathing.

19

At first the loneliness was the hardest part, because Sarah was back in L.A. and everyone was going about their lives. She hadn't told her classmates about her father. She didn't want their sympathy.

She started to skip classes. She had sex with a guy she barely knew. She cut her hair short. She hadn't worn earrings in years, but she bought a pair and jammed them through the holes. What would she do next, start to smoke, like some 1950s doctor? Get a nose ring? A tattoo? Thank God she was afraid of needles.

She was in a study group with some friends, and one afternoon they went up to the roof and smoked a joint.

"It's medical marijuana," someone said.

"That's the advantage of being in medical school," someone said. "All marijuana is medical marijuana."

"That's why I went to med school," someone else said. "Because of the pot!"

Sarah took a few hits like everyone else, but after several minutes she started to cry.

"Sarah, what's wrong?"

"I'm not feeling well." She got up from her chair and ran down the fire escape, and then she was out on the street.

Four afternoons a week, she nannied for the daughter of two law school professors. She needed the money, and it was good to get away from campus, to sit outside with Daisy by the Donnellys' pool and sun herself into oblivion.

Soon it was time for Daisy's nap—Daisy who slept with so many stuffed animals Sarah was afraid she would suffocate beneath them. She would move the stuffed animals while Daisy was asleep, like someone clearing brush.

Then Priscilla and John would come home, and they'd pack her up with leftovers: a Tupperware of pasta, watercress salad, a tureen of lentil soup.

But after she left, she started to cry again. She was spending her afternoons in the company of a four-year-old, waking up in the morning for rounds, going home to eat a stranger's food, hiding what was happening from her classmates.

She called home one day, and her father answered. She said, "I never get to talk to you anymore. Mom's a real phone hog, isn't she?"

"I'll talk to you," her father said.

"How are you, Dad?"

"I'm well."

He did sound well, better than he had in weeks.

"What's that barking I hear?"

"It's my dog," she said. "Kingsley." She'd named him after Kingsley Road, where they'd spent those Augusts in Vermont.

"You should bring him for a visit."

"First I'd need to learn how to drive." She heard a noise through the receiver, the sound of a blender being turned on.

"I used to call you Hepseba," her father said.

"So you told me." Hepseba for a girl and Habakkuk for a boy: this was when her mother had been pregnant with her. "I'm glad you named me Sarah," she said. "I don't think I'd have made a good Hepseba."

"You'd have made a good anything," her father said.

"Thank you, Daddy."

Then there was silence.

"Dad?" she said, but he didn't answer her. His breathing had lengthened. He'd fallen asleep.

———

Compared to what others had endured, what she was going through was nothing. One of her classmates had withdrawn from school with stage IV colon cancer; another had lost his mother the first week of school. It didn't matter that early Alzheimer's was rare; your pain wasn't any greater for being unusual.

On the phone with her mother she said, "How are you going to make it work? You can't afford Ginny."

"I'll manage."

Maybe, she thought, she could be like the other nannies, the women from Mexico and the Philippines, who sent cash home to their families. She would take care of Daisy so she could send money to her mother, who was paying Ginny to take care of her father, which prevented Ginny from taking care of her son.

When she'd first moved to town, she would go to the bank once a week to purchase a roll of quarters for the homeless. Now she purchased a roll of quarters only every other week. She would give just to the homeless who looked particularly bad off, raising the bar for desperation, like the government raising the poverty limit. She'd stopped eating out entirely, and in these dribs and drabs she saved some money, and she wrote a check to her mother for $400.

But a week later it was returned to her with the word VOID across the front.

She'd maxed out her credit card, and in line at the supermarket one day she was down to her last few quarters.

"I'm sorry," the cashier said. "Those are Canadian quarters."

She rifled through her pockets, but she was forty cents short. "Can't you let it go?"

"I'll get in trouble with my manager."

It was Canada, she thought: the same continent, practically the same country! The line lengthened behind her, like a handkerchief pulled out of a magician's sleeve. Impatience ran like a current through the crowd. "Come on, lady, you're holding us up!" Her face grew flushed, and she grabbed a can of beans and returned it to the shelf, swearing she would never come back to this store, but she would have to come back because the food was cheap and she couldn't afford to be resentful.

———

Finally, she told Priscilla and John what was happening. They would understand, she thought, and maybe—she hoped—they wouldn't be surprised. She'd gone back east for a couple of visits; she'd hinted that there were problems at home.

But they *were* surprised, and now their sadness had been added to hers, and she had to endure their burden.

"Do you need time off?" John said.

"We could give you fewer hours," Priscilla said.

"Or more hours," John said.

She hated how they tripped over themselves, the contortions they did to accommodate her.

She came home one day to discover that they'd paid her too much. "You made a mistake," she told Priscilla. "You gave me an extra fifty dollars."

"It wasn't a mistake. We're giving you a raise."

"Is this because of my father?"

"It's because you deserve it," John said. "It's long overdue."

But if it wasn't because of her father, then why were Priscilla and John packing her up with food—and not just with leftovers, as they always had, but with entire meals? John placed a lasagna in her arms, and Priscilla added a pound cake, and John followed suit with a quiche. As she walked out the door, she said, "This food looks delicious. And the good thing is, now I won't have to sell my eggs."

They started to hire her at night. They would go to a movie, a play, a concert, a dance recital. There were only so many restaurants in Westwood, so they drove to West Hollywood or Santa Monica. They used to go out once a week; now they were going out twice a week, sometimes even more. It was as if they were going out just to pay her.

"We could hire you for other tasks," Priscilla said. "Can you pull weeds? Are you good at gardening?"

But she wasn't good at gardening, and although she could pull weeds, there weren't many weeds to pull. Nor was there much gardening to do, because what passed for a garden was just a tiny patch of dirt out back, and another patch by the side of the house where Priscilla and John kept gardenias.

One night, Priscilla and John came home late, and John, saying he was tired, went to sleep.

"I'll drive you home," Priscilla said, but when she came into the living room she looked as if she'd been crying.

"Priscilla, are you okay?"

"I'm fine," she said. "Actually, I don't know." She sat down across from Sarah. "A couple of weeks ago you said, 'And the good thing is, now I won't have to sell my eggs.'"

Sarah nodded.

"You were kidding about that, weren't you?"

"I think so."

"People say lots of things they don't mean. I know I do. It's just…"

"What?"

"I want another baby." With Daisy, she'd gotten pregnant on the first try, and maybe that was why she'd thought it would be easy this time, too. But she'd been thirty-six when she got pregnant with Daisy, and now she was forty-one. "I guess those five years make a difference."

All at once, Sarah understood. "You want me to be an egg donor?"

"I know," Patricia said. "John said it was crazy."

"Don't people want nineteen-year-olds? Aren't they looking for blond, blue-eyed lacrosse players who are also members of Mensa?"

"That's the stereotype."

"But I'm twenty-nine."

"You're still eligible," Patricia said. "And Daisy adores you. If the egg can't be mine, you're the one I'd want the baby to be related to."

All at once, a horrible thought occurred to her. The pay raise, the free food: Priscilla and John had just been buttering her up.

———

The signs had been there all along, pasted to lampposts, on bright pink paper, and in the classifieds of *The Daily Bruin: Educated Healthy Women Ages 22–30. Help Others for Great Compensation. Make a Couple's Dream of Parenthood Come True.* One ad promised $10,000. Another ad read *Earn up to $60,000 for Six Cycles.*

Ten thousand dollars would cover more than three months of Ginny's salary. Sixty thousand dollars would cover almost two years.

Now, whenever she came to work, Sarah would take out the board games and the cards, or help Daisy change into her bathing suit— anything to avoid Priscilla and John.

A week went by, then another. When they were home, Patricia and John skulked around, and Sarah skulked around, too. A month passed, and she hadn't gained any clarity.

Priscilla and John came home one day and took her into the living room.

"I know," she said. "You want my answer."

"We've been thinking it over," Priscilla said, "and we're not sure we want you to be an egg donor."

John said, "Your relationship with Daisy is what's most important to us. We don't want to complicate things."

"Things wouldn't be complicated." The complications: that was why she'd delayed. But now that they were pulling back, she felt as if something had been grabbed from her, taken like a bone. "I want to do it," she said. "I want you to have my eggs."

"We're touched," Priscilla said, "but the more we thought about it, the more uneasy it made us. I probably shouldn't have brought it up."

"But you did bring it up." Suddenly it hit Sarah. Priscilla didn't want her eggs because the baby might grow up to have Alzheimer's.

"That's not it," Priscilla said.

John said, "Even if the baby grew up to have Alzheimer's, we'd be long dead at that point."

Not if it was early onset. And what did they care if they were long dead? No one wanted that for their child, whether they were dead or living.

Priscilla said, "We don't think egg donation is the right path for us. We're planning to adopt."

But a week later, Sarah was flipping through *The Daily Bruin* and she came across an ad for an egg donor, with Priscilla and John's phone number attached. They wanted the nineteen-year-old, after all: the blond, blue-eyed, lacrosse-playing Mensa member. They didn't want her father: he was infected, and she was, too. She didn't know how she could ever see them again. She would have to find another job.

Part V

20

It was hard, at first, with Arlo gone. The hamper felt empty without his blue jeans and hooded sweatshirts, without his cargo pants. Pru would buy too much food and watch it go to waste. She announced dinner one night, and she mistakenly called out his name.

But as the weeks passed she felt a lightening. Sarah was in high school now, off to one extracurricular or another, and Pru would go out to dinner with Spence or Camille. She'd gotten back in touch with her graduate school friends—Theresa, Claire, and Marie—and they went bowling one night, of all things, and got a little drunk.

Spence, on the other hand, was despondent. Sarah was, too. "Nothing's the same without him," she said. "I don't even know where he is."

"He's in Iowa," Pru said.

"He might as well be on Mars." On Mars, at least, he would have had reason not to write, but he was in Iowa, in the United States, and a month had passed and they hadn't heard from him.

Spence wrote him every day. Sarah wrote him almost as often. Pru wrote him, too.

"Why did we let him go?" Spence said. He should have insisted that Arlo finish out the school year. Then summer would have come, and he might have stayed for the rest of high school.

21

Ames, Iowa, Arlo thought: how in the world had he ended up here?

"What's wrong with Ames?" his mother said. She listed the town's population, spoke of its air quality, the number of Boy Scout troops, as if she'd discovered it on a list of America's Most Livable Cities, which for all Arlo knew she had. Rents were cheap, and his mother had found a ramshackle house that gave them each some privacy. And he had his music and his headphones. But he didn't care about livable. New York wasn't livable—there were rats on the subway tracks—but there was nowhere he more wanted to be now that he was gone.

He would rail against the coffee ("It tastes like piss"), and the bagels ("They're insipid": now that he'd left, he was using his father's vocabulary words), and the local bands ("They're also-rans"), until his mother said, "I lived in London these past two years and do you see me complaining?"

"What's so great about London?"

"Try Buckingham Palace and Big Ben."

Buckingham Palace? Big Ben? It was as if his mother hadn't lived in London at all, as if she'd merely seen it on a postcard.

But one night Arlo found her passport, with London's Heathrow Airport printed on the front page. On the second page was France's de Gaulle. On the third page was Portugal's Lisbon Portela. "When were you in Portugal?"

"Oliver and I traveled there," his mother said. But at that word, *Oliver*, a shadow crossed his mother's face.

"What's he doing now, anyway?"

"I have no idea. He broke up with me."

Arlo had thought his mother had come back because of him. Now he understood that Oliver had left her and she was coming back anyway.

One night his mother said, "You've changed, Arlo."

Of course he'd changed. The question was, why hadn't she changed, too? She was the same as she'd always been, only more so, as if she'd settled into a deeper, truer version of herself. She would walk around the house in only her underwear and her Toledo Mud Hens T-shirt, and when she went to the bathroom she would leave the door open, and he would have to turn away.

"Arlo, you've become a prude."

Was she right? In New York, he'd paraded around naked to get his father's goat, and now his mother was peeing with the door open and he couldn't look at her.

She found him one night with a book on his lap and said, "When did you become such a reader?"

"It certainly wasn't because of you."

"Arlo, that's not fair. I read as much as the next person."

"I didn't read when I was with you because I didn't know how to read. Mom, I'm dyslexic."

His mother just stared at him.

"You're inattentive, Mom, you know that? You've been inattentive my whole life."

She started to speak, but he wouldn't let her. "I miss Dad," he said. "I hate it here."

It was April, too late in the year to start at a new school, so his mother suggested they find jobs. They passed a bakery one morning with a HELP WANTED sign out front, and his mother went in and said she wanted the job. "In fact," she told the manager, "we both want it. It's a two-for-one deal."

"Two workers for one paycheck?"

"Two workers for two paychecks."

She must have won the manager over with the force of her resolve, because she was told to report to work the next day and to bring Arlo with her. They would be on cash register duty, the manager said.

The rest of the workers wore name badges, so Arlo reluctantly wore one, too. But he refused to wear the white baker's hat everyone else was wearing. His mother, though, took to her new uniform. She would stand beside the ovens in her baker's hat, though she was supposed to be up front at the register.

One day, when she thought no one was looking, she removed a five-dollar bill from the tip jar. A couple of hours later, she removed a ten.

"I saw you stealing from the tip jar," Arlo said.

"You can't steal from yourself."

"Those tips are pooled."

Maybe so, she said, but some workers were better than others. That woman who left the five? Arlo's mother was the one who had served her. She'd thrown in an extra napoleon, and the five had been her reward. And the man who left the ten? He liked her pretty smile. If someone else had a pretty smile, they would get ten dollars, too.

They were walking home beneath the dogwood trees, and Arlo's mother said, "Steal from the rich and give to the poor."

"Steal from the rich?" His mother was stealing from the other workers. She was stealing from him!

One day, Arlo's mother said to the bakery's owner, "Arlo has good business sense. I bet he'd have some ideas for you." She turned to Arlo. "Tell Nancy what you think."

Arlo hesitated, then launched right in. The bakery was underperforming.

"How's it underperforming?" Nancy said. On weekend mornings, the lines were out the door.

But most people bought just a coffee and a scone, then sat at a table, reading. And as the day wore on the crowds dwindled, and on weekdays they were thinner to start. "The bread's overpriced," Arlo said. He pointed at a shelf, where a loaf of einkorn bread sat behind a window like a museum jewel.

"How can you know if my bread's overpriced?"

"Quite simply. No one's buying it." Arlo drew a graph on a napkin. "Do you know about supply and demand?" As the price went down, demand went up. Nancy could still make a profit if she sold her bread for less.

Nancy closed early one day and squeegeed the windows. With Arlo's encouragement, she hired someone to make a new sign for the store. The old sign had faded, and the new letters were blockier and bolder, like a set of straightened teeth.

A week passed, and the bakery was more crowded; revenue had gone up 10 percent. Maybe it was the squeegeed windows and the new sign. Or maybe it was the sunflowers Nancy had placed on the tables. Or maybe it was the law of supply and demand, because now that she'd cut the price of bread, more loaves were selling.

"We've turned this place around," Arlo's mother said.

What did his mother mean, *we*? She was spending her days by the ovens, making a nuisance of herself. And she'd gone back to stealing from the tip jar, doing so with an impunity that unnerved him.

One night, she removed a couple of croissants and a frittole from her bag.

"Did you pay for those?"

She just smiled at him.

"Mom, you can't go stealing tips, and you can't go stealing bread."

"With everything we've been doing for the bakery, we need to ask for a raise."

"Would you stop it with the *we* already? I'm the one who needs to ask for a raise."

"Yes," his mother said. "You do."

But when Arlo asked Nancy for a raise, she said, "If you get a raise, all the workers will want one."

"I helped bring in more revenue."

"Let me think about it," Nancy said.

But a week passed, and Nancy didn't get back to him.

One day, a worker showed up wearing a T-shirt with a half-eaten doughnut silkscreened across the front and the words DOUGHS BEFORE BROS printed above it. Nancy liked the T-shirt; she thought it could be the bakery's new uniform. She ordered ten of the T-shirts and handed them out. Soon everyone was wearing the T-shirt—everyone, that is, except for Arlo, who hated clothes with words written on them. He certainly wasn't going to show up to work with the words DOUGHS BEFORE BROS printed across his chest.

And when Nancy insisted, he quit.

"Do you have another job?" his mother asked him.

"Don't worry about me." He was too big for the bakery. He was too big for Ames. If he was going to succeed, he would succeed spectacularly, and if he was going to fail, he would fail spectacularly, too.

One day, he found a pile of mail in his mother's drawer, with the envelopes sliced open. The return address said *New York, NY*. It was in his father's handwriting. He found another envelope, in his stepmother's hand. And a postcard from Sarah.

He stood in the doorway when his mother got home, holding the pile of letters. "What are these?"

His mother looked startled.

"Answer my question."

"Is that how you greet me at the end of a long workday while you've been loafing around?"

"Tell me what they are."

"They're letters, Arlo. The question is, what were you doing going through my drawers?" She grabbed the letters from him.

"You took my mail. You probably read it."

"And if I did?"

"What else are you hiding?"

"Nothing," she said. "Search me."

He thought he might do that; he was tempted to strip her bare.

"Listen, darling."

"No, *you* listen."

"What if he wanted you back?"

"Did he?"

"A person only gets one chance in life."

Arlo disagreed. His mother had gotten many chances with him. Maybe his father deserved another chance, too.

When he picked up the phone the next day a voice said, "Arlo?"

"Dad?"

"Where are you?"

"I'm in Iowa, Dad."

"Why haven't you answered my letters?"

"Mom confiscated them."

"What about my phone calls? I've been trying you day and night."

In the day Arlo had been at work, and at night his mother had told him not to answer the phone because she didn't want him talking to solicitors. Now he understood what she'd been doing.

"Put your mother on right now."

Arlo handed her the phone.

"You have no business—"

"Don't lecture me, Spence."

"I have a right to talk to him."

"Arlo and I are on our own now. Stop meddling in our lives."

22

Spence tried to catch the first plane to Des Moines, but the flight was overbooked, so he flew to Cedar Rapids, with a stopover at O'Hare, then took a car service to Ames.

"The things you'll do for Arlo," Sarah said.

"I'd do it for you too," he said. "Thank God I don't have to."

When Spence got to the house, Arlo was waiting, but Linda was still at the bakery.

"She bakes?"

"Mostly she steals from the tip jar."

"At least we'll have a few hours before she tries to send me back."

"She won't bother," Arlo said. "She's met a new man."

"Who?"

"Some guy from the bakery. I haven't seen her in days." He ushered his father into the house. "How long are you here for?"

"Just a couple of nights. I can cancel only so many classes before the dean gets suspicious."

"You canceled class for me?"

"I couldn't very well ask my students to fly out here, could I?"

Arlo thought he was going to cry. He doubted his father had ever canceled class in his life. One time, his father had shown up to class with a 103 fever. Another time, he'd hobbled on a broken ankle through a foot of snow, only to discover that classes had been canceled. "How about we go camping?" Arlo said.

"You camp?"

Arlo didn't camp. In fact, until he'd said those words, he hadn't realized he wanted to go camping.

They found a camping store, and Arlo's father bought a tent, a tarp, and two canteens. "Will your mother let me borrow the car?"

"I doubt it," Arlo said, "but she'll let me."

"Since when do you drive?"

"I'm seventeen, Dad. I got my driver's license." It was the first thing he'd done when he'd gotten to Iowa. He took out his phone to call his mother.

"You have a cell phone too?"

That was the second thing he'd done. "It's nineteen ninety-four, Dad. Everyone has a cell phone now."

"Not anyone I know."

Not many people Arlo knew either. But he had one, and that was all that mattered.

At the campsite, Arlo strung a hammock between two trees. He lay down in the hammock and closed his eyes. In his half-sleep, he could feel his father gently pushing him.

They walked through the park along the Des Moines River. Maybe they could swim there, or at least dip their feet in.

"I didn't bring a bathing suit," his father said. At the camping store, he'd bought a pair of breathable pants. He was wearing them now as they hiked along the path.

The river was filled with canoers, kayakers, and tubers, and Arlo, in his bathing suit, said, "Come on, Dad, jump in!"

But his father just stood in the shallows. He rolled up his pants cuffs almost to his knees, then stepped in deeper.

"Be careful, Dad. You'll capsize!" One time, the family had spent the weekend at the beach, and Arlo's father had gotten stung by a jellyfish. He'd cried out in pain—how exhilarating that had been, how terrifying— and afterward, Arlo sat with his father back at the hotel, saying, "Here,

Dad, I'll get you a washcloth," placing his father's foot in a bucket of ice. Was that why he'd taken his father camping? To cast him out into the elements once more, at the mercy of the rattlesnakes and bears?

Back at the campsite, they got the fire going. Arlo was wearing an oven mitt on one hand, and with his other hand he was opening and closing an enormous pair of tongs, ready to have a go at the vegetables. On the picnic bench the mushrooms, onions, and peppers were laid out in rows, like beads on an abacus. He dropped the hot dogs and hamburgers onto the grill.

It was hot out, and he removed from his bag a little battery-operated fan and let it blow air across his forehead. "Let's sit back-to-back," he said. "I could use some support. You probably could, too."

They ate dinner that way, back-to-back, sitting on the ground, hamburger juice dripping on them.

"I got you something," his father said, and he went to the car and returned with a package. "It's a little housewarming gift."

Arlo opened it. "It's your Cornell bowl." He recognized it from his father's study. It held his father's pens and pencils, his erasers, staples, and paper clips: the tools of his trade.

"My parents gave me that bowl when I got into Cornell."

"And now you're giving it to me?"

"It's had a long life. May it have an even longer one."

Arlo held the bowl in front of him.

"This way, you can think of me back home in New York."

Arlo spun the bowl around on his lap. It was strange to have it at this campground, like an animal removed from its natural habitat. "Were your parents proud when you got into Cornell?"

"Probably. Parents are engineered to be proud."

"You graduated number one from your high school, and also number one from Cornell."

"Who told you that?"

Arlo shrugged. It was just something he knew.

"Well, don't go being my publicist," his father said. "It's bad enough when Pru does it."

Arlo placed a blade of grass between his two front teeth and let it bob up and down like a compass needle. "I won't be applying to Cornell."

"You don't have to," his father said. "There are lots of good colleges out there."

"What if I don't want to go to college at all?"

His father was quiet. A man walked by with his Saint Bernard. The dog days of summer, Arlo thought, though there was still another month of spring.

"What about next year?" his father said. "Will you be finishing up high school in Ames?"

"If we even stay here."

"Where else would you go?"

"Beats me."

"Maybe Mom's new man will keep her in town."

"Just as likely, they'll break up and it'll be on to the next place."

Behind them, a man carried his toddler into the bathroom. "I got you something else," his father said, and he went to the car and returned with another package.

"It's your book," Arlo said. *Who Really Wrote Shakespeare?* His father had inscribed it to him: *To Arlo, from your loving father, thinking of you back home in New York.* In the smoky half-light, Arlo stared down at the pages.

"I hope you'll forgive me," his father said. "It's hubris to give someone your own book."

"It's not," Arlo said. "I want it."

His father said, "Pru has this artist friend who gave us one of her paintings, and we're forced to hang it up whenever she comes over, and we take it down as soon as she leaves. With a book, at least, you can hide it on a bookshelf. Or sell it for a few bucks at the Strand."

"I won't sell it," Arlo said. In the lamplight, a mosquito buzzed. "Wasn't your book on the best-seller list?"

"For a week or two."

"Mom says you don't like that it was a best-seller. That you bite the hand that feeds you."

"Well, you know Mom." Spence didn't want to be fighting with Linda, especially when she wasn't even here.

They went to sleep that night in their matching sleeping bags. Outside the tent, the moon glowed ivory. They could hear the crickets susurrating.

On the drive back to Ames Arlo said, "Pru told me you used to ride a moped. That you drove around on it with her."

"I drove around on it with Mom too."

"Where's that moped now?"

"It was turned into scrap metal years ago. I had kids at that point. It wasn't worth the risk."

"Do you miss it?"

"Every now and then, but there are other joys."

"You drove around the city on a moped, but you're afraid to drive a car?" Even now, in the passenger seat, his father was holding on to the handle.

"I'm a mass of contradictions."

"It's because of Enid, right?"

His father shrugged. "Cars are the one place I get claustrophobic. On a moped, at least, there's nothing hemming me in."

"How's Enid, anyway?"

"She's the same. She'll be the same until the day she dies."

"When will that be?"

"Five years? Ten years? Thirty years? Maybe more?"

"And Stanley?"

"I haven't seen him since the party."

"Why not?"

"I haven't known Stanley since we were kids. We wouldn't have anything to say to each other."

"But you're blood relatives."

"That goes only so far."

On the day his father was supposed to leave, Arlo's mother made them lunch. Tuna fish sandwiches. Sliced tomatoes and wedges of Gruyère. A loaf of einkorn bread, pilfered from the bakery. Without Arlo around to watch over the till, his mother was really going to put the store out of business.

Arlo's father didn't like einkorn bread: it wasn't bland enough for him. But Linda, his ex-wife, was cutting him a slice, and he didn't want to seem ungrateful.

They ate lunch on the porch while Arlo's mother sat on the swing. Her new boyfriend had mellowed her. Two weeks ago, she'd been confiscating Arlo's father's mail; now she was making lunch for him.

Arlo looked at his parents. He'd been an accident in deeper ways than that mistaken pregnancy, a product of this unlikely couple. Yet here they were, eating the bread his mother had stolen. He allowed himself to imagine that it had been this way all along, the three of them in their home in Iowa.

On the street, a man was playing the bagpipes.

"Reveille," Arlo said, thinking of a story his father had told, summer camp at the Fresh Air Fund, his father waking up to the sounds of the bugle.

They sat there for a while, eating their sandwiches and drinking lemonade. Arlo's mother fell asleep on the swing. Arlo closed his eyes, too. Then his father stood up. He needed to get to the airport.

That night, Arlo said to his mother, "Give me those letters you confiscated."

His mother handed him the letters.

March 26, 1994

Dear Arlo,

We made a mistake. Come back home. Your bedroom is waiting.

The letter went on, but Arlo stopped reading. What could it have told him that he didn't already know?

That night, he looked through his mother's drawers for more letters, but he couldn't find any. It was better that way, because the letters he already had were enough to break him, and he hadn't been able to read through them anyway. His mother was right to have intercepted those letters. They would have only set him back.

Meanwhile, his father had left: come and gone in two days.

The next morning, garbage day, Arlo dumped the letters in the trash, then waited as they got carted off.

He'd guessed correctly: his mother and her new boyfriend had broken up. So when August came and his mother said, "What do you say we move to San Francisco?" he packed his bags before she could change her mind.

23

Arlo's mother's friend Charlotte lived in San Francisco, and she told them they could stay with her until they got back on their feet. But Arlo wasn't off his feet—that was his mother's problem—and he resented Charlotte's implication. He took an instant dislike to Charlotte, in part because she took an instant liking to him, so extravagant was she in her effusions and embraces he thought she might strangle him.

The other thing he disliked about Charlotte was that she appeared trapped circa 1968, the same year in which his mother was trapped. Until they crossed the Bay Bridge in his mother's Toyota, Arlo had never set foot in San Francisco, but he felt as if his whole life had been San Francisco, so he could have been forgiven for not wanting to dip in and out of the thrift shops on Haight Street, which his mother made clear was her idea of fun. He preferred to wander through Dolores Park, then head into the Mission and Potrero Hill. It reminded him of New York, when he made his roost in the East Village and the Lower East Side, and he would think of his father, whom he was barely in touch with, and he'd be filled with pleasure but also with an abiding regret.

Three months at Charlotte's was more than enough, so they found a small apartment a few blocks away. It was too close to Charlotte's for Arlo's taste, but his mother was happy to have Charlotte nearby; she was his mother's ballast in the city. Charlotte would drop by with corn bread and chili, and though Arlo could have done without the company, he wasn't one to turn down free food.

But the real thing that happened in San Francisco was that he got into one of the good public high schools. School, that sphinx: he finally unlocked the puzzle. He used the tricks he'd been taught to decode words, only they didn't feel like tricks any longer; they were simply how he read. He was thriving at school, but if his father knew about his success—he would make sure he didn't—he would claim it as his own. There emerged in Arlo a battle between his wish to succeed—he would show his father, once and for all—and his wish to fail: he would show his father that way, too.

He graduated from high school because he was too smart to fail. The summer after he graduated, he worked at a Wendy's in downtown Oakland. He hated the job, but he wanted a photo of himself in his Wendy's uniform to send to his father. On the back of the photo he wrote, *I graduated from high school,* and he dropped the photo in the mail.

It was enough to imagine his father opening the envelope. That alone was sufficient for him to endure the work, knowing that every time he flipped a burger his father was thinking of him flipping that burger. While Professor Spence Robin was presiding over the most popular English lecture on campus, his son Arlo was working the microphone at the Wendy's drive-thru. Arlo was on his feet all day, and he smelled of cow fat and pig fat. But he could endure any humiliation as long as his father was tethered to him in his misery.

He stayed the summer at Wendy's and into the fall, long enough to get his first raise and to understand that, as much as it must have pained his father to have a son working at Wendy's, it pained Arlo even more to be that son.

So he quit his job. When he was seven, he'd helped rewire his mother's transistor radio. Now he was assisting UC Berkeley and San Francisco State students with their computer problems. Before long, he was being hired by young professionals in the East and South Bays. He worked out of his mother's apartment on Guerrero Street, but soon the space became too small, and he opened an office above a taqueria, from which free food was delivered in exchange for computer help and troubleshooting with technology. His business grew and grew, and he branched out into the more lucrative field of programming. Soon he was working at Yahoo.

But he was growing restless again. So he left Yahoo and broke his lease. He bought a one-way plane ticket to Asia.

"When will you be back?" his mother said.

"Maybe six months. Maybe never."

"I'll miss you, Arlo."

At least he kissed his mother goodbye before he left. He hadn't talked to his father in six months, and he didn't even tell him he was leaving.

24

Sarah was a sophomore at Reed, standing in line for coffee one morning, when the man behind her said, "I heard a rumor you went to this school."

She just stared at him. "Arlo?"

"Aren't you going to hug me?"

She hesitated, then gave him a hug. She hadn't seen him since that morning six years ago, when his mother picked him up in a cab. The world had evolved, and her relationship with Arlo had devolved in kind: long periods of no communication followed by much shorter periods of communication, after which she wondered whether they should have communicated in the first place. Every time they planned to get together, Arlo backed out.

Arlo had grown into his body. His hair, auburn like their father's, was cropped short. He was wearing blue jeans and a black T-shirt, and he had the beginnings of a goatee. She'd forgotten how handsome he was. Or maybe it was just that he was her brother, so she hadn't noticed. "Look at you," she said. "You've learned to like coffee."

"It's Portland," he reminded her. "If I didn't like coffee, I'd get deported." Also, he said, he'd been trying to sleep as little as possible.

"But you used to love sleep."

He shrugged as if to say he still loved sleep but he'd learned to love other things more.

"Arlo, you hold yourself the same way you used to. I recognize your walk."

He looked at her dubiously. "Would I recognize your walk?"

"Let's see." She trafficked across the café and back.

"Nope," he said. "I don't recognize your walk."

She felt strangely disappointed. Maybe he was just taunting her. He'd always been good at that. "Come," she said. "I'll introduce you to my dog." She untied Kingsley from a post. He thumped his tail against her leg, then thumped his tail against Arlo's leg; soon he was sniffing her brother's sneakers.

"Way to a man's heart," Arlo said, "but can I give you some brotherly advice? You should never leave a dog tied up. I had half a mind to steal him. He's a handsome creature."

"Thank you," she said, but then she felt foolish: Arlo wasn't saying *she* was a handsome creature. "Listen," she said, "if you want a dog, you don't need to steal one. There are thousands just waiting for a good home."

"But I don't have a good home."

For an instant she wondered whether Arlo might be homeless. But he looked carefully groomed, and despite having claimed he'd dispensed with sleep, he appeared well rested.

"Seriously, I rarely spend two nights in a row under the same roof."

"Are you an itinerant worker?"

"After a fashion. What about you?"

"Am *I* an itinerant worker?" She was a college student, which was closer to being an itinerant worker than she'd have liked to think. She moved from library to library and class to class; sometimes she made pit stops in the dining hall. "I'm a sophomore at Reed. Or a second-year, as they now call it."

"So as not to sound sophomoric?"

"So as not to call the first-years freshmen. Speaking of which, I'm going to be late for my next class. Animal studies. If only I could bring this animal along." She let go of Kingsley's leash, and again he sniffed Arlo's sneakers. "So, busy person, how will you be spending your busy day?"

"I thought I'd check out the alma mater."

"Wait a second," she said. "You went to Reed?"

A tinge of indignation colored Arlo's face. Not for the first time, she saw how quickly he turned defensive. She said, "I just figured college was beneath you."

"College *is* beneath me. I went to Reed the same way Steve Jobs went to Reed. I dropped out after a semester."

"So you're one of the millions of people who think they're going to be the next Steve Jobs?"

"Listen," he said, "I'm off for the day. How about I watch your dog while you go to class. I can show him old haunts."

"You were here for a semester and you have old haunts?"

"He can show *me* old haunts."

"The thing is, I'll be gone all afternoon."

"In that case, sign me up." Arlo spoke like someone people succumbed to, and so it was best to relent sooner and avoid all the fuss.

"My address is on his collar," she said. She handed Arlo the leash, and then she was gone, leaving Kingsley with her brother.

The sky was dark when she got back to her building, and when Kingsley saw her he nearly escaped his leash.

"He missed you terribly," Arlo said. "All day long he's been talking about you."

"Do you have time for dinner?" she said. "There's a good restaurant nearby. My treat."

She took him upstairs to meet her housemates, but then she realized she'd never told them about him. And Arlo, perhaps sensing this, said, "I'm Sarah's long-lost cousin," and he shook her housemates' hands.

At the restaurant, they ordered a bottle of wine, and through the haze of candlelight her reflection swayed in the glass. "Arlo, you're all grown up."

"I was always the grown-up compared to you."

He was right: he was her big brother. Yet she'd always considered herself older than he was. Now he'd caught up, maybe even surpassed her.

Their food came: the steak for Arlo, the eggplant for her. "Listen," she said, "you didn't have to say you were my long-lost cousin. I'm not embarrassed by you."

"And *I'm* not embarrassed by *you.*"

"Touché," she said. What a strange phrase, she thought, *long-lost cousin,* when she considered cousins almost automatically long lost. She recalled that visit to Stanley's, how hard Arlo had worked to plan the get-together, how disappointed he'd been.

It was raining outside. A man speared his umbrella at the sky while the cars came fast around the bend, spraying water at him. She had heard the reports about Portland weather, but when she visited Reed her senior year of high school it had been a sunny April day and the trees were blossoming, and campus was bathed in an almost heavenly light. That, as much as anything, was why she'd chosen Reed. How ill equipped she'd been to determine her future, to decide anything at all. "Jesus, Arlo, all I know is you dropped out of college and you're good with dogs. Tell me what you've been up to."

So he told her about Iowa and San Francisco, how he finally solved the riddle of school. "I got a fifteen hundred on my SAT."

"Jesus, Arlo, that's better than I did."

"Are you surprised?"

"No," she said, though she was.

"Those tests are stupid."

"A lot of things are stupid, but you do them anyway."

"Not me."

"Except you did. You took that test."

"And I failed it."

"I thought you said you got a fifteen hundred."

"My official score was a five forty." Acing things and failing things, Arlo said: it was the story of his life. He'd taken the SAT and answered nearly all the questions correctly: six wrong on verbal and three wrong on math. In each section, he intentionally skipped a question so that he filled in the wrong bubble. The answer to the first question he put in line two, the answer to the second question he put in line three, all the way until the end of the section. For a fee of $9.25, he was sent a copy of the test he'd taken so he could match up his answers with the correct ones. He was able to calculate his true score, the one he would have gotten if he'd filled in the proper bubbles.

"Jesus, Arlo. That's insane."

He shrugged. He'd been living in Asia, he explained, but eventually it was time to come home. Apple was everywhere, and it was true: he was determined to be the next Steve Jobs. The first step, he decided, was to drop out of Reed, but in order to drop out of Reed, he had to go there. So he flew home. When he touched down at PDX, he went straight to the airport barbershop, where, in preparation for the interview he hadn't scheduled, he got a haircut, his first in a year.

"You just showed up at admissions?" Sarah said.

"Posture," he said. "It's what gets you across the threshold and into the room." He told the dean of admissions about his travels in Asia and about his time in San Francisco as a programmer. He mentioned his poor SAT score, though not about having filled in the wrong bubbles: he wasn't there to make excuses. He saw an SAT prep book on the shelf, and he offered to take a practice test right there. He made a deal with the dean: if he got a perfect score, the dean would let him in. "And that's how I ended up at Reed."

"Well, that's quite a story," Sarah said.

"It's not just a story. It's true."

"Tell me something," she said. "You went to Reed just to drop out?"

"I can read Dante on my own time. The world was calling me."

"And what has the world taught you?"

"That I no longer want to be the next Steve Jobs. I'm happy to be the first Arlo Zackheim. I'm back at Yahoo now, but I'm thinking of starting my own company. Suffice it to say, no one has to worry about me anymore."

"I was never worried about you." It was true. She had always known he would find his way.

"I'm going to be rich," he said.

"Is that how you're going to thumb your nose at Dad? By making money?"

"It's as good a way as any."

"Have you told him this?"

Arlo shook his head. "It's been a while since we spoke."

She'd gathered as much, but she was still sorry.

"It's for the better," he said. "We weren't meant to get along."

What did that mean? They were father and son: of course they were meant to get along. And if they didn't get along, they were meant to try harder. His relationship with Arlo was the great failure of her father's life, and at the simple mention of his name, he would make that precipitous drop into melancholy.

"And do you want to know the crazy thing? Keeping my distance hasn't done me any good." Even here, Arlo said, he was looking out at the street, thinking that if his father were eating at this restaurant he would ask to be seated away from the window. Why did it drive him crazy that his father didn't want strangers to see him eat the way other people didn't want strangers to see them go to the bathroom? "I'm going to make a lot of money," he said, "but Dad will still look down at me, because if I'm not going to be a literature professor or a historian or a classicist—if I'm not going to do something no one gives a fuck about—I might as well be a plumber. When we'd be up a creek without plumbers. Dad counts on his toilet being unclogged so he can look down on people who unclog toilets."

"I didn't realize you were going into the toilet business."

"What I'm saying is, I can't eat a meal without thinking about Dad."

"Parents are burdens."

"He's earned the right to be a burden on you. Do you know how long I lived under his roof? Six hundred and thirty-one nights."

"You counted?"

"You've lived almost as long on this campus."

"Dad's proud of you," she said. "You're his son."

"He doesn't even know what Yahoo is."

"Then educate him."

Arlo shook his head.

"Listen to me," she said. "There's regret on both sides. But that doesn't have to be the end of the story. You could still be in touch."

"My mother doesn't want me to be in touch."

"Your mother? What are you, Arlo, six years old?"

"I have obligations to her. She raised me."

"What about me?"

"What *about* you?"

"I was miserable after you left. I thought about you constantly that first year."

"It's easy to miss someone when they're gone. You were a jerk to me."

"You were a jerk to me, too."

Arlo leaned across the table so that the candle flame flickered just inches from his shirt. For a second she thought he would combust; for a second she wanted him to. "Jesus, Arlo, I was a teenager." She was still only twenty, barely past being a teenager now.

Then she said it—said it before she knew she was going to say it. "Why did you chop off my hair?" She'd been waiting to ask him this question for years, even as she hadn't realized she'd been waiting to ask it.

"It's a good question," he said, but even now, six years later, he didn't have a good response. He'd scared Sarah by doing what he'd done, but he'd scared himself even more. The things he was capable of. Leaving New York for the last time, he was already rewriting what had happened. That night at the club, Sarah may not have been twenty-one yet, but already at fourteen she had the connivance of adulthood. She'd set him up, he told himself. And when he cut off her hair, she'd set him up, too.

Now he had a question of his own. Why didn't she say anything at the time? Because what still haunted him was her composure. *I cut my hair. I've always wanted it short.* Her refusal to acknowledge what he'd done, as if he didn't exist at all. That was what he found most chilling. "Were you trying to freak me out?"

Sarah laughed. She wished she were as poised as that. A memory came to her from when Arlo had been living with them, her mother reminding her that Arlo had had a hard life, that for years he'd been living with his feckless mother. There was something about that word, *feckless*, that startled her; to this day it sent shivers down her back. She felt guilty for the life she had, as if in coming along she'd taken Arlo's life away, as if life were a meal and she'd eaten more than her fair share of it. It was always food they competed over, and she thought this again at the restaurant, watching Arlo wolf down his dessert.

When the bill came, Arlo reached for it. She'd said dinner would be on her, but even that he wouldn't give her.

When they got to her apartment, the sky opened up. Rain was falling down her brother's face, and he looked both louche and fragile standing there, allowing himself to get wet.

"So this is it?" she said. "I don't see you again for another six years?"

"I don't know if it will be that long." But the way he spoke, with the curious speculation of someone observing his own life, made her think it might be even longer.

"Come upstairs with me," she said. "Say goodbye to my housemates. Say goodbye to my dog."

Her housemates were gone when they got upstairs, but Kingsley jumped up and licked her brother's face.

Arlo didn't even remove his coat. "Take care of yourself, pup."

Those were the last words he said, and they hadn't even been to her. She stood at the window as he walked down the path, until he was out of sight.

25

Sarah got to the admissions office early. Unlike Arlo, she'd made an appointment. Her posture was fine, but it wasn't getting her across any thresholds.

The dean was about fifty-five, with a full head of silver hair, and he wore a navy blazer and an open-collared shirt. He'd been a professor once, but academia hadn't been for him, so he moved into administration.

"Do you know Arlo Zackheim?" she said.

"Why do you ask?"

"He's my half brother."

The dean nodded. "I remember him vaguely."

She said, "Did my brother talk his way into Reed?"

"All our students talk their way into Reed. It's called an interview."

"But did he do it differently?" Her gaze alighted on a bookshelf, where an SAT prep book stuck out. Was that the book Arlo had told her about? "Would you be able to tell me my brother's SAT score?"

The dean laughed.

"I didn't think so."

"First of all, I don't remember your brother's SAT score. Second of all, those scores are confidential."

"He told me a strange story," she said, and she repeated Arlo's story to the dean.

"That *is* a strange story."

"So you're saying it's not true?"

"I'm saying this sounds like a family matter." The dean wrote down the phone number for student counseling and escorted her to the door.

———

As he left Portland that night, Arlo wondered whether Sarah believed anything about him. Checking out the alma mater? Well, yes, he'd gone to Reed. But the reason he'd come back was to see her again. He couldn't admit it, so he'd wandered around campus for hours until he found her at the café.

He had, in fact, done well on the SAT—not as well as he'd claimed, but well enough. That story he'd told about the dean? The truth was, he hadn't even met him. He was admitted to college the regular way. But this demeaned him, felt like an indignity.

Did he want to be the next Steve Jobs? Absolutely. But he had no idea why Steve Jobs had dropped out, and he hadn't been planning to drop out himself.

He had trouble, though, going to class; he was busy with his programming business. And it was insulting to write papers and study for exams. He got Cs and Ds that first semester. If he'd played the game and gone to class, he could have gotten As. But what if he'd gone to class and hadn't gotten As? So he cut bait before someone else could cut it for him.

He was doing well in tech, rising up the ranks at Yahoo, but the reason he was driving through the night was to be back in San Francisco the next morning for his classes at San Francisco State. Though once he got back, he slept through them anyway.

A year later, he transferred again, this time to UC Berkeley. He hated college, but he needed to graduate in order to go to medical school.

The problem was, his academic record was spotty. An A in organic chemistry, an A in physics, but Bs, Cs, and Ds in his other classes, a penchant for excellence when he set his mind to things and an almost principled resistance to doing so. His MCATs, like his SATs, were strong. The medical schools didn't know what to make of him. They turned him down, except for a medical school in Grenada, but all he knew about Grenada was that Reagan had bombed it, and he wasn't going to medical school there.

In August, he got off the waitlist at the University of Nevada. He left

Yahoo with his stock options. He could live off the money for a while, and if he didn't like medical school he could ski and prowl the casinos.

There were only sixty-five students in his medical school class, but a month into the semester he was introduced to a classmate, who said, "You go here?" He had no idea why he'd gone to medical school, or why he'd endured premed. Because of a conversation he'd had years ago with his sister, something she probably couldn't even recall? Because they'd said they'd be doctors together? In a few years, when Sarah was in med school herself, he would tell himself it was because of him, but he felt as if she were taunting him, reminding him she was the favored child.

He didn't even bother to withdraw from school: he simply left. By Thanksgiving, back in San Francisco, he had trouble remembering he'd ever been gone. Yahoo offered to take him back, but he was already working at his start-up.

26

The next time Sarah saw Arlo, she had graduated from college and was back in New York, applying to medical school. "Dad's been given a new rank," she told him over the phone. "There's a ceremony for him."

"Have the cardinals convened? I always knew Dad would someday be pope."

"Not pope," she said. "University Professor." It meant you transcended department. In theory, at least, their father could be a dramaturge now. He could teach physics, or Portuguese.

"So you're inviting me to the coronation?"

She was. But when she told Arlo the date, he said he was busy. There would be other elevations, other honors: he would try to come next time.

But as the cocktail hour started, she saw her brother from across the room. "Mom, Arlo's here."

"Does Dad know?"

She shook her head. She hadn't even known herself.

Her father, sipping a club soda, was conferring with the president and the provost. He looked up and saw Arlo. "You'll have to excuse me," he said, and he walked across the room to his son.

"Dad." Arlo had seen his father twice since Iowa, but not in the last couple of years. They hesitated for a moment, then hugged.

"Son, you're all grown up."

Arlo nodded.

"Let's take a walk," his father said. "They can elevate me in absentia, for all I care."

They made their way across College Walk, Arlo's father still sipping his club soda, Arlo with a cup of red wine. A man stood on the steps, playing the trumpet. A college kid was fiddling around with a golf club, swinging at an imaginary ball.

Philosophy Hall was dark except for the illumination from the EXIT sign and from the small lamp on Arlo's father's desk. "Have a seat," he said.

Arlo spun around on his father's chair, recalling visits to this office when he was a teenager, seated where he was now.

"If I'd known you were coming, I'd have cleaned up."

"My start-up's office is cluttered, too."

"It's the sign of an organized mind."

"That's what I tell myself."

Arlo's father tapped the computer monitor. "They've given me one of these machines."

"Dad, it's called a computer."

"That I know."

"Do you ever use it?"

"Not when I can avoid it. I still write my lectures by hand, and my secretary types them up for me."

"And email?"

"I use it occasionally. I prefer letters, or the phone. Come," he said. "Show me what's inside." He seemed to think information was inside computers the way milk was inside the fridge. "Tell me about your start-up."

"We provide restaurant reservations online. We've started in San Francisco, and we're hoping to expand around the world."

"And before that, you worked at Yahoo?"

Arlo nodded. "Yahoo you know about."

"I've heard of it," his father said unconvincingly.

"Yahoo's a search engine," Arlo said. "Now, take a look at this." He typed his father's name into the computer. "Here's your event tonight. People can know about it anywhere in the world."

"Is that how you found out about tonight's event? From Yahoo?"

"Sarah told me." Arlo pressed a few more keys, and an image of himself appeared on the screen, beneath the logo for his start-up. "That's my company. I'm on Yahoo, therefore I am. What about you?" he said. "What's new in Shakespeare scholarship?"

"Not much. There are new trends, of course, but the work I do is all about the old."

"Yet you seem to be reaching new heights."

"It's nothing."

"You always refused to brag."

"What's the point? Honors are nice, but it's mostly good fortune."

"But the work?" Arlo said. "That you love?"

"I'm committed to it," his father said. "Love—that's for family. It's for Pru and Sarah, and for you."

Arlo looked away. This wasn't what he had come for. Though what he had come for he didn't know.

"Look," his father said, "I know I was difficult."

"I was too. The thing is, you were a teenager yourself once. You probably rebelled, too."

"I did."

"You were arrested."

His father looked startled. "Who told you?"

"Stanley."

"When?"

"That day in New Jersey. He said you broke into someone's house and wrote graffiti."

His father nodded.

"Why didn't you tell me?"

"I didn't see the point."

"You always hid things from me."

"That's not true."

"You didn't tell Pru I existed. You didn't let her know you had a son."

His father was quiet.

"Were you embarrassed by me?"

"Never." It was Linda he'd been embarrassed by. He'd wanted to split custody.

"Then why didn't you?"

"She wouldn't agree."

Then the phone rang and it was Pru, saying the guests were waiting. He had to come back to deliver his speech.

They returned to the celebration, where, for a few minutes, Arlo stood in back. Then he did what he'd done at seventeen. He left without saying goodbye.

He spent the night at a hotel, and the next morning he took the subway downtown and loitered outside a club. It was daytime and the club was desolate, like a church after the parishioners had streamed out. Many of his old hangouts were gone now; it was hard to do business in the city.

He walked down Essex Street, and he didn't realize where he was going until he stepped inside. The Schoenfeld Rehabilitation Center. He had come to see Enid.

The metal detector, the divesting of wallet and keys: security was as strict as it had been last time; it was as if he were at a border crossing. There was still the same book, the same onion-skin paper, grimy and tea-stained, with the guests' names printed on it. "I've come to see Enid Robin."

"Are you an authorized guest?"

"I am."

The man flipped through the book. "Her only authorized guest is Spence Robin."

"That's me." But Arlo didn't have ID, not with his father's name on it.

He returned a couple of hours later. Eleven years had passed, but he still knew how to make a fake ID. The security guard pressed a name-tag to his chest, like someone pinning a corsage.

Enid was brought out. She had no idea who he was. Why should she have? The last time he'd been here, she'd had no idea either. She was wearing a floral-print dress, which inflated like a parachute in the breeze. She touched her hair.

"I'm Darlene," the attendant said. She looked at his father's name printed across Arlo's chest.

Then the music came on—the same music as last time, Arlo thought, as if the show had been on replay. The lemonade followed, as if it, too, had been kept on reserve. Again Enid asked if she could have lemonade, and again she was told sugar wasn't good for her. Sugar wasn't good for anyone; Arlo himself avoided it. Still, he believed life was made up of little privileges, and if he were ever told he couldn't have lemonade, he would have to kill himself. "Enid, will you sing for me?"

Enid started to sing—a Yiddish song, a plangent song—and Arlo, his eyes closed, hummed along with her. He thought he was going to cry. "Can I use the bathroom?" he asked the attendant. "I'll be back in a minute."

But he didn't come back. He still had his father's nametag on, and when he finished in the bathroom he went down to the lobby and stepped out onto the street.

Back uptown, he entered his father's building. "I'm Arlo Zackheim," he told the doorman. "Spence Robin's son."

"Professor Robin's at work."

"That's all right." All these years later, he'd kept his key.

There was still a no-shoes policy, still the shoe cubby like a bulwark in the hall. He removed his shoes and walked through the apartment in just his socks, careful not to disturb anything.

His old bedroom, at long last, had been switched back to his father's study, the bed replaced by a couch. He lay down on it and closed his eyes. He fell asleep for several minutes.

In the hallway, the charcoal map of Florence still hung on the wall. Above him, the smoke alarm blinked. The Käthe Kollwitz print hung in the living room. A couple of chairs had been reupholstered, but everything else remained the same. He sat down at the grand piano and struck a few keys, then played a song of his own devising.

He found the TV in the linen closet. It was removed only for special occasions; the rest of the year it was hidden away. His father's plaques and awards were on a ledge, next to the fitted sheets and pillowcases.

On the shelf in the living room stood his father's books. *Beyond Verona: Shakespeare's Politics and Poetics. When the Elizabethans Ruled. Humoral Musings: The Complexion of Shakespeare's Sonnets. How New Is the New Historicism? Kicking and Screaming: Essays in Renaissance Culture. Who Really Wrote Shakespeare? When There's a Will, There's a Way: Performance and Costume on the Elizabethan Stage.* He flipped through the pages, then put the books back on the shelf.

He took an apple from the fridge and ate it down to the core and tossed it in the garbage. He took another apple and ate it too. He wandered through the apartment for the last time. He put his shoes back on and closed the door behind him.

Down the stairs he went, past the Putneys and the Fitzgeralds, the Lathams and the Schwartzes and the Abner-Goldsteins, the doorman in the lobby ushering him out. He thought of school days when he was a teenager, looking up from across the street to see his father at the window, waving to him.

In another few years, his father would be sick. Even before Sarah called him with the news, he'd suspected something. That night in New York, sitting in his father's office while the celebrants waited for them to return, he thought the disease might be taking hold. It wasn't confusion, exactly, just a kind of reckoning, as if his father were ordering his affairs. And a softness in his father he couldn't recall. Was it possible the disease had made his father gentler?

Part VI

27

"I want to introduce you to my oldest friend," Camille said.

"I thought I was your oldest friend," Pru said.

"You're my closest friend. Walter's my oldest friend." Back in high school, Camille had been friends with Walter's younger brother, so she became friends with Walter, too. They'd been out of touch for years, but she ran into him last week on the subway.

"Is he a caregiver?" Pru said, because Camille had been saying Pru should befriend other caregivers. She'd even suggested Pru take a caregiving class.

"Kind of."

"He's *kind of* a caregiver?"

"Just get together with him and you'll see."

They'd agreed to meet at a burger joint, but Pru was twenty minutes late. She found Walter at a table, waiting for her. "I'm sorry," she said. She started to say something about subway delays, but Walter stopped her. He understood: when he was told he had something in common with someone, he ran the other way, too.

His complexion was so fair Pru could see the capillaries running beneath his skin. His beard cast his face in shadows. His eyes were pale green, set precariously between mourning and mirth, and he had a mass of dark hair he kept patting down as if to prevent it from ascending skyward. He was handsome, she thought, carelessly so, as if the very notion hadn't occurred to him.

He ordered them each a cheeseburger and fries. "Camille tells me your husband has Alzheimer's."

Pru nodded.

"I'm so sorry."

"And you're taking care of someone, too?"

"It's complicated," Walter said. He'd met his wife when they were seventeen, though they'd waited until they finished college to get married. "Columbia," he said, thrusting his thumb in the direction of campus.

"My husband taught at Columbia," Pru said, then wondered why she'd said that.

"My wife put me through graduate school," Walter said, "and then, after twenty-five years of marriage, she up and left me. All those clichés about not seeing it coming? Well, in my case, they were true." A french fry was pinned to Walter's fork; for a moment he just held it there. "My wife fell in love with someone else, but a few years later she got Parkinson's. Then her husband left her."

"That's awful," Pru said, though she feared she was protesting too much. Because who in the position of this man—who in her own position—didn't entertain fantasies of leaving? "And now you're the one taking care of her?"

"I'm not the main person, no, but I stop by a few times a week. She has the day nurse and the night nurse, but neither the day nurse nor the night nurse was ever married to her."

"That's very generous of you."

"She helped put me through graduate school."

"That was years ago."

"You sound just like my sons. They tell me I should get on with my life."

"You haven't been?"

"I have." He went to work every day, he played tennis twice a week, he'd been in a few relationships. But Anne had been his wife no matter what had happened, and she was the mother of his children. "If our boys visited her more, maybe I'd visit her less, but someone has to visit her." Walter ran his napkin across his face, as if to say he was through—with his meal, with his story. "What's that old joke? I've been talking too much about me—what do *you* think about me?" He laid his hands on the table. His wrists were as pale as eggshell. His knuckles were pale, too, his fingers long.

"That tie of yours," Pru said.

"This?" It was a bright red tie, the bottom strip slightly longer than the top one. "I've despaired of ever getting it right."

But she'd meant the tie itself. It was six in the evening, Walter was released from work, but he still had his tie on. "Spence—my husband—he used to say he earned three-quarters of his salary just for grading exams and he was paid in the currency of not having to wear a necktie."

"Your husband's a smart man. I think of ties as women's revenge for having to wear high heels."

"Yet you're wearing a tie now and no one's forcing you to."

Walter shrugged. "That's the power of convention for you."

At the next table, a girl extended an earbud to another girl so they could listen to music together. Walter examined his reflection in the discarded cutlery. "And there you were, staring at my tie, when I thought it was my tooth you were staring at."

"Why would I be staring at your tooth?"

Walter pulled back his top lip to reveal that one of his front teeth was slightly discolored. "It's an old basketball injury." He'd been playing one-on-two against his sons—this must have been twenty years ago—and the older one collided with his mouth. "Dead tooth," Walter said. He could have gotten it bleached, but it was too much bother, and his wife was paranoid about chemicals. He used to keep her away from the *Science Times* because whenever she read about a new disease she was convinced she had it. "And then she got Parkinson's. An old disease."

"But you're not married to her anymore. What's to stop you from dyeing it now?"

"I've gotten used to it. I tell myself it's distinguished, like gray hair."

"And basketball? Do you still play?"

Walter laughed. "Take a look at this." He lifted his pants to reveal the leg of a near-sixty-year-old, bulbous and knobby as an old tree, a tributary of veins running through it. "My war wounds. Twice-torn meniscus, torn ACL, bone chips in both ankles. Certain sports aren't meant to be played by people over forty. Even my sons have stopped playing basketball. My wife tried to get me to stop playing for years."

"You talk a lot about your wife," Pru said.

"And you talk a lot about your husband."

Actually, she'd mentioned her husband only twice. And the other difference was, she was still married to her husband.

Walter stared down at his plate, where a few bites of cheeseburger remained uneaten next to a hummock of coleslaw. A man in a black beret was mopping the vestibule. A woman at the next table kept using the word *chignon*.

It was dark outside, and through the window Pru could see a bus blundering across town. "Listen," she said, "it was nice to meet you."

"It was nice to meet you, too," Walter said.

Out on the street, Pru walked one way and Walter walked the other. She turned around to look at him as he disappeared down the block.

28

When Pru and her mother got to Camille's apartment, Camille introduced them to Bruce, her new boyfriend, who looked, oddly, like Camille herself, with his own angular jaw, his own shock of blond curls. "Happy Thanksgiving!" Camille said.

"Happy Thanksgiving!" Pru had been planning to bring Spence too, but she feared he wouldn't enjoy himself, so she arranged for Ginny and Rafe to have Thanksgiving with him.

A college girl came in and poured wine. Then she returned with plates of hors d'oeuvres: bruschetta with tomato and mozzarella, caramelized onions on fingers of toast, leek tartlets, mushroom beignets. A couple entered the living room wearing matching leather jackets, followed by a young woman in culottes and a man in a silk shirt and a bolo tie. A man sat at the piano, flipping through some sheet music. "Brahms," he whispered, and the woman beside him slung her arm across his back.

Then the doorbell rang and it was Walter.

"Oh," Pru said. She hadn't realized he'd be here.

"I thought I'd surprise you," Camille said.

Walter was wearing a dark blazer and gray chinos. He removed a hardhat from his head. "I biked here," he explained. He kissed Camille on the cheek. Then he kissed Pru on the cheek, and she blushed.

Everyone seated themselves at the table, and Camille suggested they all say what they were thankful for. Pru disliked these rituals, and she spent the minutes leading up to her turn trying to figure out what to say. Walter seemed as reluctant as she was, though he did his best, saying what everyone else was saying: health, children, relative peace on earth, at least on the tiny part of earth they inhabited. Then it was

Pru's turn, and she said she was thankful for her daughter and her husband, for the years they'd had together. "My husband's not well," she said, and everyone nodded somberly.

Someone said, "I'm thankful Barack Obama is president," and someone else said, "I'm thankful Lehman Brothers collapsed."

One of the guests asked Camille how she and Bruce had met.

"A group of us went on a camping trip," Camille said. "I forgot my toothbrush, and Bruce said I could borrow his. It made me think he might like me. Which made me wonder if *I* might like *him*."

One couple had met Israeli dancing at NYU. Which was funny, the man said, because neither of them was Israeli.

"Or Jewish," the woman said.

"Or students at NYU," said the man.

Then it was Pru's turn and she said, "I pass."

A chorus of "Come on!" rose from the table. Even the college girl, who had returned with more wine, seemed eager for her to speak. Thank God for Walter, the only person at the table who wasn't making her unburden herself, who agreed to do it for her.

He'd met his ex-wife in high school, Walter said, though they hadn't known each other at the time. That was how it went at their enormous public school; everyone stuck to their own crowd. But they had the same last name—Cohen—so they ended up with each other's graduation gown. "And out of that grew a marriage. And, later, a divorce." Growing up, Walter's wife had been adamant that she wouldn't change her name when she got married, and then she didn't have to. But it bothered her that people would think she'd changed her name, so she considered changing it to Cohen-Cohen. But then she'd have been changing her name in order to prove she wouldn't change her name, which would have defeated the purpose.

Out the window, Pru could see the tessellated sparkle of Broadway. A woman got up to play the piano. The other guests rose to walk around before dessert, which left Pru and Walter alone.

"Where did you get that?" she said. She was pointing across the room at Walter's hardhat.

"At work."

"You build things?"

"I'm a structural engineer. I make sure buildings don't fall down."

"Well, that's important!"

"You laugh, but they don't stay up on their own."

But she hadn't been laughing. It was hot in the apartment, and she wiped a dark frond of hair from in front of her face. She could hear the TV in the other room, the Macy's Thanksgiving Day Parade on replay.

Back at the table, pecan pie was being served, and the college girl brought out coffee and tea. Camille emerged from the kitchen holding a cake with a single candle lit on it. People started to sing "Happy Birthday," and Pru, not knowing whose birthday it was, sang, too. Then she heard the words *Happy birthday, dear Pru,* and she started. "How did you remember it was my birthday?"

"I've known you for almost forty years," Camille said. "Did you think I'd forget?"

"Is this a big one?" someone said.

"Big enough," Pru said. She'd turned fifty-five.

"More millstone than milestone?" someone said, and someone else said, "Now, now."

Walter handed Pru a box covered in gift wrap. "Camille told me it was your birthday, so I thought I'd get you something."

She was holding Walter's gift, fumbling with the ribbon, which was tied so tight she couldn't undo the knot.

"Here," Walter said. "Let me help you." For an instant their fingers touched.

It was a cashmere scarf, gray with a red stripe down the middle, like a filament on a candy cane. "It's beautiful!"

"Wear it well," Walter said, and Pru grew teary-eyed. She was thinking of Spence, of the nightgown he'd bought her, how he'd been afraid he would forget her birthday, and now, ten months later, he had.

It was after midnight when they left, and the streets were desolate and hardscrabble. A gust of cold air blew past. "Brrr," Pru's mother said, but it was just a show because when it came to the weather, she was hardier than Pru was.

Broadway was blanketed in darkness. The only illumination came from some fugitive streetlamps and the lights from the twenty-four-hour drugstore, where a couple of solitary figures revolved through the aisles. Pru thought of the neighborhood when she first got here, her trips to the drugstore before the chains came in, loading up on the shampoos of the 1970s: Breck and Wella Balsam and "Gee, Your Hair Smells Terrific."

On the corner, a drunk called out, "Happy birthday, Jesus!" having gotten his holidays mixed up. A sign hung in a window: BEWARE OF THE DOG. THE CAT ISN'T TO BE TRUSTED EITHER.

"I was just thinking," her mother said. "This is the thirtieth Thanksgiving I've been without Dad. And that's not counting all the Thanksgivings before him."

"May you have many more Thanksgivings, Mom."

"I don't know about many."

"Ad mayah v'esrim." Until 120: Moses' age. Her father had always said those words; if only he'd directed them at himself. He used to bless Pru and her brother Hank every Friday when the sun set. *Yesimcha Elohim c'Efraim v'chimnahsheh. Yesimaich Elohim c'Sarah, Rivka, Rachelle, v'Layah. Yevarechicha Adonai v'yishmirecha . . .* And when he died, Pru's mother took over. Even now, when she didn't keep Shabbat anymore, Pru would call her mother every Friday afternoon, and she would stand quietly with the receiver pressed to her ear while her mother recited the blessing. "Do you miss Dad?"

"All the time."

Of course she did. They'd been married for thirty-one years, and it had been a good marriage. Her mother rarely spoke about her father; sometimes it seemed as if she'd forgotten him. But she hadn't forgotten him, she was making clear now; she was just a private person. "You surprised me when Daddy died. I thought you'd drop it all. That you'd stop being religious."

"I was married to Dad for most of my adult life. Certain things stick."

"Do they?" Because when her father was alive, her mother hadn't been drawn to religion. Pru recalled when she was a girl and her friend caught her mother eating breaded shrimp.

"It's funny," her mother said, "because I must have been married twenty-five years the first time I was alone for Shabbat. Dad was away for the weekend. You and Hank were gone, too. I asked myself was I really going to observe all the rules when it was just me alone without him?"

"And did you?"

She shook her head. "I couldn't do it without Daddy beside me."

"Yet now that he's dead, you're more observant than ever."

"It's a paradox, isn't it?" But her mother was also saying it wasn't a paradox. Because now that Pru's father was gone, her mother felt more beholden to him than she had when he was living.

They were standing at a streetlight, waiting for a dump truck to pass. A woman was bent over a garbage can. "Have there been other people you love?"

"There have been you and Hank, of course. Nothing's more important to me than family."

"I meant other men."

Her mother laughed. "I was eighteen when I met Dad. Back then, high school girls didn't date."

"But after Dad. These past years."

Her mother looked bewildered. "You're asking if I date?"

"Yes, Mom."

"It's not like I have to fend the men off."

"I bet you do." Her mother was eighty-three, but she was still attractive. She had her wits about her; she was engaged with the world. "It's been thirty years, Mom. I wouldn't mind if you dated again."

"But *I* mind. I like my life the way it is." Down 81st Street, the wreckage was laid out from the parade: Horton the Elephant, Buzz Lightyear, the Pillsbury Doughboy, everyone in their holding pens. "I've been on a few dates, if you must know. This one man was interested in something more serious, but he was eighty-six."

"Eighty-six-year-olds are people, too."

"I'm not saying he wasn't a person. But my health is good. Who wants to date an older man?"

"It's been done before." Pru had done it herself—even Spence was older than she was—though she was thinking about Matthew, the man she'd dated when she first moved to New York, forty-seven when she was only twenty-two. A few months ago, she'd run into Matthew for the first time in decades. He was eighty now, but he was still quick-footed and sharp. In this regard, she'd bet wrong. Though what did she want? To be married to a healthy eighty-year-old?

Her mother said, "You're the one who should be going out on dates."

"You're forgetting something, Mom. I'm married."

"This wasn't what you bargained for."

"No one bargains for anything."

"What about Walter?" she said. "He seems lovely."

"He could be the loveliest person on earth, but that doesn't make me any less married."

The M104 was an empty canister, churning up slush as it passed. On the corner, a woman removed a pear from her bag and rubbed it vigorously against her coat.

Back at the apartment, Ginny and Rafe were sacked out in the living room, and Spence was asleep in bed. Pru removed Walter's scarf from its package. He'd held it only briefly—it was still in the box—but it smelled like him: lemon and cloves and a hint of musk.

She put the scarf away in the closet. Then, not wanting anyone to see it, she hid it under a pile of clothes.

Spence was asleep when she entered their bedroom, and she touched him gently on the neck. "Spence, darling." She balled up her socks and put them in her shoes. She folded her cardigan and laid it on the dresser, then removed her shirt, bra, and underpants and arranged them side by side.

She was naked now, their toes touching. She felt his heartbeat through his pajamas, the thrum of his pulse. A guttural sound rose from him; his breath was marshy, brackish. He was asleep and not asleep, pliant, offering up one pajama leg after the other, and she was like a tailor, hunched at his feet. She slid his pajama pants down his thighs, leg by leg, molting him, until all that was left were his legs themselves, goosebumped as a chicken. She slid her hand under his bottom so she could get at the tail of his shirt.

She untoggled his shirt buttons, going down his flank. Now all that remained was his diaper. She tugged on the Velcro and tossed it into the trash. She kissed his neck, his forehead. There was a burbling inside him, like a pot of tea. "Spence, darling." She could smell talc and turpentine, and now the vague scent of formaldehyde. A sheen of sweat clung to his stomach.

She took him in her mouth, and he hardened. A murmur rose from him, a moan, and she said, "Spence, honey, it's me." There was a nod or something like it, a tipping of the head. But then he was soft again: an exhalation, an expiration, just the salty, flaccid taste of him. She tried once more, but the blood wouldn't course through him.

She mounted him, trying to guide him into her, and this time there was a different sort of moan. She feared she was hurting him, but soon he grew silent. "Spence?" she said. "Darling?" A distant keening came from within him, the receding blare of an alarm, and he rolled onto his side.

It wouldn't happen: there was no use.

She retrieved the diaper from the wastepaper basket, but it was sulfurous and damp, so she got another one. Standing beside the bed, she tilted him like a kayak from side to side, sliding the diaper under him until she got the Velcro to fasten.

She ran her finger down his spine and brushed the hair from in front of his face. "Go to sleep, darling." But his eyes were shut and he was already asleep, still as a redwood beneath the covers.

He woke up one night, coughing in her face. The next morning he had a fever. Soon she had a fever, too. "I should sleep alone tonight," she said. "I don't want you getting what I have."

Ginny said, "The professor is the one who gave you what you have. He's already built up his immunity."

"So says the nurse," Pru said, forgetting for a moment that Ginny had studied to become one. "It's best to be cautious," she said, but it was just an excuse. Spence had lost weight, but he was heavier-seeming, a cloddish man in repose, lying there as dense as cordwood. He would roll over and be pressed to her, and even when he wasn't coughing, he was breathing in her face. The breath of him, the whiskers, the smell of bleach and disinfectant. The man who had never wanted a body, and now that was all he was, laid out like a piece of veal. She would try not to breathe, and then she would breathe, and she wouldn't be sure if she was smelling herself or Spence, or if there was even a difference.

She moved in to Sarah's bedroom. She told Spence it would be just for one night, but one night of sleeping alone and she knew she wasn't coming back. Every night, she lay down with him for a few minutes, and once he'd fallen asleep, she would get up quietly and leave the room, like a teenage lover sneaking down the hall, only now she was sneaking in the other direction.

Soon Spence was waking up in the middle of the night and careening down the hall.

"It's four in the morning," she said. "What are you doing up?" She took him back to his bed and lay down with him until he quieted once more.

What had been an every-other-night occurrence soon became nightly, and then it became twice-nightly. "You'll be exhausted in the morning," she said. "It already *is* morning, and *I'm* exhausted."

Half an hour later she heard him again, standing outside her bedroom, breathing. "Pru, where are you?"

"I'm right here."

"What are you doing in there?"

"I'm sleeping," she said. "At least, I'm trying to."

"Are you all right?"

"Yes, Spence. I'm a little tired, but I'm fine. Go back to sleep, please."

One night, he left the refrigerator door open. Another night, she heard him trying to open the front door, and she had to run down the hall to retrieve him.

She returned to sleeping in the same bed with him, but now she really wasn't getting any sleep because he was thrashing around like a dolphin. Daytime wasn't enough: she would need to hire someone for nighttime too. Maybe she could pay the night aide less: she got to sleep on the job. But only when Spence was asleep himself: maybe she'd have to pay the night aide more.

She scheduled only one interview and kept it short. Elaine was reserved and not especially friendly, but her references were good and she came to work on time. And she was strong enough to roll Spence over so he wouldn't get bedsores. And she was a light sleeper: that was most important of all.

29

The crowd swelled behind them, but in front there was no one but the players themselves. Courtside tickets: for the day, Pru had become a member of the city's elite. She felt far removed from corporate America, but Walter engineered buildings for corporate America, so he'd been given free seats.

"The Rockets are from Houston," Walter said, and though Pru knew little about the NBA, she knew this. With such good seats, Walter felt liberated to express his views about the game, and especially about the referees, who weren't, in his opinion, letting the players play. They were making ticky-tack calls, except for when they were missing the calls they should have made. "That guy's been traveling all day," Walter said. What had happened to the soft-spoken man Pru had eaten a cheeseburger with, the man who'd sat next to her at Thanksgiving? It was as if he'd become like the players themselves, fueled by the same testosterone.

"The Knicks are terrible," she said.

"They're the worst," Walter agreed. He nodded at the scoreboard, which had the Rockets in the second quarter up by seventeen.

In a break between plays Pru said, "Sixth-row seats. You must be an excellent engineer."

Walter looked at her uncomprehendingly, as if to say he hadn't *built* the seats. "I'm a good enough engineer, but the seats aren't for me. We have big clients, so we get good seats." Now Walter was talking about Stephon Marbury, the Knicks' recently departed star, whom he kept referring to as homegrown, as if he were a plant. Walter twice used the word *disappointment,* as if Stephon Marbury had personally disappointed him, Walter Cohen, which, Pru had noticed, was how a lot of people talked about sports. That was what football Saturdays had been like in Columbus: a whole town of people taking things personally.

The Rockets were up by twenty-five, and one of their players threw down a monstrous dunk and the crowd rose in grudging admiration. A Rockets fan, solitary and emboldened, screamed out. Then a former Rocket, now a Knick, threw down a dunk of his own, and Walter shouted, "Show 'em, Tracy!" before turning to Pru and saying, "Not bad for a guy with a perennially bad back."

During a time-out, the Knicks City Dancers materialized on the court in their blue tops and short shorts, and when one of the dancers did a back flip, a fan called out, "Sign her up!" and another fan shouted, "Fire Isiah!" though that had already happened.

The Knicks came back onto the court, and only then did the Rockets follow, as if trying to be deferential, with their twenty-five-point lead.

As the game wore on, the novelty of sitting so close wore off, and Pru would have preferred to be high in the stands, the way she was at baseball games, where you didn't have to worry about getting hit by a ball and you could allow your concentration to wander.

At halftime Walter said, "Do you want to go? The Knicks are getting slaughtered, and you're looking, how should I put it, a little..."

"Bored?" She went through the motions of denying it, but Walter had already reached for his coat.

They walked through the Garment District, where, during business hours, the streets were a hive, but now they gave off an air of quiet dissipation. There was nothing but the occasional taxi and the roar of the subway below their feet. The street cleaners were preparing for the end of the game, when the crowd would spill out across the avenue and down into the subway and the LIRR.

But in Times Square the streets glowed neon and the tourists revolved as they always did. "Do you have time for a drink?" Walter said.

Pru hesitated. She'd told Ginny she'd be home soon. She'd also told Ginny that she'd gone to the Knicks game with Camille; Ginny didn't need to know about Walter.

They ordered beers, and Pru told Walter she couldn't stay for long, even as a languor settled on her and the small, incremental sips she took from her beer betrayed that she didn't want to go yet.

When they got to Walter's building Pru said, "I can only stay for ten minutes."

"That's plenty of time to meet Albert."

"Who's Albert? Your manservant?"

Walter laughed. "Albert's neither man nor servant. He's my dog, and *I* serve *him*."

But when they entered the apartment, Albert wasn't there. Walter went from room to room, calling, "Albert! Albert!

"Oh, Jesus," he said when he came back inside. "I just remembered. I asked the neighbor to walk him." He slung his coat over a chair. "What's wrong with me? Fifty-eight years old, and I'm already losing my mind." He looked up at Pru and he blanched. "I'm so sorry. I didn't mean it that way."

"It's okay," Pru said, and when Walter continued to apologize, she said, "Really, it's fine."

The living room was expertly arranged: the pile of *Atlantic*s on the coffee table, the little decorative ashtrays and porcelain bowls arrayed on the side tables just so. She didn't know what she'd been expecting— not a bachelor pad, exactly, but not this either. The travel books were alphabetized—Denmark, Ecuador, Frankfurt, Maine—as if Walter were collecting the whole series.

Then the front door opened and Albert burst in. Walter said, "Easy does it, Albert." But Albert, a Labradoodle, didn't do things easy. He had his paws up on Pru's shoulders, and he was licking her face. "Albert, get down!"

Albert sniffed at her shoes, moving around to her backside, survey-ing the nethermost reaches of her, while she stood, still as a Rodin, waiting for his next maneuver.

Finally, he lay down at Walter's feet. His tail moved across the floor like a paintbrush.

Pru pointed at a cello case across the room. "Do you play?"

"A little."

"Are you good?"

Walter laughed. "You'd have to ask my teacher, but, sure, I'm good enough. I'd be better if I practiced more, but who wouldn't?"

"Will you play for me?"

"Pru, come on."

But when she insisted, Walter removed the cello and ran some rosin over the bow. "Do you like Bach?" he said, and before she could answer him—she did like Bach—he was playing Sonata Number 3 in G Minor, his body swaying with the music, his arms like an extension of the instrument, his beard a shadow across the wall.

She grew teary-eyed, and she turned away.

"Am I that bad?"

"No," she said. "You're good." She didn't know what it was. She just got so emotional. "I didn't mean to lay this on you."

"You didn't lay anything on me."

She looked at her watch. She'd promised herself she'd stay for ten minutes, and already an hour had passed.

As she left Walter's building, she checked her phone. Nine messages! And then she realized: her ringer was off.

There was a message from Ginny—and another one, and another one. "Pru, call me immediately!"

There had been a bicycle accident, Ginny explained; something had happened to Rafe.

"Is he all right?" Pru said, and then she remembered: Rafe was a hemophiliac.

"He's in the emergency room," Ginny said.

"Where are you?" Pru imagined Ginny putting Spence in a cab, the two of them racing to Brooklyn.

"I'm right here," Ginny said. "In your apartment with the professor. I was waiting for you to call me back."

"Go straight to the hospital," Pru said.

"And leave the professor alone?"

"I'll have a friend come over. Just go."

From the back of a cab, Pru called Camille. She would be home in fifteen minutes, she explained. In the meantime, could Camille go over and hold down the fort? Spence would be where he always was: asleep in his chair, *The New York Review of Books* toppled across him.

But when Pru got to the apartment, Camille said, "Spence isn't here."

"Are you kidding me?" Pru went into the living room, the dining room, the study. Her heart kicked as she rushed down the hall. "Spence!" she called out. "Come out here this instant!"

She checked the kitchen again, and the dining room. She ran down the hall, opening every door she passed. Frantically, she flung open the linen closet, as if he'd folded himself inside.

She stepped out onto the balcony above 73rd Street, then over to the balcony above Central Park West. "Spence, this isn't funny!"

There was no response.

"Professor Spence Robin, are you down there?" She turned to Camille. "Good God. He's missing."

"How far could he have gone?"

He'd been alone for five minutes, at most ten. Pru thought of him on the night they got engaged, sprinting around the block to propose to her. And now he was outside again, released into the city.

When she rang the elevator, James opened the door immediately, as if he'd been stowed away. But he'd gotten on duty only five minutes ago, and he hadn't seen Spence.

Maurice, downstairs, hadn't seen him either.

"Come with me," Pru said, and she pulled Camille onto the street. She would go north and Camille would go south.

She entered bodegas and drugstores, asking everyone if they'd seen Spence. "He's old," she said, though he wasn't. "He's confused. Demented."

A restaurant hostess asked her to describe Spence, and Pru said, "He looks like someone who shouldn't be out on his own." And when the hostess asked if she had a photo, Pru removed from her wallet the only photo she carried of him, taken on their wedding day, thirty years ago.

Then she was outside again, in and out of whatever establishments would admit her, reemerging onto the streets stunned with rain.

"No luck?" Camille said when she got back to the building, and, seeing that Camille was alone, too, Pru started to cry.

She ran roughshod through the apartment, opening and shutting the same doors. In a moment of lucidity she said, "Camille, you should go home."

"Are you kidding me? This happened on my watch."

But it hadn't happened on Camille's watch. Spence was gone by the time Camille had gotten there, and Ginny had already left. And Pru was to blame for that—not Ginny, not Camille—because she'd turned her ringer off.

When she got through to the police, she was put on hold for several minutes.

She called back and said, "My husband's missing." The officer's attention slackened; she could hear him thinking, *Another person gone AWOL.* "He has dementia," she said. "Alzheimer's disease."

"Have you checked the hospitals?"

She had not.

She said, "I'd like to file a missing-persons report," and hearing her own voice filled her with resolve.

She called the hospital and was caromed from one department to the next. Finally, she was deposited in the ER, where she was put on hold, interminably.

Then the doorbell rang, and it was Annabelle Hanson from next door. She took Pru across the hall, where her husband, Tom, was cleaning up from dinner. "He's waiting for you," Tom said.

"He's been here the whole time?"

Annabelle said, "I found him out on the street."

And it struck Pru that, even as she'd panicked that he was outside, she'd thought there had to be another explanation. "Where was he?"

"Seventy-fourth and Amsterdam."

Pru had been on 74th and Amsterdam herself, but by then he'd already been rescued.

"He'll be glad to see you," Annabelle said.

But when Pru entered the guest room, Spence, seated in an armchair, appeared neither glad nor unglad. He regarded her distantly. It was only as she stepped back that she realized he was wearing tan slacks and a flannel shirt a little long in the sleeve. And dark green socks. And fuzzy slippers. Her thoughts collided with each other. Spence had soiled his clothes and the Hansons had had to change him. He'd been wearing no clothes at all. And there was Annabelle, to answer the question she hadn't dared ask. Spence's clothes were in the dryer; he'd gotten rained on, that was all, and Pru, shot through with relief, thought, Of course. She'd gotten rained on, too. "And his shoes?"

"He was barefoot."

"Ten degrees colder," Tom said, "and he'd have gotten frostbite."

A kettle shrilled in the kitchen; a clock ticked down the hall. As she helped Spence up, Pru turned away from Tom and Annabelle, too embarrassed to look at them. "Thank you," she said. "I'm so, so grateful."

"What neighbor wouldn't do it?" Annabelle said. "I hope you'll do it for us someday."

"No," Pru said. "Of course. I mean, yes." As she guided Spence out the door, she shook Tom's hand and followed suit with Annabelle. Then she took them each in a hug. As she maneuvered Spence out of the apartment, she said, "I'll get those clothes back to you just as soon as I have them dry-cleaned."

"You don't have to dry-clean them," Annabelle said, but Pru had already shut the door.

Then Camille was gone, too, and it was just Pru and Spence. As she took him down the hallway, her coat rubbed against the wall, leaving in their wake a pop of static.

Then the phone rang, and it was Ginny.

"Thank God it's you, Ginny. How's Rafe?"

"He had some internal bleeding, but he'll be all right."

"Internal bleeding? Oh, my God."

For several seconds they both were silent.

"What about the professor?" Ginny said. "Your friend was there when you got home?"

"Yes," Pru said. "Camille." She would never tell Ginny what had happened. She just hoped Spence wouldn't tell her himself. Though she didn't have to worry about that, because when he woke up tomorrow everything would be gone, vanished like the image on an Etch A Sketch.

The next morning, Pru covered the radiators and electrical outlets. She installed safety latches on the medicine chest. She put the household chemicals out of reach. And she placed a safety lock on the front door so Spence couldn't leave. "You big dummy," she said. He'd been barefoot in the rain, his medical alert strung around his neck, and he hadn't thought to push the button. Or maybe he simply hadn't wanted to. She looked down at the tape and screws and discarded plastic, trying to tell herself it was a job well done, but Spence just sat there, as baleful as the night sky, silently staring back at her.

When Ginny arrived later that day she said, "Didn't you say Camille came over last night?"

"That's right," Pru said.

"But Camille was with you."

"What do you mean?"

"You said you went to the Knicks game with her."

"You must have misunderstood me."

Ginny stood there for several seconds. "I could have sworn..." Then she went into the bedroom to check on Spence.

30

Over dinner with Camille Pru said, "I told Ginny I went to the Knicks game with you."

"But you didn't," Camille said. "You went to the Knicks game with Walter."

"Come on, Camille. Don't you think I know that?"

"You sound like a schoolgirl sneaking around."

"I think I like him," Pru said.

"Of course you like him. He's a likable guy."

"You've been doing this for years, Camille. The last time I kissed someone new, it was Spence, and I wasn't even twenty-five."

"Kissing's pretty much the same at fifty-five."

Was it? And what if she and Walter ended up naked? "I love Spence," she said. "I'll never love anyone as much as him."

"You don't have to say that."

"You must think I'm awful."

"I don't."

Pru took a sip of water. "You were trying to set me up with him, weren't you, Camille?"

"What difference does it make what I was trying to do? Tell me what you think of him."

"He's different from Spence, that's for sure. It's not that he's low-brow, exactly. He's just not as buttoned-up. You should have seen him yelling at those basketball players. With Spence, there's always dignity to consider. Walter's a little zany. He bikes in his hardhat to work."

"And he takes care of his ex-wife. Whatever else, he's loyal."

"Unless he's just a sucker." Even if he was . . . Pru could have used a sucker for once. She let her hands drop to the table, and some tzatziki splattered and nearly got on her shirt. "My head's in the clouds, Camille. I left my phone on mute, and Spence wandered off and could have gotten killed. I probably wanted him to. I haven't even kissed Walter yet, and I already feel like I'm cuckolding Spence. And I'm cuckolding him twice over because I'm hiring Ginny to take care of him while Walter and I go out on a date. And Elaine's there tonight so I can talk to you about cuckolding him. His IRA is paying for my meal. And here I am, carrying on, when I don't even know if he likes me."

"Of course he likes you. Why else would he be spending so much time with you?"

"Maybe he finds me comforting. Safe." Again she dropped her hands against the table. "I *am* a schoolgirl, saying he-loves-me-he-loves-me-not."

The next night, Walter called. "Did you say your husband taught at Columbia?"

"That's right," Pru said.

"Spence Robin? In the English department?"

"Yes."

"My younger son, Jeremy, studied literature at Columbia. Maybe he took his class."

"I'm sure it wasn't Spence. It's a big department." She didn't want it to be Spence, even if it was only Walter's son.

An hour later, Walter called back. "It was him."

"Who?"

"Your husband taught my son. Freshman year, Jeremy took his Shakespeare lecture. He liked it so much, he took a seminar with him. He said he was the best professor he ever had."

31

They sat on a bench in Bryant Park, lacing up their ice skates. Pru had rented hers, but Walter had brought his own skates.

"So you're a real skater," Pru said. "I can't even skate backward."

"And I can't even skate forward. My daughter-in-law got me these skates. She thought if I owned a pair I might learn to skate. She used to take lessons."

"You have a daughter-in-law?" Pru said.

"Saul, my older son, got married last year."

It was a Sunday afternoon in February and there were still the remnants of the holiday crowd. Pru had gotten Ginny to watch Spence again. This time, she made sure to leave her ringer on.

"Okay," Walter said, "make way for ducklings." He wambled toward the rink, and Pru followed him. "You go on without me," he said. "I don't want to hold you back."

"You're not holding me back."

But he was holding her back, and no amount of politeness could hide it.

So Pru took off, skating confidently but not *too* confidently: she didn't want to show him up. It was true that Walter couldn't skate forward, but she'd been modest in saying she couldn't skate backward, and certainly when she skated forward she trafficked nimbly around the rink.

Walter, meanwhile, was holding on to the side, moving forward like an inchworm. He let go for a second, then grabbed back on.

"How about you join me?" she said, and she took his hand and they moved slowly around the rink until they got back to where they started.

Then she was off on her own again. "Slow and steady wins the race!"

she called out, but Walter couldn't hear her from across the rink, and with his palms out in front of him, he simply shrugged.

She stepped off the ice and got a cup of coffee. She handed him the coffee over the glass, and he took a sip and passed it back to her.

Her leg had fallen asleep, so she knocked her skates against each other and a chip of ice flew off.

They moved along the ice, holding hands, Walter with his gloves big as oven mitts. He did a swivel, and now he was grabbing onto the wall. "Maybe the wizard will give me courage."

"Don't worry," she said. "If you fall, I'll pick you up."

He skated ahead of her, faster now.

"You see?" she called out. "You're a daredevil!" But she'd barely finished speaking before he wiped out, his legs sliding out from under him.

"Let's try again," she said.

She liked his tight grip, mitten to mitten, hip brushing against hip. His legs slid out like a frog's, but he managed to right himself.

Wayworn and footsore, they got off the ice. Walter shook his head from side to side, as if trying to dislodge something. He strung his skates like a yoke around his neck.

They walked across Bryant Park, past a woman in a diaphanous dress peering into opera glasses. Someone was wearing a T-shirt that read JESUS HAD TWO DADS. A balloon was stuck in a tree, and Pru thought of the Roosevelt Island tram, hanging from the wire like a dead man.

Outside 'wichcraft, a portraitist sat in front of an easel.

Walter said, "Let's be like the other tourists and get our portrait done."

Seated beside each other, they posed for the artist. Half an hour passed, and they had the portrait in their hands.

"Not bad for twenty bucks," Walter said.

Pru put the portrait away in her bag.

She leaned against Walter and kissed him. His mouth tasted like peppermint. She unzipped his parka and rested her fingers against his side; through his sweater she could feel his rib cage. Her legs pressed against his as they kissed. She pulled him close to her.

———

Back at Walter's apartment, they kicked off their shoes and toppled into bed. Pru lifted off Walter's sweater and T-shirt. He unbuttoned her shirt and rolled over on top of her, the bedspread bunched at their feet. Gently, she bit his lip. He lifted her from behind and unclasped her bra.

Now she knew why she'd gotten off the dating track, why she'd married at twenty-four. A few kisses, an hour topless in a man's bed, set you back to being a teenager.

Walter lived on 110th and Riverside, and for the next week she got off the subway a stop before campus so she could pass his building. What would she do if she saw him? Duck behind a tree?

During her lunch hour, she walked down Broadway from 116th to 110th, then back up to campus on the other side of the street, glancing into the restaurants, the hardware stores, wondering if he might be inside. He worked downtown, but maybe he'd taken a sick day. She passed the dry cleaner and thought: does he get his suits cleaned here? She looked at the rows of pressed shirts, thinking one might be his.

She saw Labradoodles everywhere; she hadn't realized they were such popular dogs. From down the block, she saw a dog who looked like Albert and her pulse rammed against her throat.

Walter had said he would call, but he hadn't called. Or was it she who'd said she would call him?

Finally, he called, but when she saw his number on the phone she let it go to voicemail.

He didn't leave a message.

He didn't call that night, or the next morning, but the following night he called again. This time, he left a message, asking her to call him back.

Just talk to him, she told herself. But she couldn't get herself to do it.

32

She was headed home on 72nd Street when she saw a man pushing a wheelchair who looked so much like Walter she almost called out to him. Then she did call out. "Walter!"

He didn't turn around.

She crossed the street so she could see him from a different angle. It was Walter, indisputably. He was pushing a blond woman in a wheelchair. It was Anne, his ex-wife: Pru was sure of it.

She watched them from between the parked cars. Walter was bent over, whispering to the woman, so that for a moment their heads resolved into one.

A bus obscured them, followed by an ambulance, its siren like a threnody. Walter and Anne: they emerged and reemerged from behind the parked cars, moving along the street in the shadows.

Then they disappeared into an apartment building, plucked from the street as if they hadn't been there at all.

Did Walter's ex-wife live only two blocks away? Pru was returning from Fairway one afternoon when she saw Anne in her wheelchair, with her attendant. "Are you Anne?"

The woman appeared startled. Or maybe it was just the disease. She had the signature tremors of Parkinson's. Her neck vibrated forward and back.

"I know your ex-husband," Pru said. "Walter. He's a friend of mine."

Anne just sat there.

"And your two sons."

"Saul and Jeremy?" Anne's voice shook. It was hard to make out what she was saying.

"Your younger son, Jeremy," Pru said. "He studied Shakespeare with my husband."

"Who are you?" Anne said.

"I'm Pru," she said. "Pru Steiner." She took hold of Anne's hand, and now they were vibrating together. "I'm a friend of Walter's," she said again.

Anne's face didn't move. Was it suspicion, or again the disease?

The attendant took hold of the wheelchair. "Anne has to go," she said. "We have errands to run."

Then they were headed down the block, and Pru just stood there. What had she been hoping to find out?

She showed up unannounced at Walter's apartment. Even Albert seemed caught off guard.

"I saw you wheeling your ex-wife," she said.

Walter nodded.

"You never told me she lived two blocks away."

"I guess it never came up."

"What else hasn't come up?"

"A lot of things, I imagine. If we spent more time together, more things would come up."

"It's not so simple, Walter. I'm married. You want me to drop it all and move in with you?"

"Answering my phone calls would be a start."

"What do you suggest I do? Put him in a nursing home?"

"It's been done."

"Well, I'd never do it. I'm betraying Spence just by standing here."

"Come on, Pru. He wouldn't even understand what was going on between us. He barely speaks."

"How would you know?"

"You told me."

"You know nothing about my marriage. You wouldn't even know what a good marriage is."

"Pru, that's not fair."

"Listen to me. Sure, he's doing terribly, but he's not a vegetable. You can see for yourself."

She invited him over one night after Ginny had left and before Elaine was on duty: the changing of the guard.

"Spence," she said, "this is my friend Walter Cohen."

Walter reached out to shake Spence's hand, but Spence just sat there.

"Spence, honey, Walter's trying to shake your hand."

Spence extended his hand to Walter.

They were sitting in the living room, Pru and Spence on the couch, Walter in an armchair across from them. Spence was wearing pajamas. Pru had tried to dress him, but he'd refused. Now, though, he was at a disadvantage, sitting in his pajamas while they were in their street clothes. "Darling, would you like a sweater?"

He didn't respond.

"He gets cold so easily," she told Walter.

Spence tapped his slippers against the floor.

"How was your day, darling? Did you have a nice time with Ginny?"

"It was okay."

"Walter, why don't you tell Spence what you do."

Walter hesitated.

"Walter's a structural engineer," Pru said. "He helps build buildings so they don't fall down."

Walter told Spence how his firm had engineered Citi Field and had made a bid on the Hudson Yards project. "You were at Columbia, right?"

"I'm an emeritus professor," Spence said. Again Pru wished she'd dressed him in a sweater, but she couldn't force it on him now.

She went into the kitchen, leaving the two of them alone, and came back with three cups of tea. She took Spence's hand and just held it. "Should I put on the record player, darling?"

Spence shook his head.

"You should probably go," she told Walter.

Walter removed a book from his bag. *When There's a Will, There's a Way*. Spence's book. "My son studied with you," he said. "He'd like you to inscribe your book for him." He handed the book to Spence.

For a moment Spence just stared down at the cover. He reached into his shirt pocket for a pen.

"I'll get you a pen, darling." Pru went into the kitchen and came back with a pen. "Go ahead, darling. You can sign it now."

But Spence just sat there.

She could sign his name for him, the way she'd once tried to write his book. She could guide his hand across the page like someone teaching a child to write, but she wouldn't subject either of them to that, certainly not in front of Walter.

Finally, she inscribed the book herself.

To Jeremy,

Thank you for taking my class, and for reading my book, and for keeping it safe all these years.

Best wishes,
Spence Robin

Walter called a few hours later. "That didn't go very well."

No, she said, it didn't.

"I apologize," he said. "I shouldn't have come."

"It was my idea, not yours." She should have been the one apologizing—to both Walter *and* Spence.

"I have a proposal for you," he said.

She waited.

"My family owns a cabin in the Berkshires. It's free the weekend after next. I'd like you to come with me."

She didn't speak.

"Will you at least think about it?"

———

Day and night and day again, at work and at lunch, when she slept and when she couldn't sleep, when she was standing on the street corner waiting for the light to change because if she crossed against the light, she would get run over: it was all she could think about.

One morning, she put Spence's diaper on backward. She tripped over a garbage pail at work and nearly injured herself. On 116th and Broadway, she almost did get run over by a car, which would have been one way to solve her problem.

Meanwhile, a week had passed, and she'd gone back to not answering Walter's calls. The weekend he'd invited her for came and went, and so she wasn't going.

She was a few blocks from her building when she saw Walter in the window of a restaurant, sitting across from a pretty woman. A blonde, just like his ex-wife.

Gentlemen prefer blondes, Pru thought darkly. He was eating spaghetti with clams. He lifted his fork to his mouth. She stood there for a moment, watching them, then rushed down the street.

She waited a couple of days to call him, but when she did, she launched right in. "Well, someone works fast."

"Pardon me?"

"I saw you eating at a restaurant. You were on a date."

Walter didn't speak.

"You're telling me it wasn't one?"

"It was."

"You're going on dates a few blocks away from me?"

"I didn't realize you had dibs on the neighborhood."

It was early evening, and she walked across 72nd Street to the Hudson. In Riverside Park, dog feces lined the grass. A man, close to ninety, with a sharp triangle of a face, moved along the cobblestones with a walker, patches of beard dispersed across his cheeks like sod.

When she got home, she called Walter. "I want to go away with you. Is there another weekend when the cabin is free?"

33

The cabin was on a service road outside Great Barrington, set back from traffic and attached to a barn, and Pru felt as if she were being introduced to Walter afresh: to Walter from childhood, and to Walter's parents, now dead, and to Walter's brother, whom she'd heard about from Camille, who lived with his wife across the Hudson, in Parsippany, photographs of whom were strewn about the house, some in frames, some loose. Board games—Boggle, Risk, Bananagrams, Othello—lay on the floor; a single cleat was abandoned behind a bed; a pair of nunchucks sat in the game room. In the basement, the Ping-Pong table stood with the net at half-mast, the paddles beside it, as if someone had only just stopped playing, as if Walter's dead parents were about to materialize and summon the boys upstairs. "We haven't really updated since nineteen eighty-two."

"Or cleaned up," Pru said. "And you say you rent this place out?"

Walter pointed to a closet. "When the renters come we throw the junk in there. But it's true. I haven't gotten the hang of Airbnb. This could be a cash cow. If only I was better at milking it." He sat down on a bench. "Do you want to go for a run?"

"I didn't bring my running shoes."

"What size are you?"

"An eight."

"My brother's an eight. I can probably scrounge something up."

But an eight in women's wasn't an eight in men's, and as Pru made her way along the dirt road, Walter breathing steadily beside her, she felt as if she were running in clown's shoes.

They stopped for coffee at Fuel, where Walter stretched on the concrete, moving one leg forward, then the other. A couple of drops of sweat hung from his beard. A young woman walked up Main Street, her yoga mat like a baguette tucked beneath her arm.

Back at the house Walter said, "I'll drive into town and pick up some groceries. You can stay back here and freshen up."

Once he'd gone, she thought she should shower: she'd worked up a sweat running to and from town. She brought her bag into the bedroom. She wondered when Walter had last had sex. More recently than she had, no doubt, but how much more recently, she didn't want to know.

She set up her toiletries in the bathroom: her toothbrush, her dental floss, her deodorant, her makeup remover. She sat down to pee, only to realize she didn't need to. She would be here for two days: would she need to take a shit? She thought of summer camp, defecating in public, in a bunk full of girls. She got up from the toilet to make sure the door was locked. She sat down again, and this time she peed.

She checked her phone, but there were no messages. Ginny and Rafe were staying with Spence for the weekend. She'd told Ginny she was going to the country to spend some time with a friend.

In the kitchen, Walter soaked the trout in a marinade. She chopped the ends off asparagus. She shredded some romaine hearts and placed them in a bowl.

He handed her a glass of wine.

"To the weekend," she said.

"To the weekend." They clinked glasses, and she took a sip. A smudge of lipstick came off on her glass.

He stood behind her as she sliced tomatoes and mixed oil and vinegar for a dressing. He rested his hands on her shoulders. His breath was against her neck. She turned around and kissed him. His beard grazed her throat. She tasted wine on his tongue. How soft his eyelids were, the brush of his nose, his chest pressed to hers. She thought she might love him. Was it possible she was falling in love? She said, "I got lipstick on you," and she ran her finger across his chin.

Upstairs, she brushed her teeth and gargled some mouthwash. She cupped her hand over her mouth so she could smell her breath.

They kissed beside the bed. Then their shirts were off and kicked across the floor and she was yanking off his pants. Her bra was lassoed over the bedpost. She pulled his boxers down to his feet. His tongue was in her ear, and they were rolling over, and he was on top of her. He shucked off her underpants. He still had one sock on, and she tossed it across the room.

He kissed her breasts, running his tongue over her nipples. He was hard against her thigh. She touched his scrotum. She went down the length of him and took him in her mouth, but after a minute he stopped her. "I don't want to come yet."

She squeezed his leg and he shuddered. Her breath came out in jagged spurts.

They lay together when they were done, their ankles touching.

In the bathroom, she stood behind him while he peed, her hands running through his hair, her chin resting on his shoulder. Back in bed, she wrapped her arms around him, and soon they fell asleep.

She woke up suddenly at four a.m., thinking she heard a cell phone ringing. But no one had called. She had no text messages either.

She got back into bed but she couldn't sleep. Walter was on his stomach, breathing quietly beside her, the corner of the pillow tucked into his mouth.

She stood at the window and tried to see the road, but it was as dark and desolate as the tundra.

Back in bed, she started to cry.

"Pru, what's wrong?"

"I want to go home."

"Are you kidding me?"

"Walter—please—take me back to the city."

"It's five in the morning."

"Don't make me take the bus."

Great Barrington to West 73rd Street. The trip took two hours and twenty minutes, but on an early Saturday morning the Taconic was deserted, and they made it back in two hours. They didn't even stop for gas. "Coffee?" she said, thinking he was going on little sleep, but he said, "I'm fine."

When they got off the highway, she started to cry again. They were stopped behind a truck on 72nd Street, and she wiped her face clean.

Walter pulled up to her building.

"I'm sorry," she said. "You don't deserve this."

He didn't contradict her.

She kissed him long and hard, the windshield clouding over from their breath. A tear came off her face and traveled down his nose. The neighbors could see them, but she didn't care.

She was outside the building fishing for her keys, and when she turned around he was gone.

When she walked into the apartment Ginny said, "What happened, Pru? Why are you back?"

"It was cold up there. I hate the country."

"Look who's home, Professor. Your wife came back from her trip."

But Spence just stared at her distantly, as if he hadn't realized she'd been gone.

One morning, as Pru was leaving for work, Ginny stopped her in the hallway. "What's this?" Ginny held up a piece of paper.

Pru's heart lurched: it was the portrait of her and Walter. How had Ginny found it? "That's me," she said calmly. "I got my portrait taken with an old friend."

They were sitting in the kitchen, and Spence, eating his grapefruit, looked down at the portrait. "That's Pru's other husband."

"What?" Pru said.

"I met him," he said. "That's the man you're going to marry when I'm dead."

Part VII

34

They were staying in Georgetown, in a short-term rental. Arlo had found them the house, just as he'd gotten his father into the drug trial. He was rich now, and he invested in biotech. Zenithican was the most promising Alzheimer's drug to come along in years.

A drug trial? Pru had thought. Spence already resisted taking his medicine. Sometimes, when she wasn't looking, he would spit out his pills, and she would have to start the process over again. Other times, she would find the pills coagulating between his teeth and gums, secreted there like chewing tobacco. Why should she put Spence in a drug trial? So he could have his blood drawn, his vital signs measured, so he could be given injections, like a chicken or a cow? Zenithican was an experimental drug: there was no telling what it might do to him.

Meanwhile, he was getting worse and worse. The other week, she let her attention idle, and he inserted the remains of a red pepper into his mouth: the stem and core, the seeds. As she tried to remove the food from his mouth, he looked up at her, startled, his eyes welling with tears.

He'd bitten her, and she ran her hands under the sink, thinking he had rabies, that he was a dog and had mange. He'd eaten the pepper scraps, unable to distinguish the wheat from the chaff, the food from the rot, the garbage. What would happen next? Would he chew on electrical wires? On shoes?

Of course he was getting worse and worse. Did she think he was going to get better and better?

"Darling," she said, "do you want to take a drug that might help you?"

"Yes."

"You do?"

"No."

There were so many questions she should have asked back when she could have asked them. If she believed in this drug—if she believed in any Alzheimer's drug—she wouldn't have hesitated: anything to save him. But she didn't believe she was saving him, and maybe she was doing him harm. "Okay," she said. "We'll talk about it tomorrow."

But he would be no more able to decide tomorrow than he was today.

So she quit her job and moved them down to D.C.

Arlo's office was in a big glass building, where, from the reception area on the fourteenth floor, Sarah could see the nation's great edifices: the White House, the Washington Monument, the Supreme Court. She was doing her medical residency now, and she'd been given two weeks' leave. She wanted to be in town at the beginning of the trial so she could guide her parents through the protocol.

She was shocked that Arlo had landed in D.C. He was an entrepreneur, and he hated government. Yet he'd moved there anyway, as if to say, *You don't know me.* And she didn't. She wouldn't have been surprised if he'd moved to D.C. just to flummox her. He'd left Silicon Valley, cashed out right before his company's IPO. If he'd stayed, he would have been obscenely wealthy; this way, he was only very wealthy. He wanted people to know he didn't care. She thought of Arlo's maternal grandfather, the kosher butcher, moving the family from outpost to outpost; thought of Arlo's mother, wanting to poop in all fifty states. And there was Arlo, her brother, the third generation of Zackheims who couldn't sit still.

It was July, and D.C. was as advertised: hot and damp as the inside of a dog's mouth. Arlo's office was long and rectangular, larger than most of the apartments she had lived in, and it was decked out in the spare, unreflective manner of a young MBA. A leather couch. A leather recliner. An enormous flat-screen TV. In the corner stood a fish tank in which tropical fish appeared to be doing laps. There was a lot of metal and glass, and what wood there was had a metallic sheen, so that everywhere she looked her reflection was cast back at her. Nothing sat on the desk save for Arlo's iPhone. It was as if paper were beneath him: he dealt only in the lofty currency of ideas.

"So the prodigal daughter returns."

"For two weeks." Then it was back to her own life. Growing up, Arlo used to compete with her over who was the better child. Now she competed with him over who was the worse one.

"I assume you know about Zenithican."

She did. The drug was in phase 2, and it was generating excitement. There was a new theory that Alzheimer's was related to the microbiome—a gut-brain relationship—but that theory was dismissed by most researchers, and whatever drugs arose from it were still years away. Zenithican, on the other hand, was a plaque drug; it was, Sarah believed, their last, best hope.

Pru hadn't seen Arlo in six years, not since that night at Columbia when Spence was elevated to his new post. Arlo was thirty-three now, but the boyishness hadn't dissipated, and the skittishness of his face. He stood across from her: Spence's son, the boy her husband had fathered, the boy her husband had loved, the boy she herself had grown to love. For a moment, she was overcome. "Arlo." She hugged him.

"Where's Dad?"

"I'll take you in."

But Ginny came out first.

"I'm Arlo," he said.

Ginny shook his hand. "We've been waiting a long time for your visit."

Arlo understood that. Sarah had called him. Pru had called him. He wouldn't have been surprised if Ginny had called him herself. *Come visit*, they said. *Come see your father while you still can.* Every time he said he would come, and every time he didn't. How could a visit mean anything to his father when his father wouldn't remember it after he'd gone? But Arlo would remember it, and it sickened him. The chest-beating, the deathbed apologies: he wouldn't be a part of any of that.

Who was Spence Robin to him, his nominal father, the man he'd been delivered to like a care package, a week here, a few days there, a smidge of time during summer vacation before he was returned to his rightful owner, those two years, not even, when he'd been given lodging in their apartment, quartered like a horse? That was no way to treat a son; someone should have called Family Services.

He looked at Ginny, and at Rafe. Why did all these people care about his father? Why did he not care enough? "He was a bad father," he told Ginny.

"My son probably thinks I'm a bad mother, too."

"You're an excellent mother. I've heard about you."

Rafe just stood there, not saying anything, listening to his mother speak about him.

"Let's go, Rafe," Ginny said. "The professor's son has come to visit. We should leave them alone."

In preparation for his father's visit, Arlo had looked at horrific photographs—burn victims, children ravaged by starvation, survivors of bombings and war—but he wasn't prepared for what he saw now, this man who looked twenty-five years older than he was, shriveled as a fig. "Pop."

His father didn't respond.

A magazine lay on the table, and Arlo was brought back to when he was a boy, reading to his father from *Deadpool vs. X-Force* and *Kingdom Come*, drawing the letters in the air. "How are you, Dad?"

"I'm all right."

"You're here for a drug trial, Dad. We're going to make you better."

"Thank you," his father said.

"Zenithican," Arlo said. "It's the most promising Alzheimer's drug to come along in years. I got you into the drug trial, Dad."

"Thank you," his father repeated.

Arlo looked at his father. Who cared if he didn't visit? He would arrest the course of his father's disease. That was how he'd be a good son.

———

That night, unable to sleep, Arlo removed the folder from his desk. The words were written in his hand, composed when he was still a teenager, living in his father's apartment. *All together vs. Altogether. Continual isn't the same as continuous. Learn the difference between infer and imply. Between you and I is wrong, though even Bill Clinton made that mistake. He said, "Give Al Gore and I a chance." When used as an adjective, it's blond, not blonde, even for a girl. Forbear vs. forebear, forgo vs. forego. Invaluable is not the opposite of valuable. It's a stationery box, not a stationary box, though presumably it's a stationary box, too. Lie vs. lay vs. laid vs. lain. Sleight vs. slight. It's home in on, not hone in on, like a homing pigeon. Principle vs. principal. The principal is your principal pal. Spell these words correctly: supersede, minuscule, idiosyncrasy. Flout vs. flaunt. Grizzly vs. grisly. Mantel vs. mantle. Desert vs. dessert. It's anticlimactic, not anticlimatic. Marquis vs. marquee. Discrete vs. discreet. Aggravate is not the same as irritate. Taught vs. taut. Leech vs. leach. Hark vs. hearken. Whet vs. wet. Peek vs. peak vs. pique. Loan is not a verb. Tic vs. tick. It's free rein, not free reign, unless you're the king. Demur vs. demure. It's duct tape, not duck tape. Already vs. all ready. Bizarre vs. bazaar. An acronym is different from an abbreviation. And never, upon pain of death, use the word impacted, unless you are a dentist.*

Even now, reading through the list—*perusing* it—sent Arlo's heart lurching. He thought of the things he hadn't known, and now he knew them. Even when he didn't know something (did *spendthrift* mean you spent or you were thrifty?), he reminded himself it didn't matter. He could spit on the difference between *lie* and *lay*. He could use *impact* as a verb and be no worse for it. He remained a bad speller—he still couldn't spell *minuscule*, or *idiosyncrasy*, or *supersede*—but he'd earned the right to misspell those words, to mangle the English language with impunity. A lot of good it had done his father, knowing the difference between *discreet* and *discrete*. His father, who could never accept his son's limitations; who would say, *Focus* and *Try harder* and *Bear down;* who had wanted to understand Arlo's learning disability but hadn't been able to. What good had his father's vaunted language skills done him? He was but a shell of himself, and Arlo, meanwhile, had risen and risen.

In the bathroom, taking a pee, Arlo recalled a joke his father had once told about a British person and a French person arguing over whose language was superior. The punch line was that *impertinent* wasn't the opposite of *pertinent*. Arlo hadn't understood the joke, and he was left with only the memory of it, and the accompanying feeling of embarrassment. He still didn't understand the *pertinent* vs. *impertinent* joke, only now his father couldn't understand it either. The famous steel trap had become porous. Arlo didn't want to see what his father had become; he didn't even want to imagine it. But he did imagine it, and he felt relief.

Dawn was ascending; daybreak would be coming soon. Maybe the Zenithican would save his father. Then his father would appreciate him. But his father had never appreciated him, and if he made his father better, his father would go back to not appreciating him.

Arlo got down on the floor and did two hundred push-ups.

When he was done, he stood by the window as daylight spilled in, stood shirtless, in his boxers, scrutinizing himself. I'm alive, he thought. I'm alive, I'm alive, I'm alive, I'm alive—the words coursing through him as he got dressed and waited for the car to take him to his office.

35

The first part of the drug trial would last two months. Three days a week, Pru would take Spence to Georgetown Medical Center for an injection. He'd be monitored by doctors and have his blood drawn, given EKGs and cardiac echos. And when the summer was over, he would return to New York for the maintenance part of the trial, where he'd be given a pill once a week.

That first day, Ginny accompanied Pru, Spence, and Sarah to the hospital. She and Rafe had moved to D.C. for the summer; Arlo had found a house big enough for them all. But once they got to the hospital, Ginny let Sarah take over.

There were forms to sign, and Sarah had Pru sign them. A few side effects had been observed in phase 1: sleeplessness, agitation, diarrhea. A couple of subjects had experienced a drop in blood pressure, but that had been rare and non-life-threatening.

"I'm a doctor," Sarah explained, and the nurse, taking out a blood pressure cuff, said, "It's good to have one of those in the family."

Sarah supposed it was. But there wasn't much she could do besides explain to her mother the purpose of these tests. "They want baseline levels," she said. "They'll be looking for adverse reactions."

"Okay," the nurse told Spence, "you're good to go," and Spence pushed himself up from his seat before the nurse said, "Good to go, meaning you're ready for your injection."

With a cotton ball, she rubbed alcohol across Spence's arm and removed the syringe.

Spence looked away, and so did Pru. Ginny lowered her head like a penitent. Only Sarah stared straight-on. Hazard of the job, she thought, making sure everything went as it was supposed to.

"Do we have to do this every time?" Pru said.

"The injection?" the nurse said. "That's why you're here."

"I meant the blood work."

"That's just at the beginning," Sarah said. "Though periodically they'll want to repeat the tests."

"In the meantime," the nurse said, "keep an eye on him."

"I'll be watching him like a hawk," Sarah said.

"I'm already watching him like a hawk," Pru said.

"I am, too," Ginny said.

"Three hawks are better than one," the nurse said, and this time Spence rose from his seat and led them out of the hospital.

Back in their temporary home on P Street, sitting in someone else's living room with the twill cream slipcovers and the Eames lounge chair, seeing Spence lugubrious and depleted once more, Pru became downcast. "What if he doesn't get better?"

"Be patient, Mom. Give it a chance."

What else was she doing besides giving it a chance? She'd quit her job and moved them down to D.C. She'd uprooted them both.

"It could take months before we see improvement."

If they saw it at all, Pru thought. They were guinea pigs, these subjects. And it was a double-blind study, which meant Spence could be getting a sugar pill. In which case, he wasn't just a guinea pig but a fool, and she was the biggest fool of all for having brought him down here.

Over breakfast one day, Ginny showed Rafe a map of the Smithsonian. "An entire mall of the world's greatest museums, and you don't have to pay a cent."

"I hate museums," Rafe said.

"Do you know what the world be would like without museums?"

"It would be a world in which I didn't have to go to them. I want to be a doctor someday. What does going to museums have to do with that?"

"You think doctors don't go to museums?"

"Not this doctor."

"There could be a passage about museums on the SAT."

Rafe would be taking the SAT in December. He'd brought his Barron's book down to D.C. and he'd agreed to study an hour a day, but Ginny wanted him to study more. She wanted him to read too, because that was the best way to build his vocabulary.

"Don't I get a break over the summer?" Rafe was hoping to explore D.C. with his friend Carlton, whom he'd met at chess camp, and whose family had relocated to D.C.

"You can explore D.C. when you're done studying."

So Ginny and Rafe came to an agreement. Every morning, Rafe would spend an hour studying for the SAT followed by three hours of reading, after which he could do what he wanted. Ginny even made him a reading list—*1984, To Kill a Mockingbird, The Adventures of Huckleberry Finn, Narrative of the Life of Frederick Douglass*—and she took him to the public library to borrow the books.

When Spence was home taking a nap, Pru and Sarah would stop by Arlo's office.

"How's he doing?" Arlo said.

"About the same," Pru said.

"Is there anything I can do?"

"You've already done everything."

They just stood there, Pru and Sarah in this huge office with the tropical fish doing their laps, and it became clear that these updates were making everyone uncomfortable and Arlo had, in fact, done what he could.

"Call me if you need anything," Arlo said, and they told him they would.

When Pru was out running errands, Ginny, who at the hospital deferred to Sarah, would, when they were home, take charge. She wouldn't rebuke Sarah, exactly, but she'd correct her ways. The professor liked his grapefruit divided into sections and cut smaller; his hamburger needed to be mashed so he wouldn't choke. One time Ginny said, "The professor prefers his applesauce strained."

Oh, does he? Sarah thought. On what authority did Ginny base this—Ginny, who had known her father for a couple of years, whereas Sarah had known him her whole life. But Ginny was right: her father did prefer his applesauce strained, the fact of which Ginny knew because she was the one who made it from scratch, which Sarah had never done.

Another time Sarah poured her father tea, and Ginny looked on disapprovingly.

"He takes his tea light," Sarah said. "'Just a little colored water' is what he says."

But it wasn't the color that concerned Ginny, but the heat. "The professor's hands shake. The tea needs to be lukewarm or he'll burn himself." She dropped a couple of ice cubes into the tea, and only then did she let him drink it.

Still another time, Sarah gave her father a hard-boiled egg, and Ginny said, "He doesn't eat lunch until noon."

"What difference does it make?"

"He needs to be on a schedule."

"Why?" Sarah said. "He's not in the Marines."

"Aren't you supposed to be back in L.A.?" It was clear Ginny couldn't wait for that to happen, which made Sarah unable to wait for it, too.

Then Sarah was gone, and Pru was lonelier than ever. She'd been checking email once a day; now she started to check it twice a day, even more.

Dear Walter,

I'm in D.C. with Spence. The drug trial is . . . a drug trial. They give you some chemicals and see what happens to you. The scientists find it fascinating. So far no improvement, but the good thing is he doesn't seem worse. D.C. is as hot as advertised. I've been turning on the A.C. while Spence is asleep. He's always hated wasting electricity. And he gets so cold, even when it's ninety-five degrees out. So I wrap him in blankets while I walk around in shorts. We're like some bad version of Jack and Mrs. Sprat. I hope New York isn't quite as hot, and that you're enjoying your summer.

Fondly,
Pru

Pru—

It was good to hear from you. It's like they say, the two great inventions of the twentieth century were penicillin and A.C. I'm sorry about what you and Spence are going through. I wouldn't wish it on my worst enemy.

—Walter

I wouldn't wish it on my worst enemy? What was this, Pru thought, some sympathy card? But her email had sounded like a sympathy card, too. *Fondly?* She'd never used the word *fondly* in her life.

Did she think she and Walter were going to be friends? They were long-distance now, and there was a reason for that. She didn't email him back, and he didn't email her either. That was it: she was alone.

She woke up one Saturday and went to shul. Maybe here in George-town, at Kesher Israel, she would find her community. Or maybe she could commune with God.

A man was chanting from the Torah when she arrived. Someone announced the Blessing for the Sick, and the congregants lined up to say the names of their loved ones. Was she really going to do this, say a prayer for Spence, the legendary atheist, and she, an atheist, too, prostrating herself before the God she didn't believe in, in the company of a congregation she didn't know?

But as the other congregants approached the bimah, she got in line too. *Me she'bayrach avoteinu Avraham Yitzchak v'Yaakov, Moshe v'Aharon David oo'Shlomo, hoo Yivaraich v'yirapai et ha'cholim.* She reached the front of the line, and the man reciting the prayer asked whom she was blessing.

"Spence," she said.

The man looked at her.

"Shulem."

"Shulem ben who?" the man said, and Pru remembered: when you blessed the sick, you said the name of the sick person's mother. She racked her mind for Spence's mother's name but couldn't come up with it.

As the man leaned forward to chant the words, his tallis brushed her arm. Then his voice rang forth. "Shulem ben Sarah."

Later Pru would recall that when you didn't know the mother's name you said Sarah, the Matriarch, but at the time she forgot, and she stood beside the bimah, poleaxed, thinking the man was referring to *her* Sarah, and how in the world did he know?

"Your mother's name is Ruth," she said when she got home. She'd remembered it the instant she walked into the house.

Spence just stared at her.

"I tried to bless you," she said, "but I couldn't remember your mother's name."

He was quiet.

"Oh, darling, I wish I knew your parents."

"You did know my parents."

"I didn't, darling. They died before we met. I have no idea where you come from."

"I come from the Lower East Side."

"I meant the people you come from." She took his hand.

"Where did you bless me?"

"In synagogue."

"You used to go to synagogue."

"That's right." Why did Spence remember some things and not remember others? Why could he tell her what had happened years ago but couldn't tell her what had happened yesterday?

"When did you go to synagogue?"

"When I was growing up," she said. "And when I met you."

"Why?"

Why did she go? Why did she stop? Why, she wondered, did she no longer believe? "I'm sorry for forgetting your mother's name."

"I forgive you," Spence said.

She started to cry.

36

One morning, Spence looked down at his plate of scrambled eggs and said, "This meal seeks."

Could he possibly have meant his meal *sucks*? No, Pru thought: he'd never spoken that way in his life. The word *sucks* was vulgar—it was boorish, it was crass—and no disease could ever change that.

But Spence kept saying *This meal seeks,* becoming more agitated each time. Finally, he lowered his head to the table and didn't say anything more.

At the end of the day, Pru realized something. "Darling, you meant your meal *reeks*! You didn't like the smell of your scrambled eggs!"

Then something remarkable happened. Spence had been in the drug trial for a month, and suddenly he was improving. Maybe he hadn't said *reeks,* but he'd started to use other higher-order words. At dinner one night he said the word *quotidian.* "Do you think he's doing better?" she asked Ginny.

"He might be," Ginny said.

Pru called Arlo. She called Sarah too.

Another week passed, and it became clearer: Spence was improving, indisputably. He was staying awake until ten at night, having a go at *The Washington Post.*

He was moving better, too. He walked with Ginny to K Street and back and barely used his cane.

There had been improvement, too, in his manual dexterity, in how he wielded a fork and knife. There were shades of the old Spence: clean, fastidious, the dabbing of his napkin to his mouth.

One morning, Pru let her gaze fall on the *Times* crossword. *Late Missouri Senator Thomas.* She hadn't realized she'd spoken the clue aloud, so she was startled when Spence said, "Eagleton."

She reached out and touched him. "What did you just say, darling?"

"Eagleton," he repeated.

She very nearly leapt out of her seat. Thomas Eagleton, longtime senator from Missouri! George McGovern's vice presidential nominee, forced to withdraw because of electroshock therapy! "Spence, you did a crossword!" And it was Friday, late in the week, when the crosswords were harder.

A minute later she tried again. *"Late Missouri Senator Thomas."*

Spence just stared at her.

"Come on, darling, you said it before. What's the last name of the late senator from Missouri whose first name is Thomas?"

Spence was silent. Finally, he said, "Why's the senator late?"

But it didn't matter, because a minute ago he'd gotten the answer right. They said if you put a chimp in front of a typewriter, eventually he'd type *Hamlet.* But if you asked a chimp who the late Senator Thomas from Missouri was, he would never, in a billion years, say *Eagleton.*

37

Ginny had made two rules: in the morning, Rafe had to read and study for the SAT, and he had to be home by six for dinner.

One night, Rafe came home at seven and Ginny was waiting at the door. "Where were you, young man?"

"I got confused."

She just stared at him.

"I'm tired of being under your thumb."

"When you're an adult you can stop being under my thumb. We made a deal that you'd be home by six."

"I want to renegotiate."

"Deals don't get renegotiated."

"Sure they do." Rafe invoked the names of several pop stars and a couple of professional athletes.

"Here's what's being renegotiated. You're grounded."

"For how long?"

"Three days. And if you sulk about it, it will be longer."

When three days passed, Rafe was allowed to go out again, provided he was home by curfew.

He followed the rule for several days, but on Saturday six o'clock came and went, and there was no sign of him.

Ginny stood at the window.

"It's the weekend," Pru said. "You should give him a grace period." And when Ginny gave her a look, Pru said, "I'm sorry, it's none of my business," and Ginny gave her another look to say she was right.

Six thirty passed, then seven: Ginny was starting to get worried. She called Rafe's cell phone, but he didn't pick up. She called Carlton's cell phone, and he didn't pick up either.

It was eight thirty when Rafe got home. Ginny was about to say, *You're two and a half hours late, young man,* when she saw Rafe and gasped. There was dirt on his face, and his hands were scratched. "What in the Lord's name?"

"I fell."

"Where?"

Rafe walked past her, but Ginny grabbed his arm. "Sit down and tell me what happened."

"I got into a dustup."

"A what?"

"A fight."

Now it was Ginny who had to sit down. "Are you trying to kill yourself, Rafe? You're a hemophiliac, in case you forgot."

"I don't care what I am. Ground me all you want. I hate it here."

When Pru woke up the next morning, Ginny had already packed their bags. "We're going home to New York. It's not working out for Rafe down here."

Rafe, chastened by a night's sleep and having cleaned himself up, said, "I'm sorry, Pru. I know you need my mom. I promise I'll do better."

Ginny said, "It was foolish to come down here in the first place."

"I like it here," Rafe insisted. "I want to stay."

"It doesn't matter," Ginny said, "because in another few weeks you have to be back at school."

It was true, Pru thought. At the beginning of September, she and Spence would be going home, too. The first part of the drug trial would be over and the maintenance part would begin.

All at once, she realized something: what if, come September, Ginny was no longer available? What if she found another job?

"I'll pay you not to work," she said.

"What do you mean?"

"I'll pay you in New York as if you're working here."

"But I'm not working here."

"Technically."

"I'm not going to be paid to do nothing."

All Pru could do was hope—hope that Ginny would find temporary work so she could come back to her job.

38

Over the next couple of weeks, Spence declined. He was back to how he'd been before the drug trial; he might have even been worse. Pru blamed Ginny for his decline, then blamed herself for blaming Ginny.

She was alone with Spence in this city she didn't know, the gawkers gawking at the White House and the Supreme Court. She could have enlisted Arlo's help, but Arlo wasn't cut out for the kind of help she needed, and he'd already done more than she'd asked.

She thought of going back to shul, but she couldn't pick and choose her worship times.

But she did go back, taking Spence with her because she couldn't leave him alone. He grew agitated during the service, and she grew agitated, too, sitting across the mechitza from him. She hated Orthodox Judaism, where you couldn't even sit with your own sick husband.

When the Torah reading started, Spence began to moan, and she crossed over to the men's side to collect him. She thought of waiting until the Blessing for the Sick, but that wasn't for another twenty minutes. She didn't want to bless him while he was standing right there, arrayed before the congregants, on display. What was the point, besides? If the drug hadn't worked, then praying wouldn't work either. It didn't matter that she now knew his mother's name.

One evening, Spence began to cough. He sounded like the city buses, their pneumatic doors wheezing closed. It was three in the morning, and Pru took the stethoscope Sarah had left her and pressed it to his chest.

"I hear a crackle," she told Sarah over the phone.

"It sounds like pneumonia," Sarah said. "You should take him to the ER."

But Pru didn't want to take him to the ER. She'd signed a DNR order; she refused to have him intubated.

In the morning, though, his breathing was worse; he was making gasping sounds, like a fish on a dock.

This time Sarah insisted. "Pneumonia's not..."

What? Pru thought. A good way to die? She hadn't encountered one of those yet.

At the hospital, it was confirmed: Spence had pneumonia. He was given antibiotics and put on a ventilator.

Sarah flew in. Arlo came to the hospital, too.

In the waiting room, they sat in front of the TV, taking breaks to check on Spence, buying Popsicle after Popsicle from the cafeteria, letting the sticks pile high.

"This could be it," Pru said.

"Have faith," Sarah said. "Dad's stronger than you think."

They went outside, where Pru leaned against a car and drank a cranberry juice, watching the city conduct its affairs.

Back in the waiting room, Judge Judy was yelling on TV.

Sarah was right: by the end of the day Spence had rallied, and when Arlo showed up, he rallied even more.

The next morning, he was off the ventilator. The morning after that, his breathing was back to normal. Two days later, he was allowed to go home.

As they left the hospital, Sarah said, "Dad needs to rest." Moving forward, they would have to treat him with greater caution.

But Pru was thinking something else. In the coming months—in however much time he had left—she would let him do whatever he wished. He'd always wanted to go to Nepal. Spence, who had forded snowdrifts to get to class, who just might have tried to climb Mount Everest if she'd let him—Spence, who probably didn't know what Nepal was anymore and certainly couldn't have located it on a map: Spence probably still wanted to go to Nepal, and she would allow him to do it. She made a proposal to the sleeping Spence. "Let's go to Nepal, darling. We'll leave the rest of the world behind us."

———

Sarah was about to fly back to L.A. when she got a call from Arlo. "There are problems with the drug trial."

"What problems?"

"Other patients have gotten pneumonia, too."

Two days later, the news broke in the *Times* and the *Post*. A statistically significant elevation in heart attacks and strokes among the patients on the Zenithican compared to the patients on placebo, and an even bigger jump in pneumonia. The trial was being suspended.

"That drug almost killed him," Sarah told her mother.

But Pru refused to blame the drug.

"I was an idiot," Arlo said.

"You weren't," Pru said. She had gone to his office, leaving Spence in Sarah's care.

Arlo handed her the newspaper article. She knew what it said, but she hadn't been able to look at it. Even in the last two weeks, as Spence had gotten worse, she'd been holding out hope.

She handed Arlo back the article.

"It's my fault," he said.

"It's not." She was the one who had brought Spence down. What difference did it make, besides? Spence was falling like a meteor, he was diminishing like a candle, but that had been true before he'd gotten the drug, and so the only thing dashed were her hopes, and they'd been unreasonable hopes, anyway.

"I'm so sorry," Arlo said.

Pru was, too.

Arlo hired movers to pack their bags. Then he called a car to drive them home to New York.

Part VIII

39

"And this is the dining room," Pru said, "and this is the kitchen and this is the hallway, and this is the bedroom where you'll sleep." Spence had already slept there—four weeks and counting—but every day she had to start over. The new building was handicap-accessible, and as if to acknowledge this, Spence had started to use a wheelchair. This heartened Pru—she no longer had the strength to do battle—but it depressed her, too, seeing his resolve flee like a thief.

She'd had to sell their apartment. She wasn't working anymore; already these last months they'd been living off savings. Spence, if he'd understood, would have been relieved; he'd hated being a property owner.

As soon as she put the apartment up for sale, she started to look for rentals. Maybe their old place on Claremont Avenue would be available; being back where they'd started might jog something in Spence. But the apartment was being rented by a young sociologist and his wife who weren't planning to have children. And the man, Pru reasoned darkly—he was in his early thirties—was twenty-five years away from even early Alzheimer's, so they weren't getting their apartment back.

She could have rented in one of the big condos, with a gym and a party room, where the elevator rocketed you straight to your door and the doorman ran out to greet you. But she didn't want to be accosted as she entered the building, forced to surrender her groceries when she was capable of carrying them herself. So she settled on a three-bedroom on 112th and Riverside, where the doorman got on at four and off at eleven, and the rest of the time you were left alone.

The apartment was big enough to hold their grand piano. She had played it growing up, and for a time she'd hoped Sarah would play it, too, but except for some sporadic banging on the keys, it had spent the last twenty-five years unmolested. The beached whale, Spence had called it, though he liked to sit on the piano bench, listening to Mozart on the old Victrola, like those fans at Wimbledon in their tennis shorts.

Pru was lucky: Ginny had taken a temporary job, so she was able to come back and take care of Spence. And Elaine was available to cover nighttime.

When Pru closed on the apartment, she raised their pay to twenty-two dollars an hour, and she paid off Sarah's medical school loans.

"We're back in our old neighborhood," she told Spence, but even as she wheeled him past College Walk he seemed not to realize it. He was lost now, a puppet cut loose from his strings.

Watching him sleep, Pru told herself he wasn't in pain, and maybe this receding even brought him pleasure. She recalled fevers as a girl, lying in front of the TV with her hot-water bottle and ginger ale, that feeling of being locked in her own body. Now, again, she was so rooted in herself she would lose track of where she was. What month was it? What year? Whole parts of her life were lost to her.

The first time Spence wet his pants and, months later, the first time he soiled them, the stink was such a humiliation she went mute. But as the months passed it happened more and more until it became a matter of course. It was better not to be ashamed of what couldn't be avoided, but there came with this accommodation its own kind of loss. When they were around, Ginny and Elaine cleaned him up, but on weekends the job fell to her, and she went about the task with grim efficiency.

Early on, when he was sufficiently himself that she almost wouldn't have known anything was wrong, the bad moments were made worse because she had his old self to compare him to. That was when she would rage at him, when she would tell him to try harder, to concentrate. Afterward she would rebuke herself and think maybe her impatience was the problem because nobody liked to have the pressure put on. Now, though, he was so far gone that to rage at him would have been like raging at a stone. What a year ago had been a bad day would now have been so good it was unimaginable. A good day was when he could string a few sentences together, when he could respond directly, if tersely, to *How are you?* Finally, she was able to be kind to him in a way she hadn't been before.

Looking at him as he slept, she told herself she wouldn't forget him. But in a way she'd already forgotten him, forgotten what he'd been like before he got sick, even as it was all she could think about. She wondered whether this was what she would remember, these last years of diminishment. She persuaded herself that when he was gone the end would fade and the man she'd first known would remain, accompanying her through the lonely days, through the years of solitude that lay ahead of her.

In the morning, she helped him to the toilet and stood outside the door. Even now, when there was little dignity left, she wanted to give him some privacy. When he was done, she came inside and squeezed the toothpaste onto his toothbrush.

He was brushing too hard, jabbing himself in the gums. "Go easy on yourself, darling."

He kept brushing too hard.

He'd left the water on, and she said, "Rinse up, rinse up, there's a water shortage here," though she'd gone running last week and the reservoir looked full to overflowing. There was probably enough water for them to brush their teeth from now until they both shall live.

She laid his slippers on the floor and watched him struggle to put them on. "The brain controls everything, doesn't it?"

He stared silently at her, and she wished she hadn't said that. But she needed to talk to someone; there was only so much talking she could do to herself.

The soap kept sliding out of his hands. She could get him liquid soap, but that probably wouldn't be any easier. He had only the hot water on, and she recoiled at the touch. "Jesus, darling, you're going to burn yourself."

But he was already drying off his hands, his palms as red as rib eyes. Perhaps this, too, was part of the disease and he was losing his sensitivity to heat.

She had started to shave him, and it brought her back to childhood, watching her father shave. She placed the shaving cream on his face, a patch on one side, a patch on the other, as if he had muttonchops.

"You're hurting me."

So he could still feel pain. And she hadn't even begun to shave him yet. It was the cold he felt—that was what he was most sensitive to— and he shivered at her touch.

She ran the razor down his right cheek, moving along the slope of his jaw. "Lift your chin, darling."

But he lifted his whole body instead of his chin, when what she wanted was for him to tilt his head back so she could get at the sensitive skin along his throat.

The bristles on his neck were as fine as a baby's brush.

She pointed at the two of them in the mirror. "That's you and me, darling." Eventually he would stop recognizing her; there would come a time when he wouldn't know who she was. She didn't want to be there for that, but she would be there for that, as she would be there for everything. For now, though, she had the opposite problem: she would go into the kitchen and he'd be calling out to her, forgetting she'd just been in the room.

"Should we finish up? Call it a shave?" She ran the razor under the water, and now she was going over the last patches of skin, mopping up the final clumps of shaving cream like a Zamboni. As she moved the razor in that sensitive trough between his nose and upper lip, he flinched. She had cut him: a drop of blood rose to the surface like a pomegranate seed. "Darling, I'm so sorry." *Hazard of the job,* he would have said, but it was she who had nicked him, and as she wiped the blood away, she said, "You almost got through unscathed," the lightheartedness like a screen to cover her true feelings, which were melancholy and self-reproach.

———

For years, he'd asked her to bake kichel for him, but she'd always refused. Kichel! It was peasant's food! Now, though, she finally agreed.

She followed the recipe devoutly, refusing to improvise, as if to wash her hands of the affair. Six eggs, half a cup of oil, half a cup of sugar, half a teaspoon of salt, two cups of flour. She poured the ingredients into a mixing bowl, like bath salts into a tub.

More and more, he would refer to people she'd never heard of, friends from childhood, the Lower East Side. Often he talked in Yiddish, but the only Yiddish she knew was the Yiddish everyone knew. She knew *chutzpah* and *putz* and *kibitz* and *macher* and *schmooze* and *shtick* and *pisher* and *tush*. She knew *boychik* and *traif*. She knew *nebbish* and *nosh* and *shpilkes* and *punim* and *schlep*. She knew *yenta* and *zaftig* and *kvell* and *klutz* and *kishkes* and *naches* and *bupkis* and *farklempt*. Watching Spence eat his kichel, she tried to put the words into sentences. *Okay, boychik, sit down and eat your kichel. That takes chutzpah, you big macher, not thanking me when I schlepped all the way home just to bake these for you. Let me wipe your face, you klutz; you've left kichel dust all over your punim.*

But there was no point: it made her farklempt just to try. She grew teary, and she took the napkin and dabbed her eyes, leaving kichel crumbs across her face.

40

"It's Ginny's birthday," Spence said one morning.

How like Ginny, Pru thought, not to mention her birthday, to be embarrassed she even had one.

"Ginny's birthday is next year," Spence said.

"Well, yes," Pru said. Ginny's birthday was this year and next year and the year after that. It was an annual occurrence.

When Ginny came into the living room Pru said, "What's this I hear about a birthday?"

"Oh, that," Ginny said, seeming to regret she'd let word slip out.

"When is it?"

"Next week."

"When exactly?"

Ginny sighed, the force of which lowered her onto the couch. "My birthday's next Saturday, if you must know."

"And what would you like?"

"I'd like you to stop talking about my birthday."

"I'll stop talking about your birthday when you tell me what you'd like."

"I'd like to go to the Botanic Garden," Ginny said. "I've lived in Brooklyn for thirteen years, and I've never been there."

"It's November," Pru reminded her. "Wouldn't it be better to go in the summer?"

But Ginny didn't care what month it was. She wanted to go to the Botanic Garden, and she wanted Pru and Spence to come along. Rafe could come, too, if he wanted. They could spend her birthday, all four of them.

They moved slowly down the hill at the Botanic Garden, Spence silent in his wheelchair.

"He's not having a good day," Pru said.

"Just give him a little time," Ginny said. "He'll rally."

But Pru knew, and Ginny knew, and Pru knew that Ginny knew, that if Spence wasn't doing well in the morning, he'd be doing even worse in the afternoon, because the passing hours marked a depletion, like gas leaking out of a tank.

Rafe stood across from them in his jeans jacket. Ginny had tried to get him to dress for the weather, but to no avail. "You see?" Pru said when Ginny lifted Rafe's collar to protect him from the cold. "You're a Jewish mother, after all."

A tour was gathering on Cherry Walk. The topic was deciduous trees of winter: how organisms responded to the changing seasons and how to use sunlight to keep the blues at bay. Seasonal affective disorder, Pru thought—or, as Spence had once called it, seasonal effective disorder, effective as it was at selling sunlamps. But then all diseases, Spence believed, were effective at selling things; it was why they'd been invented in the first place. "How about it?" Pru said. "Should we take the tour?"

Spence, glancing at the crowd clustered at the visitor center, said, tersely, "No, thank you."

"It's a Madurodam of trees," Pru said. They were wandering among the Bonsai now, and Pru was recalling a family visit to the actual Madurodam when Sarah was a girl.

"Sounds good to me," Rafe said when Pru told him about their trip. "I'd like to travel around the world."

"If you're able to afford it," Ginny said, "be my guest."

"I'll be able to afford it. And if you're nice to me, you can come, too."

"I'm always nice to you. In the meantime, take a look at this forest."

But it wasn't much of a forest, if you asked Rafe, just a smattering of denuded trees in their glass terraria, like something you'd bring home from a fair. "What good is a Christmas tree if it's going to be miniature?"

"You know what they say," Pru said. "Good things come in small packages."

"They may say it," Rafe said, "but it isn't true."

Outside the Palm House, Pru said, "Does this look familiar?" and when Spence didn't respond, she said, "We got married here."

"Yes," he said, unconvincingly. It had been a warm Sunday in August, decades before everyone had started to move there, but she and Spence had spent the first few hours of their married life in Brooklyn before decamping for the more familiar climes of the Upper West Side. Spence had wanted a small, simple ceremony. Pru had wanted that too; she just had a different idea of what was small and simple. Spence suggested City Hall, the clerk's office, but Pru thought that was too close to eloping. In the end she prevailed because she always prevailed with Spence, and they got married in front of thirty guests, where they were standing now.

"What about you?" she said to Ginny. "Where did you and Rafe's father get married?"

"In a church."

"Where?"

"In Kingston." And that was all Ginny was going to say. She lowered her hat over her brow.

Outside the Garden's entrance, Ginny said, "It was a lovely outing, Pru. Thank you for taking us."

And Rafe said, "I'm going to try to learn to appreciate small trees."

Rafe and Ginny turned to go, but Pru said, "Not so fast, you two." She'd borrowed a friend's car and would drive them home. "It's your birthday," she reminded Ginny. "I baked a cake for you."

Ginny and Rafe lived in the basement of a brownstone, down half a flight of steps that had been suctioned of weeds. "We'll come inside and sing 'Happy Birthday,'" Pru said. "We'll stay just long enough for you to blow out the candles."

"I don't have birthday candles," Ginny said. "Also, the apartment's a mess."

Rafe snorted. "I *wish* that apartment was a mess. I leave a shirt folded on my chair, and my mom's bugging me to put it away."

"We all have our standards."

Rafe snorted again.

"I'll bring you the leftovers tomorrow," Ginny said. "Rafe and I can't finish this cake on our own." She lifted the cake box in gratitude.

She was halfway out of the car when Rafe said, "Do you know why my mom doesn't want you to come in? Because we have all your stuff."

"What stuff?" Pru said.

Rafe listed the items Pru had given them: the bread maker, the toaster oven, the clothes, the VCR. "My mom doesn't want to be a charity case."

Ginny just stood there, one foot in the car, one foot out of it, looking mortified. Then she reared back and slapped Rafe across the cheek.

Pru was so startled, her breath caught. Even Spence blanched. Ginny herself looked shocked. "I'm so sorry," she said, and Pru didn't know whether she was apologizing to her or to Rafe, and Rafe, still stunned, stood beside his mother, the blood rising to his face, while Pru sat there a moment longer before she stepped on the gas.

On Monday, Ginny arrived early to apologize. "There's no excuse for what I did."

Pru tried to object—what parent didn't do things they regretted?— but Ginny wouldn't tolerate excuses from others and she certainly wouldn't tolerate them from herself. People said if you spared the rod you spoiled the child, but she'd never subscribed to that way of thinking. "You won't see me doing that again."

"It's all right."

"I apologize," Ginny said. "It was inexcusable."

41

Pru came home one day to find Spence agitated, tapping out some rhythm she couldn't decode.

"Who's that?" he said, pointing at Ginny.

"Darling, you know who that is."

"Who is she?"

"It's Ginny, darling. Come on."

"It's okay," Ginny said. "Don't embarrass him."

"Your shift's over," Pru said. "You should go home."

But once Ginny was gone, she felt no better.

It was cold out, and as she wheeled Spence down Broadway, she touched her mitten to his face, trying to keep him warm, while she navigated the wheelchair with her other hand. But the wheelchair zigzagged along the street, like a sled gone loose down a hill.

At West Side Market, she wheeled him around like one of the grocery carts, and it was into the basket at the bottom of his wheelchair that she placed lettuce, oranges, bananas, avocados, grabbing whatever she passed. She wedged a carton of milk between the wheelchair and his ribs.

In the dairy section, by the rounds of Gouda, she saw Walter. He was standing with his grocery cart. "Pru."

She just stood there.

"I'm going shopping." He pointed at his grocery cart.

"This is my husband, Spence," Pru said, forgetting that Walter had met him.

"And these are my sons," Walter said. Two young men materialized from the produce aisle.

It must have been Jeremy who stepped forward, drum-chested like his father, but without the beard. "Professor Robin," he said. He shook Spence's hand.

"I'm pleased to meet you," Spence said.

"And this one," Walter said, putting his arm around Saul, "says he's planning to make me a grandfather."

Saul pointed at his cart. "It's like they say. My wife is eating for two."

They stood there for a few seconds, Pru holding on to Spence's wheelchair, Walter with his grocery cart. Behind Walter, a woman was tasting the cornichons. A man walked by clutching a fistful of mustard packets. A cat emerged from behind the avocados and ran across the aisle.

Pru laid her hand on Spence's shoulder. "We probably should get going. Spence has had a long day." Spence had had a long life, she wanted to say. Though not, at the same time, nearly long enough.

She wheeled him toward the exit, nearly colliding with another shopper, and it wasn't until she was outside that she realized she hadn't paid for her groceries. The produce was still in Spence's wheelchair, the carton of milk still wedged to his side. But it was too late—she couldn't go back—so she moved quickly up Broadway, hoping she wouldn't get caught.

She was in the kitchen, making Spence his tea, when she heard a thunk in the living room. "What happened?" she called out, but by the time she got inside, Ginny was already bent over him. "The professor tripped," Ginny said helplessly. She was kneeling next to Spence, and now Pru was beside him, kneeling, too. "I was trying to get him into his wheelchair, and he tripped over my feet."

Pru took one of his arms and Ginny took the other, but he just lay there. "Let's try from a different angle," Ginny said, but she couldn't lift him up.

"I'll go get help," Pru said.

But Ginny insisted they could do it on their own.

Spence flipped over like a fish.

Pru bent down as low as she could, reminding herself the body's strength was in the legs, and she got him halfway up before she lost purchase.

"Elaine will be here soon," Ginny said. "I'm sure the three of us…"

"Elaine will be here in an hour. What's he going to do until then? Lie on his back?"

"He lies on his back all day."

But he didn't lie on his back as he was lying now, didn't lie there without recourse.

Ginny returned from the bedroom with a stretcher. She tried to slip it under Spence, but he wouldn't move his legs. Pru lifted one leg and Ginny lifted the other. They raised him six inches off the ground, but he teetered like a canoe.

"We can't do this," Pru said. "He's going to fall again." She lowered the stretcher onto the floor.

"Be careful," Ginny said. "You're going to hurt him."

"*I'm* going to hurt him?" She wasn't the one whose feet Spence had tripped over; this hadn't happened because of her.

"What's wrong with you, Professor?"

"What do you mean, what's wrong with him? What's wrong with *you*, Ginny?"

"I'm tired," Ginny said. "That's what's wrong with me. This job isn't easy. My back keeps giving out."

"I thought you did shot put."

"I did shot put thirty years ago."

"You lifted me," Pru said. "That's why I hired you—because you were strong."

"Well, I'm not strong any longer."

Over Ginny's objections, Pru called the porter, and he lifted Spence and deposited him in his chair.

The next day, Ginny kept her distance, but an hour before she was supposed to leave, she sat Pru down. "I can't do this job anymore."

"Of course you can. There's not a person on earth who's better at this job than you."

"I'm giving you my notice."

"Ginny, come on." She hadn't meant what she'd said yesterday. She hadn't hired Ginny because she was strong. She'd hired Ginny because she was Ginny.

Ginny shook her head.

"Was it because of what happened the other night? When Spence didn't recognize you?"

Ginny shook her head again.

"Is it money?" Pru had raised Ginny's salary to twenty-two dollars an hour, but she could raise it even more. Did Ginny want back pay? Name your price, she thought, and she would give it to her.

"I've been thinking about this for a while," Ginny said. She and Rafe needed to get out of the city. They'd moved to New York, planning to stay for a couple of years, and now they'd been here for more than a decade.

"And I've been here for three decades," Pru said. "With any luck, I'll be here for three more."

"Listen to me," Ginny said. Her mother was still living in North Carolina. She was getting older—she'd be eighty next year—and she'd fallen, too, just like Spence. It was time for Ginny to move back to North Carolina, time for her to be with her mother as she aged. And it was time for Rafe to be with his grandmother; she wanted him to get to know her while he still could.

What could Pru say? That Rafe shouldn't be allowed to get to know his grandmother? That she herself hadn't really known her grandmother and she'd turned out all right?

"Also, I need to keep Rafe out of trouble. There are gangs in East New York."

"And Rafe's in a gang? What kind of gang? A chess gang?"

"You don't understand."

No, Pru said, she supposed she didn't, but she didn't believe Rafe was in a gang.

"Rafe's not in a gang," Ginny admitted, but there had been little things, and little things could become bigger ones. She wanted Rafe to go to college, and then to medical school.

"It will happen," Pru said. She wasn't a betting person, but she would bet on Rafe.

"I can't just bet on him," Ginny said. "I have to make it happen."

"And you have," Pru said. "You will."

"There's also my husband," Ginny said.

"What husband? You're divorced."

Ginny shook her head. She was separated from her husband, but they'd never officially gotten divorced. He was starting to tire of Kingston, and he was open to returning to North Carolina. If that was how Rafe would get to know his father, she was willing to give it a try.

"So when do you leave?" Pru said.

"I can give you three weeks' notice."

"Three weeks?"

"If it wasn't for the professor, I'd leave tomorrow. I can't wait anymore."

All at once, Pru understood. Ginny had been waiting for Spence to die. And all the while she'd been doing her burrowing and reconnoitering, sending out her flares into the night.

"Spence is going to die soon."

"You don't know that," Ginny said. "The professor's will is something else."

Pru thought, He's going to die when you leave, Ginny. He's going to die of a broken heart. "So what happens now?"

Pru expected Ginny not to have an answer. But Ginny always had an answer. Elaine had said she could take over during the day and someone else could cover the night. Or Elaine could continue with the night and someone else could do the day. And if that didn't work out, Ginny would help Pru find someone else. It was a big city.

Until Elaine could switch her schedule, Pru hired someone to cover the day. But Pru came home one afternoon to find Judith asleep in the front of the apartment and Spence calling out in back.

Another time, Judith was on the balcony, smoking a cigarette.

"There's no smoking in the apartment," Pru said. Judith was supposed to be taking care of Spence, and how could she be doing that if she was out on the balcony, smoking?

"I'm a smoker," Judith said. "Do you want me to go outside and leave your husband alone?"

No, Pru said. She wanted Judith not to smoke.

She replaced Judith with someone else. That person didn't smoke, but she showed up late, and she treated Spence with barely concealed truculence. So Pru switched her to nighttime and had Elaine do daytime. But Elaine was more suited to nighttime, to the curt efficiency that accompanied diaper changes, to the silent negotiations between two people who wanted to go back to sleep. Daytime required conversation, and Elaine was a brusque conversationalist, especially with Spence, who couldn't keep up his end of the deal. "You should try talking to him," Pru said, but she knew what Elaine was thinking: why talk to someone who wouldn't talk back?

"The professor enjoys your company," Pru said. She was starting to refer to Spence the way Ginny referred to him. Maybe this was her way of reminding Elaine who Spence was. Or maybe this was her way of missing Ginny.

But no matter how many times Pru called Spence the professor, Elaine kept calling him Spence.

And she handled him roughly, like a flank of beef.

"Go easy on him," Pru said. "He's delicate."

"He's fine," Elaine said.

"The professor enjoys your company," Pru said, hoping if she insisted on it, it would become true.

Spence, meanwhile, had started to call Elaine Ginny. He called the nighttime person Ginny. A woman who came on weekends he also called Ginny.

"It's okay," Pru told Elaine. "He calls *me* Ginny sometimes. Half the time he talks to me he thinks I'm Ginny."

"It's fine," Elaine said. "It doesn't bother me."

But it did bother her, and one day, Elaine threw down her dish gloves and said, "Call me by my right name for once, goddamnit!" and Spence started to cry.

42

Pru was in the kitchen when the doorbell rang. She hadn't been expecting anyone, certainly not Arlo, but there he was, standing on the threshold when she opened the door.

She'd been hoping he'd visit, even as she hadn't dared hope. She hadn't seen him since she and Spence had left D.C. "Dad's in the dining room," she said. "You can go inside. I'll give you some time alone."

Spence was seated at the table. *The New York Review of Books* lay beside his plate. "Pop."

Arlo's father was silent.

"What are you reading?"

He didn't respond.

Arlo picked up *The New York Review of Books* and read aloud to his father from an essay by a man named Ronald Dworkin about another man named Leszek Kołakowski. But his father wasn't listening, so Arlo put the journal away. "It's me, Dad. It's Arlo." Then Arlo called himself by the name his father used to call him whenever Arlo entered the room. He called himself *Butchy*. Arlo's father was the only person allowed to say that word. And now Arlo was saying it for him, hoping to jar something loose.

A flutter of recognition crossed his father's face, a flicker of candle-light, but then it was doused.

Arlo returned with his father's lunch, but his father paid no attention to it. "Don't you want to eat, Dad?" He had an image of his father feeding him as a toddler, spinning the spoon around like a propeller, saying, "Zoom, zoom, zoom, into the landing field," as he inserted the food into Arlo's mouth. Arlo forked bananas, applesauce, hard-boiled egg, and crackers onto his father's plate. He kept each item separate, recalling a cartoon about childhood horrors, a drawing of a plate with all the food touching. That was what he was like: to this day, he hated having his food touch. His father had been the same way—fastidious, compulsive—but now he was raking his fork through the food, mixing it all together. "Eat up, Dad." But his father just sat there. Arlo placed the mashed bananas onto the fork and moved them toward his father's mouth. He did the same with the applesauce and hard-boiled egg, the macerated crackers, feeling revulsion at the smell of the food, at the smell of his father, but he kept on scooping it up. "Sit up straight, Dad." But his father just sat there, limp as a linguine.

Arlo handed his father his pills, and his father squeezed them so tight, it was as if he were trying to mash them up too.

"Okay," Arlo said, "give them to me."

His father unclenched his fingers and opened his mouth.

One by one, Arlo dropped the pills into his father's mouth, giving him some milk between each pill. "Talk to me, Dad."

Arlo's father was silent.

"Come on, Dad! Talk to me!" Arlo's gaze fell on *The New York Review of Books*, and a memory came to him from years ago: standing in the shadows at a dinner party, unnoticed among the guests. Someone was making fun of *The New York Review of Books*, calling it *The New York Review of Each Other's Books*, and Arlo's father just smiled, as impervious to insult as Arlo was pervious to it. Because Arlo's father had written for *The New York Review of Books* and he'd had his books reviewed by them. He could afford to be impervious: he was a member of the club.

Arlo bent over to tie his shoelaces, and his father spoke for the first time. "Bunny ears."

"Dad?" When Arlo was five, his father had taught him how to tie his shoelaces. Most people tied their shoelaces with only one loop, but it was easier for a five-year-old to use two loops. And the loops did look like bunny ears. Even then, it had been incongruous to hear those words coming from his father's mouth, though no more incongruous than to hear them coming from his own mouth, because Arlo Zackheim, thirty-four years old, worth millions of dollars, continued to tie his shoelaces with two loops, and every time he did so he still heard the words *bunny ears.*

He thought of his father's shirt, which he'd slept with as a boy. His security blanket, his mother had called it, on those cold nights when he lived with her, his father countless states away, a voice on a telephone, a line gone dead. A white Oxford shirt, but now it was shredded from all the nights he'd slept with it. And a wallet-sized photo of his parents together, his father resting his elbow on his mother's head. Arlo secreted that photo in his dresser next to his list of vocabulary words. He would raise that shirt to his nose, and he would see that photo of his happy parents, and it would, for a time, make him happy, too. "Should I put on some music for you, Dad?"

Arlo's father was quiet, so Arlo turned on the Victrola, and the sounds of Chopin came through the room.

His father was trying to speak.

"What is it, Dad?"

"Play." His father was pointing at the closet, and all at once, Arlo understood. His father wanted him to play the ukulele.

The problem was, Arlo's ukulele wasn't in the closet. The only instrument in the closet was Sarah's violin.

So Arlo took the violin, and acting as if it were a ukulele, he plucked away at the strings. He played "Yankee Doodle Dandy" for his father.

This was what he would remember: The smell of Mennen antiperspirant, the empty cans of Fresca piled outside the back door. The all-caps emails. The closetful of neckties hanging from their hooks like tongues. The sound of his father's voice when he picked up the phone, the "*HEL*-lo!" as if projected into a bullhorn—his auburn-haired father, his face paisleyed with freckles, who continued to call the stereo the Victrola, the TV the boob tube. There were people to see, stairs to walk, and he took those stairs as if he were on a reconnaissance mission: two at a time, three at a time, sometimes even four.

Arlo could hear Pru walking down the hall, coming to rescue him. But he didn't want to be rescued; he wanted another minute alone with his father. He allowed himself a moment's regret, longing for a life that was no longer his—that had never been his, really—those school breaks and summers, that restive, fitful, unfortunate two years when he'd tried to make a go of it under his father's roof, but it hadn't worked out, he hadn't been able to make a go of it.

He looked across the table. This was the last time he would see his father. He would never see his father again.

Then the footsteps were upon him: his stepmother, backlit, had entered the room. "You can stay longer if you want."

But Arlo was already standing up to go, preparing, as always, to make his getaway.

43

It was March in Columbus, and out the window of Pru's childhood bedroom the pallets of snow were stacked to the ground. Pru had flown out with Spence for her mother's eighty-fifth birthday. Sarah had come, too. Even Hank had flown in. How strange, Pru thought, that Hank was her brother. He was six years older than she was, and he'd moved to Hong Kong when she was still in college. Years ago, when he'd worked at the World Bank, she'd said, "That's all we need, a bank that runs the world," and Hank said, "Do you even know what the World Bank does?" The fact was, she didn't. "Opinions, opinions," Hank liked to say; he considered Pru a limousine liberal. Though Hank was the one who was taken to work by limousine and picked up by limousine again at night. Pru recalled playing Twister with Hank, six years old and he was twelve, how for two hours she'd contorted herself until, exhausted and exasperated, she'd given up.

"Tell me about Spence," Hank said now.

What was there to tell him? Spence sat before them, on display.

"I knew it was bad…"

"But not *this* bad?"

Hank was quiet. "Is there anything I can do?"

Pru touched his wrist. "Thank you, Hank." She took it for what it was, an offer, not insincere, coming from someone far away from her.

In the dining room, Pru's mother laid out pastrami sandwiches. She'd gotten a banh mi tofu sandwich for Sarah, who ate it dutifully, though she didn't like tofu. Her grandmother wasn't alone in thinking that if you were a vegetarian you had to like tofu, as if it were an obligation you'd incurred.

Spence, for his part, was eating broccoli. All his life, he'd hated broccoli, but the disease had dulled his taste buds along with everything else. The senior George Bush didn't like broccoli either; it was the one thing he and Spence agreed on. When Bush became president and broccoli was banned on Air Force One, when broccoli sales plummeted across the nation, Spence forced himself to eat broccoli. In the name of his opposition to George Bush, to the appointment of Clarence Thomas and the invasion of Panama, to the pardoning of Robert McFarlane and Elliott Abrams, Spence ate a vegetable that, under other circumstances, would have made him throw up, just as George Bush had thrown up, sitting beside the Japanese prime minister. Even after he left office, that was what George Bush was remembered for: not for invading Panama or appointing Clarence Thomas or pardoning Robert McFarlane and Elliott Abrams, not for Saddam Hussein and the first Gulf War, but for throwing up next to the Japanese prime minister, which, if you asked Spence, was exactly the problem with this country.

"It's good for you," Pru said, cutting up his broccoli, hearing how foolish she sounded, telling a dying man to eat his vegetables.

The next day, Pru and Sarah went to the cemetery, to pay their respects to Pru's father. Pru had hoped Hank would come, too, but he begged off.

"Hank doesn't like death," Pru said.

"Not many people do." You discovered that as a doctor if you didn't know it already.

They walked among the tombstones, and after a few minutes they found Pru's father's grave.

SEYMOUR STEINER

JUNE 4, 1926—SEPTEMBER 19, 1979

"He was only fifty-three," Sarah said. She'd known this, of course, but it had a starker cast spelled out this way. Her grandfather had died before she was born. In the photos in her grandmother's living room, he bore a mystical air, everything dark: his eyes, his fedora, the beginnings of a black beard. Even in stories he remained vaguely adumbrated: elusive, apart. Apparently, he'd been that way in life too—a man of few words, hardworking, not unkind, but it had been difficult even for his own children to get to know him. "It's strange that he was related to me."

"It's funny," Pru said, "because in my mind you two are connected." She recalled a yahrtzeit from years ago, getting up early to say Kaddish, holding Sarah in a sling.

"Why do Jews put pebbles on gravestones?"

The truth was, she'd forgotten. She had become a Jewish ignoramus.

"At least you once knew something," Sarah said. "You had a foundation."

"You did, too. You went to Hebrew school."

Sarah laughed. Sandy Koufax and Albert Einstein, famous Jews I call my own: that was what Hebrew school had been. She wished her parents had sent her to Jewish day school; she would have liked to reject what her mother had rejected—to make a choice—but as it was, she wasn't in a position to reject anything. And she had spiritual leanings, a craving for something bigger than herself, and she didn't know what to do with it. A friend at Reed had offered to take her to church, but she didn't want to go to church. She wasn't a believer, but the God she didn't believe in was the Jewish God, and the house of worship she didn't pray in was a synagogue, and the person who wasn't her spiritual guide was a rabbi. For a time, she thought of going back to synagogue, but the only synagogue she liked was her synagogue in New York, and she'd stopped going after her Bat Mitzvah. There was a Greater Portland Hillel, which served Portland State, Lewis & Clark, University of Portland, and Reed, but it took four colleges to make one Hillel, and what she'd liked about her synagogue was being part of a large group. On Friday nights at B'nai Jeshurun she'd been one of six hundred, and she feared that at Hillel she'd be one of six, and she didn't want to be a trailblazer, especially when she didn't know what trail she would blaze. "What about Dad? Are we going to bury him here?"

Her mother gave a start.

"He *is* going to die, Mom."

"I know." Now that his death was getting closer, Pru spoke about it more and more. But she half believed that talking about it inoculated her, as if treating it as inevitable might make it never come. Now Sarah was mentioning burial—the practicalities—and what had been abstract became tangible once more.

"I thought you might have a family plot."

They did have a family plot, but it was in one of the big Jewish cemeteries across the George Washington Bridge. It would be better to bury Spence close to home so the people who loved him could come visit.

"Will you say Kaddish for him?" Sarah said.

"Of course." If she'd said Kaddish for her father, she'd certainly say it for Spence. Though it perplexed her—angered her, even—that you said Kaddish for a parent for eleven months but only thirty days for a spouse. "What about you, darling?"

"It's hard to imagine him wanting me to say Kaddish." The world's greatest atheist, Sarah thought: he credited the Torah for inspiring Michelangelo and Rembrandt, but otherwise he thought it was a waste. And she, an atheist herself: it would seem doubly duplicitous. *Spend my yahrtzeit in the museum of science.* That was what her father would have said.

"It's funny," Pru said, "because the last few months Ginny was with us, she started to take Dad to church." She thought of those quiet Sundays when she got a few hours to herself, Spence in his jacket and loosely knotted tie, coming home in the afternoon with the smell of incense on his clothes, humming some vaguely recalled hymnal.

She ran a cloth over her father's tombstone. "I wish I'd had someone to share Grandpa's death with."

"You had Grandma."

"I meant a sibling."

"What about Hank?"

She shrugged. Hank lived far away, and they'd never been close. "Sometimes I wish I had more siblings." A bird landed on the tombstone. "What about you?"

"Do *I* wish I had more siblings?" Often enough, she'd wished she had less. "Now that you mention it, why didn't you and Dad have more kids?"

"We thought about it," Pru said. Or, rather, she'd thought about it, but Spence hadn't wanted another child. They already had Sarah, and their apartment wasn't big enough for someone else, with Arlo coming and going. And it was easy to want something when the other person didn't want it back. She'd told Spence they should give Sarah a sibling, but she was simply saying what she was supposed to say—everyone believed children were better off with siblings—mimicking other people's words without making them her own.

And then she got pregnant by accident.

"Jesus, Mom. When?"

"You must have been three or four." She'd miscarried at eleven weeks. She was ravaged at first, but soon she realized she didn't want another child. She was happy with Sarah and with Arlo's punctuated visits, happy with the life they had.

"Why didn't you tell me?"

"Miscarriages are a dime a dozen. Almost a quarter of pregnancies end in them." She rested her hand on her father's tombstone. "What about you?" she said. "Where are you going to be buried?"

"Mom, I'm thirty-one years old! I don't even know where I'm going to live, much less where I'm going to die."

"Where *are* you going to live?"

"In L.A. for now."

"And after that?"

"My boyfriend's from L.A., so we'll have to see."

"Your what?"

"I know."

"When did this happen?"

"Last fall."

"And you weren't going to tell me?"

"You waited almost thirty years to tell me you had a miscarriage. I only waited a few months."

"Are you going to marry him?"

"Mom, come on."

Why? Pru thought. She'd gotten married to Spence after only nine months. "What else haven't you told me?"

"I finally got my driver's license." She'd already been stopped twice for speeding. She drove like a teenager. It was as if she had to pass through some pupal stage before she became an adult.

"Come back to New York," Pru said. "You don't need to drive there. And the city's a great place to raise kids. You just put them on the subway and off they go."

"They aren't even born yet and you're already putting them on the subway?"

"I'm just saying."

And Sarah was just saying, too. "Slow down, Mom, slow down."

"If you don't come back, I might have to move to California myself."

It was hard for Sarah to imagine that. But then it had been hard for her to imagine moving to California herself, and she'd gone ahead and done it.

Pru said, "The world is filled with people whose grandchildren live across the world."

"L.A.'s not across the world."

"Whatever else, it doesn't have a subway." There would be other consolations for her grandchildren, but right now she couldn't think of any. "I'll fly out to baby-sit," she said.

"There's no one to baby-sit, Mom."

"Plan, plan." That had always been her way. She cleaned off her father's tombstone one last time. Then she took Sarah's hand and they headed to the car.

44

The memorial was held at Columbia, in the same auditorium where Spence gave his lectures—filled to the bleachers, everyone used to say, though Spence, ever modest, downplayed those accounts. He was a humanist, besides, and he didn't believe in numbers. Pru recalled their disagreements over how many people to invite to their wedding. "Why would I want people at my wedding?" he said. "They can come to my memorial if they insist."

And, it turned out, they had.

Back in Ohio, Spence had turned her mother's birthday celebration into a wake. Because when Pru and Sarah returned from the cemetery, they found him in bed, struggling to breathe.

"Walking pneumonia," the doctor said, and Pru should have known to be suspicious, seeing as he couldn't walk.

The next day he was worse and he was admitted to the hospital. The day after that the doctor said, "I think we're nearing the end."

Pru didn't want him to die in the hospital, but she refused to let him die in her mother's home, in the house she'd grown up in, so she told the doctor, "Just make sure he's not in pain."

He'd already stopped eating; soon he stopped drinking too. He allowed the nurse to insert a wet washcloth between his lips, but before long he'd locked his jaw. He was still Spence: still stubborn. Pru asked everyone to leave. She was alone with Spence, as she'd been at the beginning. She got into the hospital bed and lay there holding him, and she just lay there and lay there and she held him and she lay there.

She chartered a plane to fly the body home. It was just the two of them and the pilot on their own private jet, which would have been enough to kill Spence if he hadn't been dead already. "Finally, darling, we get to fly corporate."

They went straight from Newark to the cemetery, to the family plot across the G.W. Bridge. Afterward, she covered the mirrors and did the ceremonial ripping of the shirt, and she sat on a low stool with Sarah and Arlo in their private rendition of shiva.

Complications of Alzheimer's. That was what the obituary said. How she hated that term. There were no complications. It wasn't complicated at all.

"Do you want his wedding ring?" the undertaker had asked.

How anomalous that Spence had worn that ring—Spence, who took a dim view of jewelry on men and didn't like it much on women either. In junior high school, when Sarah pierced her ears, he said, "Why put holes in your body just to dangle something from them?" But for Pru he would wear jewelry.

Now, at the memorial, she wore his ring around her neck.

The speeches were laudatory and interminable, and she remembered none of them. Afterward she stepped outside. It was June and summer school had started; the students were frescoed across the grass. As she looked up, she saw Ginny standing across from her, in her blue dress and pillbox hat.

"Ginny, what in God's name are you doing here?"

"It's the professor's memorial," Ginny said. "Am I not allowed?"

"Allowed?" Ginny should have been the one up at the podium, delivering a speech.

They left the mourners to their club soda and iced tea and settled themselves on the steps of Low Library.

"How are you, Ginny? How's Rafe? You should have brought him with you."

"If I'd brought him with me, he'd have never gone back."

"Why? Does he miss New York?"

"He thinks it's the only place worth living."

"So he hasn't adapted?"

"Oh, he's adapted just fine. Our first week in North Carolina, he climbed a tree and landed in the emergency room. Count on the hemophiliac to court danger. I tried to remind him he's not a squirrel, or a cat." He was doing well at school, Ginny said, and he was making friends. But he missed the things everyone missed about New York: the crowds, the midnight pizza, the bodegas open at three a.m. And when Ginny reminded him that he hadn't been eating pizza at midnight or going to bodegas at three a.m., he said, "At least I knew they were out there. You were the only thing getting in my way." He blamed Ginny for the accident. Of course he was climbing a tree: what else was there to do in North Carolina? But mostly he was trying to make a point. Ginny had said East New York was dangerous, but there were far more dangerous places than East New York. "The real problem is the people," Ginny said. "Rafe thinks they're boring."

"Are they?"

"Some are boring and some aren't. Just like here."

"It takes a while to find your people."

"I tried to tell him that, but he said, 'Mom, do you really think there are people like the professor here? Do you really think there are people like Pru?'"

"Oh, Ginny, I miss Rafe, too." A Frisbee sailed past them. A professor walked by, trundling her books. "What about you?" Pru said. "Have you found your people?"

"I already have my people. I have my mother and I have Rafe."

"And your husband?"

"You'd have to ask him."

"So it hasn't worked out?"

They were in a holding pattern, Ginny said. She knew all about those: her flight had gotten in an hour late; they'd been perched high above Central Park, waiting for the go-ahead. The view was astonishing—for a minute she could have sworn she saw Pru and Spence's old apartment—but it also felt like a taunt: New York, here we come, but not quite yet. She'd been so busy with Rafe's homesickness that she hadn't realized she was a little homesick herself. "My husband's still in Kingston. He has some work to wrap up."

"And then he moves north?"

"We'll see." He had come for a few visits and they'd gone well enough, but once he left, Ginny was relieved. She was beginning to think the promise of a relationship—the threat of one—was superior to the real thing. She wasn't cut out for love, at least not love of the romantic sort. She was better suited for frustrated love, like the lovers in those nineteenth-century novels Rafe was reading at school. She was too busy at work, besides. And with Rafe, and with her mother, who, unfortunately, had fallen again, and so, for now, she was a caregiver for them both. "Rafe wants to come to New York for college."

"Will you let him?"

"If it's okay with the admissions office, it's fine with me. He still talks about having you adopt him."

"I'll even include you in the deal."

Ginny laughed. "I'll be long settled at that point. There are other things in my life besides Rafe."

Maybe there were, Pru thought, but Rafe trumped them all, just as now that Spence was gone, Sarah trumped everything. Pru had been serious when she said she might move to L.A.

Ginny looked at her watch. "I have to go, Pru. I have a flight to catch."

"I'll come visit you sometime. I'll fly down to Charlotte if you'll have me."

"I'd like that," Ginny said. "We'll have a more leisurely get-together."

Pru stood there for a minute, watching Ginny recede down College Walk, until, at long last, she was gone.

45

Pru was headed down Broadway when she ran into Walter, and all she could manage was a startled *Oh*. She hadn't seen him since that night at West Side Market.

He started to hug her, then stepped back. "I'm sorry about Spence."

"So you heard?"

"I was at the memorial."

"Oh, Walter. You should have come over and said hello."

"I thought about it, but the room was stuffed and you were busy. Those speeches, though, they were something else."

"It's like they say. Never speak ill of the dead."

"Actually, I've been hoping to run into you."

But now that he had, he didn't know what to say, and she didn't know what to say, either.

Finally, she said, "I was cleaning up the other day and I came across your brother's running shoes."

"Why do you have my brother's running shoes?"

"Don't you remember?"

It took Walter a minute, but then he did.

"I must have taken them home by accident. I'll get them back to you."

"When?"

She made a show of checking her calendar. "Are you around tomorrow afternoon?"

When she got to Walter's apartment, Albert greeted her, as always. He did a circle around her, then circled back.

She heard an infant cry—a wail, low at first—start to percolate. "Your neighbor's baby is making noise."

"That would be news to my neighbor."

When Walter returned he was holding a baby, and all at once Pru remembered. "Walter! Your grandson!"

"Pru Steiner, meet James Cohen." Walter lowered the baby onto Albert's back and led him around like a matador. "James likes to ride Albert."

"What about Albert?" Pru said. "Does *he* like it?"

"Albert doesn't mind."

Maybe he didn't, but at the moment Albert was just standing there, with the resigned aspect of a mule.

"Albert is used to having babies around. James is the least of things."

"You had *another* grandchild?"

"Albert had puppies."

"Wait a second," Pru said. "Albert's a girl?" She knew Charlies who were girls, and a couple of Georges, but Albert?

"Nope," Walter said. "Albert's a boy. He got the neighbor's dog pregnant."

"How?"

Walter sighed. "The way anyone does it." He had a history of being lax, going back to when his sons were in high school and he let their girlfriends sleep over. *Two feet on the floor* had been the house rule, but dogs could have two feet on the floor and still be up to no good. "Albert's taking responsibility," Walter said. Wasn't that how things worked these days, men standing beside their wives, saying, *We're pregnant*? Back when Walter was procreating, men didn't exaggerate their role in the affair. Albert, inasmuch as he was Walter's dog, agreed. He would take responsibility for what he'd done, but he wouldn't pretend to have carried the litter. "People kept telling me to have him neutered, but I didn't want to deprive him."

"Deprive him of what?" Pru said. "Sex?"

"Oh, who knows?" Walter sat down on the couch. "Now I have a litter of puppies on my hands. You're not looking to adopt a puppy, are you?"

Pru laughed. Some things would change now that Spence was gone, but this wasn't one of them. She handed Walter his brother's running shoes.

"So you've been cleaning house?"

"In my own way." She'd been emptying the closet of Spence's blazers and neckties, of his slacks with their creases stiff as oak tag. She'd offered Sarah her father's clothes—she thought Orson, Sarah's boyfriend, could wear them—but Orson was taller and broader than Spence; if he put on Spence's clothes, he'd look shrink-wrapped. "I figure it's better to clean up now. I won't have much time once I'm studying."

"Why would you be studying?"

"I'm applying to law school."

"You?"

"I know." She was thirty-five years late to the ball. Back in her twenties, law school had been where people went when they didn't know what else to do. Camille had gone to law school. Now Camille was marrying Bruce, and Pru was applying to law school: they were switching lives. "I should become a real estate lawyer," Pru said. "I've already had to hire one."

"Why?"

"It's a long story." A couple of months ago Arlo had visited, and he'd handed her a set of keys. "I changed the locks for security's sake, but everything else remains the same."

"What locks?" Pru said. "What remains the same?"

"Your old apartment," Arlo said. "I bought it from you."

"What are you talking about?" She'd sold the apartment to an LLC.

"*I* was the LLC," Arlo said.

"I don't understand."

"You don't need to. What matters is I'm the owner now, and I'm selling the apartment back to you. The price is a dollar. I've already had a lawyer draw the contract up."

"But that apartment would go for over a million dollars." It had already gone for over a million dollars.

"Then you're getting a good deal."

"Arlo, why are you doing this?"

"Because I owe you." Arlo removed from his bag a yellow legal pad and showed her the numbers he'd written down, all the money his father had spent on him.

"You don't owe us," Pru said. "*We* owe *you.*"

But Arlo was pressing the keys into her hand.

"You don't expect me to move back there, do you? It's where your dad and I used to live."

"Then rent it out. You could always put it on the market again, but then I'd have to buy it back from you."

So she was stuck with the apartment—stuck with it forever.

She was, in fact, renting it out. At least, Spence wasn't around to witness this. She could hear his voice. *Good God, Pru, you've become a landlord.*

"Will you go to Columbia?" Walter said now.

She shook her head. Columbia was Spence's school. She was hoping NYU would admit her. Or if not NYU, then Cardozo. "What about you?"

"Am *I* applying to law school? I'm applying to baby-sitting school, is what I'm doing." Between Albert and James, Walter spent a lot of time with one mammal or another slumped across his lap.

"It sounds like things are going well for you."

"In some ways."

"Not in others?"

Walter shrugged. "I've been seeing this woman."

"Oh," Pru said. "Is that not good?"

Walter hesitated.

"Seriously, Walter, I'm happy for you." She was, in a way, and she thought saying those words would make her feel them. She hadn't expected him to wait around for her. Still, she hoped he would keep the details to himself, leave her to her quiet speculation.

"The thing is, it's not working out."

"Why not?"

"I don't like her enough. My heart isn't in it."

Did she allow her own heart to swell? She looked at Walter across the couch from her. "We should get coffee sometime. Or maybe dinner."

"We *should*?"

"Meaning I'd like to."

A clock beeped in the kitchen. Albert stretched out his paws. Walter said, "Does this mean I'm back on your holiday card list?"

"If only I wrote holiday cards."

"You could start."

"Please, Walter, don't make me write you a holiday card. And while you're at it, could you get me to stop watching so much TV?"

"You hardly watch any TV at all."

But that had been when Spence was alive—Spence, who'd been a television teetotaler. Now Pru had been untethered, and though she still didn't watch much TV, she watched a lot more than she used to.

"Then come over sometime and watch Jon Stewart with me."

The fact was, Jon Stewart was one of the few shows she liked—Jon Stewart and PBS, her regular dips into *Masterpiece Theatre*. In college, she'd subsisted on a steady diet of *Upstairs Downstairs*, an exotic, costumed world for an Ohio girl. She missed the days when there were only ten channels and half of them were shot through with fuzz. Now TV gave her choice fatigue. One time, she asked Sarah to sign her up for a cable package that provided only PBS and Jon Stewart.

"PBS isn't a cable channel," Sarah said. "And have you ever considered streaming Jon Stewart?"

She hadn't, not least because she didn't know what streaming was. Spence would have had something to say about streaming, all those perfectly good nouns turned into perfectly bad verbs. Oh, how he'd hated what had happened to the word *impact*. Ginny used to talk about toileting Spence, and Pru, under Ginny's influence, had once used the word herself. Afterward, she thought the only redeeming thing about Spence's disease was that he could no longer be pained by how people spoke. It was bad enough to have to be toileted, but to hear his own wife use that word?

Walter had one hand on James's head, the other hand on Albert's. He looked as if he were blessing them, the way Pru's father used to bless her on Friday nights, one hand on her head, the other hand on Hank's.

"Look at these two," Walter said, staring down at his sleeping dog beside his sleeping grandson. "King James and Prince Albert." And

Walter himself was just a serf. Which was how it should be. Grandparents were meant to serve others. Pru would find this out soon enough.

"Hopefully not too soon." She was thinking of Sarah's words. *Slow down, Mom, slow down.* "I'm too young to be a grandparent."

"That's what everyone says until they become one." Walter stood up. "Here," he said, "I'll take you downstairs."

On Riverside Drive, Pru held James while Walter removed an orange from his pocket. "Do you mind if I eat this? I feel the low blood sugar coming on." Walter started to peel the orange, but Pru stopped him. "Just watch," she said, and she handed James back to Walter. When she was small, Sarah would demand that she peel the orange in one piece, then reassemble it without the fruit inside. Pru's family had its strange ways with fruit in general. She was thinking of her father eating those apple pits, leaving nothing but the stem.

"Come visit me again," Walter said. If Pru didn't find him at home, she'd find him in the playground at Hippo Playground: James loved to sit on that hippo. "It must be in the blood," Walter said. When his sons were small, they'd loved that hippo, too.

As had Sarah. She used to barnacle herself to that hippo, on the days when she tired of Central Park and she convinced Pru to trek over to the Hudson.

Walter sniffed his fingers. "I should go upstairs and wash my hands. I can't walk around smelling like citrus."

Pru sniffed her own hands, which smelled like citrus, too. As she turned to leave she thought of Spence, who wouldn't have been in her predicament. All his life, he'd resisted eating on the street. He'd maintained his decorum until the end, believing certain things were private.

46

The moon dilated and the moon diminished and you could count on Spence every other Sunday visiting Enid in the nursing home. But a few years ago he stopped visiting, embarrassed by what he had become.

"Enid," Pru said. "It's me, Pru." They were sitting in the cafeteria, and a querulous look came over Enid's face; something bobbed in her throat.

"I'm Pru," she repeated. "Spence's wife."

"My baby brother," Enid said. "He doesn't come here anymore."

"Spence can't come here anymore. He died, Enid. He's no longer with us."

Enid's eyes glazed over; Pru thought she was going to cry. Then Pru started to cry herself. "I'm so sorry, Enid." She was sorry about everything, but mostly she was sorry for having brought the news, because all it had done was upset Enid.

Pru removed Spence's eyeglasses from her purse. "These were Spence's," she said. "I want you to have them."

Enid took off her own glasses and put Spence's on. Spence and Enid didn't look alike, but now, wearing Spence's glasses, she looked as if someone had combined brother and sister, like that television show where they put one person's head on another person's body, combined the left side of someone's face with someone else's right. Trick photography, they'd called it, back before all photography had become trickery.

"I brought you something else," Pru said. She handed an envelope to Enid. It was a letter Spence had written Enid in Yiddish when he'd first gotten sick. Pru didn't know why he'd never sent it.

טײַער שוועסטער,

איך טראַכט אַ סך וועגן דיר, און וועגן דער טאַטע און די מאַמע אויך. איך
געדענק ווי דער טאַטע פֿלעגט אהיימקומען פֿון דער אַרבעט מיטן ריח פֿון
די לעדערנע שיך. פֿון צײַט צו צײַט פֿלעג איך גיין אין געוועלב נאָר ווײַל
איך האָב געוואָלט זײַן נאָענט צו זײַן ריח און צו די מאַמע בײַ דער קאַסע.
איך טראַכט וועגן די קינדער וואָס האָבן זיך געשפּילט אין האַנטבאָל אויף
אָרדזשערד סטריט. איך געדענק ווי דו האָסט מיך געטראָגן אויף דײַן פּלייצע
אין דעם אַלטן געגנט.

Dear Sister,

*I've been thinking about you, and Papa and Mama too. I
remember Papa coming home from work, smelling of shoe
leather. Sometimes I'll go into a shoe store, just to smell him in
there. And Mama behind the cash register. I think of the boys
playing handball on Orchard Street. I remember you in the old
neighborhood, carrying me on your back...*

Enid read the letter. It was hard to tell what she understood. She
folded up the letter and placed it in her dress.

47

Pru walked downtown. On 59th Street, outside Central Park, the carriage horses were waiting for their load, eating from feed bags that hung from their throats like appendages. The pigeons paraded across the cobblestone, daring her to get out of the way. Smoke rose from a chimney, and from a steam pipe jerry-rigged to the ground, and from the grill where a vendor was roasting chestnuts. Across the street stood Essex House and Hampshire House. And the Plaza Hotel, home to Eloise—and to Sarah, who, when she was Eloise's age, started to dress like Eloise and talk like Eloise and insisted that her parents take her to brunch at the Plaza.

In a store window the dresses hung, and the words came to Pru, *Pick a dress, any dress,* like the three-card monte dealers who used to assemble in Times Square when she first moved to New York, saying, *Pick a card, any card,* bilking the tourists.

She headed back up to Morningside Heights, thinking of their first apartment, on Claremont Avenue, Spence coming home with flowers for her. She thought of the old Woolworth's on 110th Street. And next to the old Woolworth's the old Sloan's. And across from the old Sloan's the old Daitch Shopwell. She missed them all, the way she missed the neighborhood's seedier days, when her friends were afraid to come uptown at night and Spence told her to carry pepper spray.

Past Koronet Pizza she went; past Famiglia, past the West End Bar, though it, too, was gone now. Past the old chocolate store, which had been there so long it might have been formed from the primordial muck. And, finally, the corner of 116th Street, where Chock full o'Nuts used to be. It was the Chinese place now, where the college kids went for takeout.

She didn't have dinner plans, so she went inside and ordered some Chinese food.

A breeze passed through as she walked down the hill: a relic from last winter, a herald of winter to come. A young woman careened up the block with a license plate around her neck like a charm.

ACKNOWLEDGMENTS

I owe a huge debt of gratitude to many people. Jason Dubow, John Fulton, Eve Gleichman, Bret Anthony Johnston, Ernesto Mestre, Brian Morton, Julie Orringer, Eileen Pollack, and Ted Thompson all read early drafts of this novel, and their insights helped me immeasurably to improve this book. For their expertise on everything from Shakespeare to Yiddish to neurology to chess, I am indebted to Irene Tucker, Anita Norich, Mitchell Elkind MD, and Jacob Kaplan. Thank you to my MFA students at Brooklyn College, whose work and commitment always inspire me.

At Pantheon and Knopf, thank you to Reagan Arthur, Kelly Blair, Katie Burns, Michiko Clark, Tatiana Dubin, Kristin Fassler, Chris Gillespie, Amy Hagedorn, Altie Karper, Pei Koay, Lisa Lucas, Emily Murphy, Sarah New, Tom Pold, Nora Reichard—and especially to my brilliant editor, Lexy Bloom, for her keen editorial eye and general guidance; I'm so fortunate to have her as my editor. Finally, a special thank-you to the late Sonny Mehta, whose support was so important to me over the years.

At Sterling Lord, where I have found a true home, thank you to Szilvia Molnar and Danielle Bukowski in foreign rights, and to Maria Bell. And, most of all, to my amazing agent Doug Stewart—a man who, among many other things, is so quick on the draw he answers my emails before I've even sent them. Thank you as well to my film agent Rich Green at the Gotham Group for his commitment and support.

Thank you to my family: Alice Henkin, David Henkin, Daniel Henkin, Alisa Henkin, Sammy Henkin, Dahlia Henkin, Ariana Henkin, Sharon Berkowitz, Jerry Berkowitz, Randi Berkowitz, Jon Regosin, Talia Berkman and Greg Berkman, Shachar Berkowitz-Regosin, and Burt Berkowitz-Henkin. And, in particular, to Beth, Orly, and Tamar, without whose love none of this would matter. Finally, to my late father, Louis Henkin (1917–2010), whose love and influence are imprinted on every page of this book, and whose memory endures, now and always.

Joshua Henkin is the author of the novels *Swimming Across the Hudson,* a *Los Angeles Times* Notable Book, *Matrimony,* a *New York Times* Notable Book, and *The World Without You,* winner of the 2012 Edward Lewis Wallant Award for American Jewish Fiction and a finalist for the 2012 National Jewish Book Award. His short stories have been published widely, cited for distinction in *Best American Short Stories,* and broadcast on NPR's *Selected Shorts.* He lives in Brooklyn, New York, and directs the MFA program in Fiction Writing at Brooklyn College.

A NOTE ON THE TYPE

The text in this book was set in Miller, a transitional-style type-face designed by Matthew Carter (b. 1937) with assistance from Tobias Frere-Jones and Cyrus Highsmith of the Font Bureau. Modeled on the roman family of fonts popularized by Scottish type foundries in the nineteenth century, Miller is named for William Miller, founder of the Miller & Richard foundry of Edin-burgh. The Miller family of fonts has a large number of variants for use as text and display, as well as Greek characters based on the renowned handwriting of British classicist Richard Porson.

Typeset by Scribe
Philadelphia, Pennsylvania

Printed and bound by Berryville Graphics
Berryville, Virginia